A Great Day To Live

Cynthia,

always stay
obedient to God.

Dela
Taylor

A Great Day To Live

An encouraging tale of overcoming obstacles, making memories and not letting anyone stand in your way.

Damali Keith

GOGG-GiftOfGabGirl Publishing

This book is dedicated to my gifts from God, my mother and my daughter.

Damianna I LOVE AND ADORE you kiddo.

Mom, thank you for being a magnificent mother, great grandmother, righteous role model, encouraging cheerleader and a super support system. To say I love and admire you is an understatement. I'm exceptionally proud of you. You have achieved something many have tried and failed. You absolutely, unequivocally mastered the art of parenting. You are my courage, my encouragement and the epitome of leading by example. In fact, you are by far the strongest, sweetest, most awesome person I know and one of the greatest leaders I have ever even heard of. If I am half the mother you are, I will be a huge success.

Heavenly Father thank you for all of my wonderful blessings!

Mom & Damianna,
God's plan is my plan!

CHAPTER
ONE

The Devil had his hands around my throat and I could feel his strong disgusting grip choking the life right out of me. I didn't know if I would live to tell my story or more importantly if I would survive to raise my daughter God had blessed me with only four months earlier.

Things like this aren't supposed to happen in such an upscale community. After all, I was standing in a 12,000 square foot home. It is a dream house by just about anyone's standards. Every home in this pristinely manicured neighborhood is. The slate temperature-controlled floor felt warm and inviting underneath my feet here in the breakfast area like it has so many times before. I could see the large, dark cherry wood, stainless steel, marble and granite filled kitchen so elegant and picturesque. It looked like a snapshot from a fancy magazine. I love to cook and eat, so the kitchen was always one of my favorite rooms in this magnificent mansion I had grown to love. There was no intruder. So why were things so different, so strange, so surreal? Why is my life in danger, here of all places? Everything felt so weird in this massive beautiful brick home that I had so enjoyed, before now. I had felt safer here in this house, in this neighborhood, than in my own home but not on this night. I could see blood on my hands from his face. My fingernails...

"Wow. My nails look really pretty. I should be a hand model. I'm glad I chose this nude color. Coney Island Cotton Candy it's called. Nail polish names are so cute. This one shows off my manicure nicely".

What in the world am I thinking? I was literally in a fight for my life and the same things I always think about are, as usual, dancing around in my head in that whimsy way that only my thoughts can. Apparently even in a matter of life and death I am still just me, Daffodil Annalisa Keigh, a TV News Anchor and Reporter in Houston, Texas. My mom thought it was a happy name. Just as my namesake, the vivid beautiful flower, happiness seems to not only seep from my very pores but also roll off of me and grab anyone who comes near. I had never been in a fight before. Violence isn't part of my life or the lives of my loved ones. The majority of letters I receive from viewers compliment me on my kindness and beauty.

"When you're beautiful inside that shines for the world to see," one woman wrote. I was proud of being that person whose caring character could be seen a mile away but couldn't this guy see that? He was so violently, yanking me this way, pushing me that way and choking me until I couldn't breathe. I felt as though my brown eyes were being squeezed right from my face. There I was begging him to stop and trying to knee him in the groin, to give him additional incentive to let me go, but even as I tried to fight back to get him to comply, my pleas and my attempted punches didn't seem to faze him.

I was confused. There are no strangers here. I looked at the faces in the room. There was my mother, Phoebe Keigh hanging on to my tiny daughter Daniella for dear life, my daughter's dad Oxford Orlando and his mother Gerta Orlando. Only the five of us are here. So who is this vicious monster that seems demon possessed as he yanks my hair? My head flicked back, over and over. I didn't know how much more I could take. I thought one more pull and he'll snap my head clean off my body. I was exhausted, out of breath, pushing and pulling trying to get away.

"Just let us leave your house, please. I'm begging you. Just let us go. What are you doing? Why are you doing this? Just let us go." I absolutely pleaded with my daughter's dad, a man who had said he loved me countless times before this. A gentle giant I thought, who seemed so caring.

"PLEEEEEEASE Oxford. Ox please!" I certainly wasn't too proud to beg. "Just let us go please". Not a chance. His grip on my neck told me so. There's no way I can beat him up. I'm 5'10" and sure I still have MUCH of the baby weight on my side but my 150-pound frame seemed flimsy in his hands. More goofy thoughts crossed my mind.

"Gosh how long has he been at it, this whole beating me up thing? Whew. I need to start working out. Boy, I am really out of shape. Isn't he getting tired too?"

Apparently, the answer was no. Oxford put his hands back around my throat and out of instinct to defend myself I clawed his face again with the nails I have loved to grow out and keep well-manicured since I was a teenager. I forced my fingers into his face clinging on and digging deep with a grip I sometimes used to open a too tight jar of pasta sauce. I dug in and dragged my nails from forehead to chin. I looked at my caramel colored hands again. This time I wondered, would his soon be like mine? Would he too have blood on his hands? That terrified me because that would mean... I couldn't even finish the thought.

My mom and his were in the battle with me. However, all three of us were no match for this 6'5" 295 pound former Hollywood superstar. His name, Ox, was certainly fitting. He had been a highly sought after stuntman, turned awardwinning actor, turned tremendously successful screenwriter. He was still very much in shape wearing muscles I had openly admired a time or two. He still looked exactly like the super human muscleman character from one of the biggest roles of his career and he was certainly acting like a madman from a movie. We were all yelling, begging him to stop. I, only by God's grace, broke free. I turned toward the fancy back door that would put many front doors to shame. He can't reach me. Thank God. So he grabbed our daughter from my mother. You've got to be kidding me.

"Give her to me. Don't you hurt her. Ox you wouldn't hurt her. You wouldn't hurt our baby." I pleaded. It was half a command, half a question. Daniella looked so pretty in her pink jammies and I could smell her soft baby scent. The fragrance and the fact that she was in her own father's arms should have comforted me. Under the circumstances I felt anything but. I had been praying silently. Now everyone could hear.

"Jesus please protect us. Father I come before you as humbly as I know how. Give me strength. Get me and my baby and my mom out of here alive. Please God". Before I knew it my daughter was in the air, over her dad's head as if he was going to throw her. Really God? This seems far from the protection I just asked you for. I've had a great relationship with God for decades. So talking to him is second nature. He's my Father, my savior. I was praying he would save me this day. My heart broke when my daughter started crying uncontrollably and there was nothing I could do to comfort my four-month-old baby girl. I couldn't get to her no matter how hard I tried. Her little pale yellow face was now bright red. In this moment I felt I had failed as a mother, a failure only four months in. How could a dad do this to his own daughter? His behavior made my stomach turn. It made me angrier than I have ever been. Ox's mother now stood closest to him begging him to hand over the baby.

"No.   They're not leaving.   They're not going anywhere," he yelled. He instructed me to go to his bedroom and he would give me the baby. So he's violent and delusional. Did he really think I would go to his bedroom or anywhere with him? Wow, this guy is crazy. Somehow my baby was in Oxford's mother's arms, then in mine and I was running holding her tightly right behind my mother out the back door. I was bolting toward my Land Rover SUV but where is my key? Before I could figure it out Ox was once again grabbing me by my hair. I yanked away leaving him with a hand full of my brown bobbed shoulder length haircut. When he saw what he could do he yanked over and over again trying to snatch away handfuls at a time. There was such pride in his face at being able to rip my hair from my scalp. It was a pride in his eyes that I had never seen before, not even when our daughter was born. How could he enjoy hurting someone, inflicting pain on people he supposedly loves? The hands that had been so loving, that had touched me gently many times before were now choking the life out of me. My body was going limp and someone took my screaming daughter from my arms.

"Mama everything is fine. Just go in the house" he instructed his mother. Everything is fine? Really? You're trying to kill me and "everything is fine"? When you're choking the life out of someone, how is it possible to calmly turn to another person and tell her 'everything is fine'? This newly discovered skill of his terrified me. Then another me moment came to mind as the palm trees swayed and danced gracefully in the wind. It looked as though we were in a tropical oasis.

"Whoa what a beautiful, warm January night. Houston certainly has a way of blessing its residents with wonderful weather even in the winter. (With my eyes closed I turned my face toward heaven and enjoyed the breeze on my cheeks. A kiss from God is what I liked to call it since childhood.) Feeling a whisper of wind on my face is one of the things I have enjoyed most in this world since I was a girl".

I can't believe I keep having all of these 'normal' thoughts in such an abnormal situation. Maybe it's because this is a place I normally feel safe and after all I was with people who are supposed to be my loved ones. What do the neighbors think jumped into my mind? I had been yelling for some time for someone to help me.

"Jesus help me please." I screamed. He seemed to think it was amusing as if he wanted to ask "Oh is He here"? These are not touch-my-neighbor's-house-from-my-side-window homes. There is plenty of land for tennis courts and full basketball courts like the one I was currently being choked on. I didn't know if anyone could hear me. Had anyone called the police? I was hoping and praying so. Then he started dragging me to the pool. We had plenty of pool parties and good times here. There was always lots of good food involved. Oxford loves to cook even more than I do and I love to eat. So it was the perfect combination. When we were swimming, there was always fresh fruit, shrimp, crab legs, steak, cabbage and potatoes. It was my favorite meal and he would even cut the crab from the shell for me. All I had to do was dip the long strips of crabmeat in the waiting melted butter flavored with just the right amount of fresh squeezed lemon. We were also in the pool surrounded by those platters of fantastic food plenty of times during my pregnancy. I have a framed picture in my house of a very pregnant me wearing sunglasses and a bikini standing by this pool. In the photo my fingers are forming a heart around my expecting, protruding belly button. Ox and I had such a great time the day of that picture. I'm not sure which is brighter in the snapshot, my smile, my glow from a wonderful pregnancy or the sun that shined so bright on my bronzed skin. We had also prayed countless times out here together by the pool blessing the food and thanking Him for our many blessings.

Now I was poolside and praying in a very different way. I found myself interviewing his mother as he manhandled and choked me. I was in the grips of evil and I still found time for a discussion. That's the journalist in me I guess. It wasn't your run-of-the-mill, sit-down-in-two-chairs chat with a producer, perfect hair, lighting and make-up that I was accustomed to but I needed answers, right then, apparently.

"Is this the person you raised? Has he done this before? I don't recognize this stranger. Is this a stranger to you? This is foreign to me. What in the world happened to him, in his life that would make him think this behavior is ok? Did you teach him this is ok? Did you teach him beating up women isn't ok? I don't understand. Did you indeed raise a boy who grew up to become a man who beats up women? Is this who he is or has he gone insane?"

The thoughts were jumbled in my head and tumbling from my mouth. I must sound like a crazy person. Certainly not crazier than her son but mad nonetheless. I found myself getting louder, not yelling but she didn't seem to hear me and he hadn't heard me since he started this madness. I just wanted, needed clarification. In that moment I really did expect her to answer my questions and I didn't understand why she wasn't. From the look on her face she thought I was angry with her. I wasn't. I just want to get out of here alive. She never answered my questions. I'm not sure what made me begin conducting an interview in the midst of mayhem but, again, I chalk it up to second nature. That's who I am. That's what I do including in the face of danger, apparently. I wasn't thinking, only doing. I was still trying to get away and understand what was happening. His mom seemed frustrated at his behavior but not surprised. The intense pressure of his hands around my throat interrupted my thought. He's squeezing so tight on my neck. I could hear gurgling. Is that me?

"I can't see. Why can't I see? Please God don't let it end this way. Please don't take me away from my daughter and leave her to be raised by a madman. Stop it Oxford". I was trying to speak but I don't know if anything came out.

He was dragging me closer to the swimming pool. A pool he used to have to drag me out of. I had always loved to swim. Give me a pool or a beach and I'll find hours of fun. Then another funny thought popped into my head, which would have been perfectly fine under normal circumstances, not as I was being dragged to what may have been my death.

"Me not wanting to get into a pool? This is definitely a first".

TWO

We had driven by this swimming pool for years. I had waited a lifetime it seemed, to jump in. It was our community center pool in Wayne, Michigan. There in my hometown winters could be brutal with blistery snowstorms and temperatures so cold my toes would be numb for an hour after coming in from outside. You would think I developed a passion for skiing but that didn't happen. Who could afford skis? This particular summer I was determined to play in that pool. It was 1977 and I was five years old. It was a sweltering Saturday and like many people in Michigan we did not have air conditioning in our small apartment. The sun was beaming and it was a beautiful day. My older cousins told me to get dressed to play in the water sprinklers. I was shocked and excited when we, along with several kids from the neighborhood started heading for the pool instead.

The lady at the community center desk was really nice until we approached the front of the line. She was colder than any Michigan winter. We paid our money and walked through the gates. After we emerged from the small building to the outdoor pool the whole world stopped and stared. Parents called to their children to get out of the water and barked it was time to go.

"I said now," one father yelled. The parking lot on the other side of the fence was clearing out faster than a shelf of freebies. It only seemed a little odd in my five-year old mind but I was focused on playing in this pool.

"This is something I have waited to do my whole life," I thought.

As I tried to pull away from my Cousin Nora's hand she held tight. I didn't understand the problem. The older kids I had come with asked one another quietly "should we leave?"

"Nooooo we can't leave" I whined loudly. "Please. Let's swim. I don't want to leave". My cousin who was six years older tried to whisper.

"Well, Daffi, it hasn't been long since black people were even allowed to swim in public pools. I don't think they want us here. Maybe we should go," Nora said. Just then my hand slipped from hers as I walked toward the water.

"No. Let's stay. Anyway, we're brown. I don't know why those black people can't come in but we can," shouted my mouth with its five-year-old logic. I saw a little girl I wanted to play with. She was standing with a group of fair-haired children and they all had pretty blue eyes. I thought her big cousins must have brought her just like mine had.

"Hey! You're it. Last one in isn't a princess," I laughed as I tagged her and ran toward the water. We both giggled and she ran behind me. We both jumped in the water with pink floaties on our arms but everyone else was standing around.

"Come on in" we shouted. Sometimes kids can teach us plenty and adults should be smart enough to learn, even from children. My cousin Matthew who was very protective of me motioned for me to just come out of the pool. 'No way Jose' I thought. This was fun and I wasn't going to leave anytime soon. My cousin Josh held a football he brought with him underneath his arm. They all stood frozen with horrified looks on their faces. Josh has always had the physique of a football player even as a child. He's three years older than me and was always very athletic and had a way of towering over everyone else.

Finally someone started moving. One of my new friend's family members was walking toward my cousins. He was even bigger than Josh and he started saying something to him. He pointed right at Josh.

"Hey if you're choosing sides for a little water football. I'm on your team".

Before you know it the squads were chosen and the guys were in the water having a ball. Well, most of them. My cousin Nora and her best friend Paige are about as beautiful as they come. They could always attract boys who would flutter around them like bees to flowers. Their light beige skin was toasting in the sun as they relaxed and seemed so cool even in all the heat. Their reclining pool chairs sat mostly upright as one polished her nails and the other thumbed through a magazine. My cousin Morris taught me to swim that day. We, and our new friends, closed the place down. It was almost dark and the summer sun was nearly just a memory when we walked back home and told our moms we hadn't been in the sprinklers but at the pool. They had already figured that out and we were mildly in trouble. Not me, of course. I was an only child and the youngest of a bazillion-cousins. Being the baby had its perks.

My mom had never learned to swim and she was terrified for me to get into the water but there was no stopping me. That pool became the place where I created wonderful childhood memories. It was also the first place where people would be aggravated at the very sight of me. Unfortunately it would not be the last time my presence would make others agitated. Just like that day, it took me a long time to figure out why just seeing me could be such an aggravation for some.

THREE

That's just the way it was when I was a child. Inside our apartment my mom and I had tea parties, I combed in her hair for fun and read plenty of books. Inside was where I felt safe and very much loved. We had good times, one another and lots of peace. I came to appreciate that early on. Sometimes visiting other homes there was yelling and arguing. That never happened in my house and that is something I valued. It was home. I practiced my violin as much as I could, which wasn't exactly music to my neighbors' ears. Sometimes they responded by banging on the shared wall demanding me to stop. I guess that explains why I developed a love for reading and writing. I could do those things quietly.

In the winter there was a nearby pond that would ice over. My mom would take me ice-skating on it. I didn't grow up in the best neighborhood so that's a funny thought for me now. Here I was this nerd-princess ice-skating with my leg kicked back like Dorothy Hamill or Debi Thomas and there were drug dealers and gunrunners slithering around the neighborhood. I would dream I was skating better than everyone else in the world and going for the gold. I knew other

Olympic hopefuls likely had better training facilities but hey ice is ice.

I was afraid there in my neighborhood in certain circumstances. Once when I was sitting outside on a bench with freshly painted nails my 14-year-old hands were crossed on my lap as the pretty pink polish dried. For some reason a guy who was about 19-years-old came over. The look on his face and the tone in his voice told me he meant business. He puffed his chest at me and snarled.

"Uncross your hands. Who do you think you are sitting out here like this, like you're somebody? You ain't nobody."

Was he kidding? I didn't ask. I think I caused near hurricane force winds I uncrossed my hands so fast. I was terrified. I sure would like that coward to try it now.

Then there was the time Tony Butler was beaten to a pulp by another neighborhood boy right in front of me. Tony, another Tony, my mom and I had been outside sitting on my porch talking and laughing. The boy came out of nowhere and set his evil sights on Tony Butler. He turned into a madman, punching, kicking and even slamming Tony onto a fire hydrant. I thought sure his spine was smashed. There was blood everywhere. Screams, cries and pleading with that guy weren't enough to stop his wicked attack. Tony himself even begged the lunatic to stop. He repeatedly threw his helpless victim onto the concrete. My mom decided it was an audience this psycho was after. We couldn't get to Tony Butler. So she forced the other Tony and me inside our apartment, closed the door and called the cops. I begged her not to leave poor Tony out there but she was right. The psychopath stopped beating Tony Butler and left him there severely injured in front of our home and he ran away. I was maybe 15 years old. The Tony's were two years older and the vicious attacker was a 16-year-old boy. The lunatic was never charged but I'm sure he went to jail for something else not long after.

In that type of neighborhood it's typical to have residents ranging from richly endearing to poor excuses for human beings. Crime-riddled communities are a melting pot of people. Unfortunately when it comes to buying a home it doesn't matter how hard you work or how intelligent you are. If you don't get paid much money, you don't get much to call home. I carried the guilt of not being able to help Tony well into adulthood. The assault wasn't for any particular reason. They hadn't argued. I knew I never wanted to cross paths with that nut or anyone like him ever again. No such luck. I would find that out years later.

That's how I learned to love things like a breeze on my face, leaves on trees dancing in the wind and the colors in a sun setting sky. Those were some of the only pleasures I had outside in my neighborhood. God had blessed me with beautiful things to admire even in the midst of crime and criminals. God's works of art were not only beautiful but an escape. The nature he was blessing me to love was the same he gave to everyone else in the world no matter how much money they had and I didn't. I knew He loved me. The beauty of a breeze, the sun, stars, moon and sky told me so. They were His gifts to me that I would hold dear forever. Sometimes, as a little girl, I would look out my second floor bedroom window at the night sky. The stars were like shiny, silent, singing fireflies. I don't know why I equate stars with music but I always have. I would peer into the darkness wondering who I would become and what I would be doing in twenty years underneath this same beautiful blanket of stars. Whatever it was I had no doubt God would be right there with me.

My mom made our home so comfortable, peaceful and inviting. It was spotless, clean and well decorated with crafts she was proud to make herself. We baked, cooked and ate together. She was always there, at my school, outside when I played, laughing with my friends and me. She spoiled me with what she had. Love. She gave me plenty of that.
She worked hard but never made much money. While most people swing by a fast food restaurant on a whim, she would

get out her calendar and show me which month she would be able to take me to McDonald's. She was always so excited at the thought of having enough money to buy me a treat. We didn't have a car. She was actually too shy to even get a driver's license. Maybe that's how I became shy because of my mother or maybe it was the mean kids in my neighborhood. How do you become outgoing in a community of kids who are unapproachable? Not all of them but there were enough big bad bully kids to go around. I fortunately found plenty of friends, many who remained special to me even when we were all grown up. I know what you're thinking. Shy and becoming a TV News Journalist don't go together. In college I decided I didn't want to be shy anymore. I thought being shy had held back my intelligent, hard-working mother from her full potential. There at Clark Atlanta University in Atlanta, Georgia I tried to be as outgoing as I could. It worked and if God can bring me out of my shyness He can do anything.

I went away to college with one of my best childhood friends but I didn't lean on her as a crutch. I made it a point to introduce myself to new people. "Hi I'm Daffodil. Yes, like the flower but most people call me Daf or Daffi." I would smile and say. By the way, the night before my best friend and I were scheduled to drive my brand new 1990 Chevy Cavalier to college it looked as though I might not make it. I thought my neighborhood would finally succeed at making me fail. I always felt the community was trying to keep me. I was determined not to let that happen. That night, my mom and I had loaded all of my stuff in my car so I could leave early the next morning. It was a bright red beautiful graduation gift that my mom worked hard to help me buy. I had worked since I was 14 years old. So I had a little money but not nearly enough. My mom was more than willing to help. Anyway, the car was finally packed and I jumped in the shower. I heard yelling and my mom was pounding down the steps of our two-story apartment. BOOM, BOOM, BOOM! It sounded as though she was wearing sledgehammers on her feet.

"What's going on? Mom?" I jumped out of the shower, grabbed my towel and ran downstairs too. By the time I made it to the front door my mom was outside yelling at a scraggly man who looked like he smelled. He was standing next to my car where he could clearly see it was packed with goodies, which he apparently was trying to claim for himself. The car had a safety measure. When you pull the locked door handle the inside light comes on. So, of course, the man was standing there at the door and the inside light was on in the car indicating he had been pulling on the locked door handle trying to open the door.

"You get away from her car. Get away from there right now. That's not your stuff," my mom yelled. This is a tiny little lady who has to tippy toe to stand taller than five feet nothing. I was hanging out the screen door still wet from the shower and dressed only in a small towel.

"Mom, just come back inside". I knew that guy could really hurt my mom and me, take my keys and my car but her bravery paid off. The guy retreated as if my mom was a big burly body builder. I got dressed, said my goodbyes to my mother and that is how I spent my last night ever at the home where I grew up. That night I stayed at my best friend's house in the next city over, where my car would be safer in her parents' driveway. We left for college early that July morning. I was 17 years old. By God's grace I never moved back home.

I met plenty of people at school and joined a bible study group in my dorm and of course I worked. I tried to pull my mom out of her shyness too but even when we could afford to eat at restaurants she wouldn't even order from the menu. She would tell me what she wanted and ask me to order for her. Once, after I became a local TV news anchor in Houston I was the Mistress of Ceremonies at a dinner for area business owners. My mom was visiting from Michigan and she went to the event with me. When we arrived at the convention center we ducked into the back room with the organizers to go over my script and the evening's agenda.   When we left the room to start the program the hall was packed with people dressed formally sitting at fancy tables ready for the fun to begin. I was walking toward the stage telling my mom over my shoulder she would be seated at table number one just in front of the stage. Since the dinner hadn't started some people were still standing and mingling. I made it to table one and the person I had been talking to all this time was nowhere in sight. Turns out, I had been walking with my beautiful emerald green silk gown flowing behind me, heading toward the front of the room with my perfect pinned up hair and expensive dangling earrings, talking to myself the whole time. I didn't see my mom or her long beautiful red dress anywhere. I couldn't find her. Where was she? I started back tracking and she was still there at the very back of the room looking elegant and wearing pearls and a very nervous face.

"Mom your seat is at the front of the room, table one," I explained to her.

"Daf I don't want to walk in front of all those people," she whispered wide-eyed.

"Mom I'm the one who has to talk. You don't even have to say anything. What are you nervous about?" She didn't know. She laughed with me and walked to her table at the front of the room and she survived. Mom actually left a lot of her shyness there with the used napkins and empty dinner plates that night. I was and am so very proud of her.

FOUR

My childhood was shared

with a woman who did everything possible to show me love. She never even spanked me. She didn't believe in that. Neither do I. My mother ruled using what I call the disappointment factor. She spoke highly of me to anyone who would listen. Her friends, family members and strangers had to hear about how smart and awesome I was. To hear how proud she was of me made me proud of myself. It was a small town. Surely if I was doing something bad I would run into someone who had earlier heard about how terrific I was. I didn't want to make a liar out of my mom. I didn't want to embarrass or disappoint her. The disappointment factor is so much more effective than spankings. There's no comparison.

While I was growing up in a loving home in Michigan, I would find out many years later, my daughter's dad had a different existence in Texas. There in Sugar Land, Texas days after I had my daughter and brought her home from the hospital Ox's mom stopped by to see Daniella. During her visit she told me something I wasn't expecting and frankly I would never be able to prepare myself for something so awful. I couldn't believe she was actually saying the words out loud. She asked if Daniella was sleeping in my bed.

"Well, her crib is upstairs in her bedroom which is so far from my room. So I set up Daniella's bassinet by my bed downstairs. I don't let her sleep with me. That can be dangerous. I've covered stories on parents who have rolled on top of and suffocated their baby. Sometimes at night I watch my little Daniella sleep. She's a good baby." I said like only a new and proud mother could.

"Suck 'em slept with me in my bed until he was nineteen years old and I get so hot at night I always sleep nude," she said with a smirk. Suck 'em was what she always called Oxford. I had never heard her call him Oxford or Ox. "Nude, wait nineteen?" I couldn't believe my ears. She must have misspoken. "Nineteen?" I repeated. "Most teens, especially boys, would choose to gauge their own eyes out rather than sleep with their naked mom," I said in horror.

"He loved it and so did I. He loved sucking on me until he fell asleep. That's why we call him Suck 'em. He would sometimes rush home from school begging for it and we would go to bed early," she smiled.

"Suck on you? Suck on your what?" Gerta stared me right in my eyes and she smiled.

I couldn't find the words. I simply got up from the couch with my baby in my arms, left my family room, went into my bedroom, closed the door and cried. When we, before that day, ran into his family members who called him Suck 'em, he told me they were saying Sock 'em. He said his grandmother made up Sock 'em because he looked tough like a rock 'em sock 'em boxer, wrestler or football player. Wow how would you tell someone the truth about that nickname? That wasn't a mother allowing her child to simply sleep in her bed. I think the law has a very different name for that.

Ox once stayed awake all night after telling me his cousin's half-sister sexually assaulted him when he was a child. He, however, didn't call it rape. He said they fooled around. He was only 12 and she was 22. Later at 14 years old he had a baby with a 26-year-old woman. Tragic incidents he dismissed, "Oh I was always big for my age". Looking like a man and being one are two very different things. Those women knew what they were doing but so many years later I don't think he fully realized what they'd done to him. It left him angry and made him hate women, including his mother but he couldn't tell her that. I don't think he could even tell himself what his mom had done. It would be too painful. Denial was easier. I would soon be added to that list of women he hates.

When we first started dating he described a loving, nurturing mother who he was very close to. She, he told me, loved church and spent her whole life worshipping several times a week. He said he never even remembered her with a man.

"She never dated?" I asked. "Why not?"

"She was a devoted mother. She worked hard to raise my two sisters and me," he answered.

When I told him my mom had never spanked me he said his hadn't either. We laughed at how our moms must have the patience of Job. We agreed we share our mothers' view. Whipping isn't something we believe in. There are better ways to discipline, effectively raise and give direction to children. We seemed to always be on the same page.

A mutual friend introduced us to one another. The first night Oxford called me we talked on the phone for hours. That was a trend that lasted two weeks then he asked if he could cook dinner for my cousin and me at his house. I thought to myself how cute he's going to try to cook. Boy I was in for a scrumptious surprise. My cousin Naomi and I arrived at what seemed more like an estate than a house. A black wrought iron fence enclosed the whole beautiful manor. The large iron gates that folded across the driveway had his initials encircled in the middle in fancy metal letters. They weren't pearly but they sure felt like the gates of heaven opening up to us, as they swung open to allow us inside. We hit it off right away. After eating the absolutely fantastic meal he cooked we all went upstairs to the game room to shoot pool. Ox and I were inseparable for months.

The first time we went to the movies we stood in the parking lot after the film talking for hours. I remember like it was yesterday. I was wearing my super sweet silk peach Balmain tank with massive silk flowers lining the neck and matching Balmain peach, super edgy, moto jeans. Good conversations are so important to me. I thought "Wow this is really going well".

I got really sick about three months after we met. I mean ugly sick. I'm talking sore throat, nose plugged up, can't eat anything, can't get out of bed, hair matted, lips chapped, looking and sounding like a germ sick. So sick the next symptom on my cold medicine box may have read "barely alive". Even though I was this-far-from-cute sick he insisted I stay at his house. He took SUCH good care of me. He cleaned my nose when I no longer had the strength to reach up and blow the gross, peeling thing. He gently fed me hot soup. He brought orange juice to me and held my straw so I could drink. It took days to nurse me back to health but he did it, gladly. He was always smiling and trying to make me feel better. He even tried to kiss me on the lips. Yuck and he said I was beautiful. I thought the guy was in love not insane. I guess I should have known better.

He had made a habit of massaging my feet, shoulders and my back and running a hot bubble bath for me with lit candles surrounding the massive Jacuzzi tub, complete with red rose petals in the water. When I said I didn't feel comfortable taking a bath at his house when I didn't have a change of clothes, he fixed the problem. The next time I went to his house he walked me into his neat massive closet and showed me a whole wardrobe of business suits and casual attire, with the tags still attached, that he so thoughtfully bought just for me. He said I never had to leave if I didn't want to. Seriously? And this guy is single? How is that possible? I would too soon find out.

FIVE

Before I would learn the answer to why Ox was still single, we read the bible together many times. He would recite verses to me out of the blue and we always prayed together but I thought it was weird he didn't take me to church or even go to church. He had a reasonable explanation for it and a pretty plausible justification, believe it or not, for having three children with three different women, without being married. He told me his first son was born when he was fourteen to a woman who was twenty-six years old. He was clearly the victim there. His second was with a woman he had a ten-year relationship with. I questioned why they would date for ten years and not marry but I thought at least he was in a long-term relationship and didn't just recklessly have a child with some woman he didn't know. His third son, he told me, came after he had made a promise to God. He wasn't going to fornicate anymore. He was going to find a wife. He had been celibate almost two years. Then one night temptation got the best of him with a woman who had, until this point, simply been a good friend. That one night produced his third son. He was 6-years-old when I met Ox. His sons were wonderful boys and he seemed to love them so much. I also love children. So I looked forward to getting to know his kids. I told him how seriously I take parenting and that his behavior had been less than responsible. He told me he had been counseled by his pastor, was older and wiser and had learned from his mistakes. I bought it.

Oxford had previously told me of his recent financial difficulties. He said he had fallen into a deep depression before he met me and I was helping bring him out of it into some of the happiest times of his life. He asked for just a little more time to get over his shame and bitterness at his financial losses and he would start taking me to church. He was still sorting things out with God and trying to get his self-esteem and get himself back, he told me. He left Hollywood after writing a very personal screenplay about his life and then couldn't get funding, couldn't get support to get the film made. He took it personally. That was five years before I met him.

I thought if only he had something he could once again accomplish, that would be perfect to pull him out of his slump. I wasn't worried about finances. I was working in a career I loved. We were both young, healthy, able-bodied adults and if we were obedient to God we wouldn't have to worry about Ox being able to find work too. I convinced him to start his own landscaping company. He loved working in his yard. I had even come home from work one day to beautiful rose bushes and palm trees planted in my yard at my modest 3,000 square foot home in a gated community where I had lived alone for years. Guys had given me flowers plenty of times but no one had ever surprised me with whole rose bushes planted in my front yard. They were beautiful red roses, yellow ones and an amazing looking peachy colored hybrid rose. I was super surprised and excited. He was scoring major points.

The same day I encouraged him to start his company, he bought all the necessary supplies. He purchased a couple of big riding mowers, a pick-up truck, trailer, a sign for the truck and a bunch of hand tools which were more like toys he loved telling me about. Yes, he could afford those things. I tried to tell him his financial difficulties were a far cry from the tough times that struck the rest of us in the working world. He hired a crew of four men and scored contracts with all of his neighbors, their friends, their friends' friends and even a few of my neighbors who would see him taking care of my lawn. I went on a number of "jobs" with him and he often called me to come by and take a look at his handy work once he finished. He was so proud of turning a green lawn into a masterpiece complete with stones, mulch, trees, plants, flowers and fountains. I loved seeing his picture perfect, postcard like landscapes he came up with. I always told him so and made a big deal over what a great job he was doing. I took plenty of pictures and started a portfolio of his work. His business grew like wild fire. Ox's clients not only included homeowners for residential lawn care but also business owners for commercial landscaping. He was excited about life again.

We had plenty of talks about getting married. He even bought a ring. It had more carats than a veggie tray and it was beautiful. As much as I would have loved seeing it on my hand I knew we weren't ready for that. He said we were.

"Daffi I know everything about you. I know who you are. I know your heart. I know how much you love God. I know how much I love you. I've never known anyone like you. I have never loved anyone like I love you. I want us to spend the rest of our lives together Daf," he told me.

It had only been a few months and we were still getting to know each other. Like the time he told me about a high school basketball incident. I was shocked. He just didn't seem like that type. He said the other players on the team thought he was such a jerk, such a bully, they took a vote and told the coach. He was voted out and thrown off the team. Really? Seriously? You would really have to be a jerk to get voted off a basketball team by players you've known your whole life. He was so kind and gentle. A jerk? Not him. I didn't see it. Yet.

When he told me he'd had a vasectomy after his last son. I was crushed. I was 33 years old and I so very much wanted to get married and have children. He assured me I didn't have to worry about it because the procedure could be reversed. We could get married and have kids he told me. Wow, was this really my soon to be husband? He had told me "I love you" first, long before I told him. So I felt maybe I wasn't ready yet to say I could marry him but in time? Hmmm maybe he was going to be my husband. Maybe I didn't have to worry about if the vasectomy could indeed be reversed.

Then I noticed stories about his childhood that he previously mentioned were changing. Now he was laughing about how his mom spanked him until he was black and blue but he had said she never whipped him. He recently told me of a time that crushed him to the core. His mom had chosen her boyfriend over him but earlier he told me she didn't have boyfriends. I got the feeling that may have been one of the first times she put a man before him but I felt it wasn't the last. He said he was a small boy and he had come inside his house after playing outside and there was a strange man in the house who wasn't wearing a shirt. He told the man who he was and asked 'who are you?'

"You don't need to worry about that," the man half answered.

"Well, why don't you put some clothes on? Why are you in my house half dressed? Where's my mother?" he asked the man. The guy started yelling at him.

"Don't ask me all these questions. You don't tell me to put clothes on. You're not running anything around here. You don't tell me what to do."

His mother came out with a scowl on her face.

"You're in trouble now sucker," he said to the man but he was wrong.

"Get out of here. You're not grown. You don't come in here trying to act like a man. You want to be a man? Get out and don't come back tonight." His mother's words and actions were clearly inappropriate. Oxford learned a lot of things that day and none of them were the correct way to behave. The nine year old left the house where his mom had chosen this low life over him and he didn't come back until late the next day.

SIX

I kept thinking about that story as he and I sat having dinner with his mom and his sisters one night. Then things got even worse.

"Remember that woman I said was your mother?" Gerta asked Ox.

"Which woman? That last one?" he asked.

"Yes. Well, she isn't and I knew she wasn't your mother when I told you." She spoke in a tone that could have been as uneventful as if she was talking about the seasoning on the meat. I couldn't believe my ears. My heart was breaking. Was anyone else at the table hearing this conversation? Why did I seem to be the only one who was horrified? He and his sisters actually started laughing. They joked about how Gerta has been telling Oxford a different woman is his mother since he was a just a little boy.

"You never tell me who my dad is, Mom. Will you tell me who my father is?" Ox looked broken as he peered right into Gerta's eyes. His tone, gloomy eyes and painful facial expression begged her for the information and do you know what that mean old witch said?

"I'll tell you this about your father. Your daddy didn't want you any more than that mammy of yours did." I wanted to jump right over the table at her and punch her lights out or at least grab her by the collar and shake her until she told him the truth about his parents and that's saying a lot because I don't normally long to attack people. Wow, you never know how someone was raised. You never know what's going on behind closed doors. Oxford's sisters, then Oxford started to laugh.

"That isn't funny, not even a little bit," I said slowly as if the sentence was too big for me to handle. They all briefly stopped and stared at me as if I was the one who was saying hurtful, evil things here. Then they started laughing again.

"It's not a big deal. Gerta is my sisters' mother but she actually took me in when I was a baby. She raised me as her own son." Ox explained as if he was telling me the difference between the rib eye and the T-bone steaks on our plates. I was shocked. My mouth hit the floor. I had no idea.

"It is sort of an inside joke when it comes to my biological mother." Ox laughed.

"Oh. Ok. So you do know who your mother is?" I asked.

"No" he shook his head.

"Then her lies aren't funny." I said in the nicest voice I could muster. His mom, friend, neighbor, liar, baby napper, whatever you want to call her, she cut me off.

"The woman who was your mother is dead. She died a few days ago. Her name was Leona Johns." Dead? As in now he'll never get to ever even have a conversation with her? He'll never look her in the eye, give her a hug or kiss or ask her any questions? This is devastating and Ox was devastated. We talked about it for days until he went to the woman's funeral. The day of the service Gerta arrived at Ox's house shortly after I did. Ox was still in his suit after attending the funeral. His handsome face was as solemn as I had ever seen it.

"Boy, what you sad about? That wasn't your mother. You actually went to that woman's funeral? What's wrong with you?" Gerta shouted at him.

My mouth hit the floor again. Ox had already told me about how he had gone to the funeral and told everyone there the woman was his mother. The mourners' grief had been replaced by the shock of their lives. I imagined all of them still standing there, stunned and frozen at a funeral that ended hours ago. Gerta had, again, told him yet another lie about a woman who isn't his mom. It would be difficult enough not knowing your own mother, then to have the woman who's supposed to be your mom, who's supposed to love you as if you were her own son, frequently lie to you about your real mom. That would be almost unbearable. She gave Oxford several different names of women who were supposedly his mother, just in the first few months that I knew him. Was she crazy? Who would do that especially to someone they raised since childhood? What kind of person could be so cruel? Hadn't this church going woman ever heard of thou shalt not lie?

Now I was ready to run for the hills and Ox knew it. By this point I had been a journalist, a communicator for twelve years and communicate I did, personally and professionally. I had become very straightforward. I didn't have a problem verbalizing what was on my mind. I could say what I mean and mean what I say quite easily but this situation was new for me. I felt I would be kicking a man when he was down if I simply walked away right then but perhaps I should have. In addition to the really messed up childhood he had endured there was one incident that should have been a red flag for me long before this. Early on when we were dating he took me out to The Cheesecake Factory. We had a great time, magnificent meal, a shared dessert and our usual perfect conversation but when we were leaving the restaurant it happened. There was an older lady standing outside waiting for her husband to pick her up at the door. Clearly she was used to being treated like a lady and respected as such. Oxford was telling me a story about something someone had said. Just as we reached the lady, Ox was at a part in the story where he blurted out a curse word. Profanity is like nails on a chalkboard to me. I especially feel very disrespected when I'm in public and some stranger completely disregards me and uses such awful language. I think it's ignorant, disrespectful and despicable. So when he said that right in front of the woman I quickly responded.

"Shhhhh. Quiet down a bit. That lady is right there. She can hear you," I said quietly thinking maybe he just didn't realize she was there. We took a few more steps in silence. Then when I felt we were out of earshot of the woman.

"Ok then what happened?" I asked with a smile thinking he would simply continue his story.

"Don't ever shush me. I'm a grown man. Don't ever talk to me like that." Oxford's words and tone shocked me.

"No, hang on a sec. I just feel so disrespected when people do that to me, when they use that profanity right in front of me as if I'm not even there. I try to be respectful of others not only at home but also in public. That was just plain rude to use profanity right in front of that lady like that. Don't you think so?"

"Oh so this is about your job. I know where you work Daffodil. So you're trying to correct me like I don't know how to behave in public because of your job because she might recognize who you are?"

"What are you talking about? This doesn't have anything to do with where I work and everything to do with respect and how I was raised. I was being respectful of others long before I worked in TV news and I'll continue to be respectful long after." I smiled with confusion.

He was actually starting an argument with me because why? He wanted to be able to disrespect women in public and use profane language in front of strangers. I didn't get it. He was now loud and yelling at me.

"Hey. You know, I'm not upset and I really don't think this is anything we should argue about. If that's your thing and the type of thing you do then I'm sorry for correcting you. I just don't hang out with people who behave that way. I had a great time. It was nice to have met you. If you would just take me home now I would really appreciate it." I said pleasantly.

He took me home apologizing the whole way.

"No really. You don't have to apologize. It's not a big deal. We're just different. Different doesn't mean bad." I said. We arrived at my house and he walked me to my door.
He asked if he could come inside to talk.

"I want you to know that is not the way I behave. My mom taught me better than that. I have really just been under a lot of stress lately. I'm not a millionaire anymore because of poor investments and an awful, if not criminal, financial staff I had working for me. That's tough to deal with. It makes me feel less than and when you told me to be quiet it was another blow to my self-esteem and it shouldn't have been. I feel like because I don't have a lot of money anymore you think I don't know how to behave. I'm sorry and nothing like that will happen again. I know it doesn't make sense and I'm talking with my pastor about it to get it behind me. Please hang in there with me. You have my word, I truly apologize and nothing like this will happen again," he promised.

I talked with my two best friends about it. Nora and Paige who had been BFF's since childhood now allowed me to hold the title as well since our six and three-year age differences no longer mattered. They thought I should give him another chance. His explanation seemed reasonable and three educated, intelligent women decided the story was plausible. So I continued seeing him but that day after the made-up-mother's-funeral I didn't need re-enforcement, I was done. Now how do I go about telling him that? I had plenty of sympathy for what he was going through but I didn't want to go through it with him. Does that sound cold? I just thought he had far too many things he had to face and needed help with before he was ready to get married to anyone. I was growing more concerned about the lies, or should I say about the far-fetched fantasy Oxford previously told me regarding the "wonderful woman" who raised him. This fantastic nurturing, nice and loving mom was downright fictional, a figment of his imagination. A great mom? Gerta didn't even come close to being that. How could he call this woman his mother?

SEVEN

After his "mother" left that night I think Ox had a plan. He urged me to stay. Although, it was pretty clear I wanted to be anywhere but here. He really seemed to need me and I felt guilty for not wanting to stay. After washing the day off with warm showers in a bathroom larger than my biggest guest bedroom, we crawled into his king size bed. I have been a Christian my whole life and I have always tried to live life doing the right thing but sometimes I gave in to temptation. As huge as the bed was you wouldn't know it. He cuddled up right next to me and we talked for a long time about him going to the funeral and Gerta lying about all these women being his mother. He didn't like when I said she was lying. Oxford said it was just a joke.

"A very bad, not funny, hurtful lie isn't a joke." I told him. Before the night was over he talked me into getting intimate with him.

"If you think it's a sin Daffi then let's just get married. I love you Daffodil. I bought the ring. You haven't accepted." He coaxed.

"Get some protection please." I whispered nervously finally giving in.

"I need to be close to you. It's been a tough day Daf. Why do you always say that? Are you seeing another man? You know I had a vasectomy. What are you concerned about?" Tears filled his eyes. "So you're seeing someone else?" He asked me again and again. Of course I wasn't seeing anyone else. After quite a bit more discussion or more like his emotional accusatory monologue, he wore me down. I wanted to just go home, instead I agreed to what he was asking. What was I thinking? Apparently I wasn't but that's what happens when you plan to only kind of, sort of, sin. The devil clouds your thinking. He has a way of putting manure in front of you and making you think it's a delicious fudge chocolate cake. You are already beyond second helpings and well into thirds, it's all around your mouth and you're in it up to your elbows before you ask, "What kind of crap did I get myself into?" literally.

Over the next few weeks I was spending less time with him trying to get some space between us. My plan was to leave the relationship. I was on vacation from work and went home to Michigan for two weeks for the holidays. There, sleeping in my old yellow and pink pastel bedroom with New Edition posters now rolled up in the closet instead of hanging on the walls, I knew I was pregnant. A picture of my three best friends from high school and me still stood framed on top of my dresser.

"Oh my! My ponytail in this picture is perfect. So adorable and look at my face. My skin was so young and flawless." I stared at the photo for a long time.

"Am I the woman this little girl was supposed to grow up to be?" Had I worked so hard to achieve so many titles, honor student, college graduate, intelligent, educated, writer and journalist, just to now become a single mother? I looked at a different picture of myself when I was in seventh grade. That little girl in the photo had such big dreams and high hopes. She deserved to be someone's wife and then start a family when they chose to. Parenting is hard work. Looking into the eyes of the seventh grader in the portrait I knew she deserved to have a husband who loves her to help her raise a little one, to have family dinners with at night, to take vacations with on holidays and to sit in church with on Sundays. The baby would deserve to have both parents in a loving home.

Was I now a disappointment to this little girl in the picture? I couldn't help but feel like the answer was yes. That girl had worked hard her whole life. She had been complimented and achieved such high distinctions, now this. "Am I the woman this little girl had hoped and worked to become?" Was I having a baby with a pathological liar? I seemed to have a million questions and not many answers. I was in as much denial about Oxford telling me he had a vasectomy as he was about having a wonderful mother. I couldn't bring myself to even think about it. Has this guy really been telling me in many different conversations he had a vasectomy and he really didn't? Who am I dealing with? Who am I pregnant by? I don't even know this guy if he lied to me about something as serious as having a vasectomy. If he blatantly deceived me, then what else has he lied to me about? I certainly hadn't been with anyone else. I was either pregnant by a liar or immaculate conception by God and the latter just didn't seem likely. So I pushed the vasectomy thoughts right out of my mind. It was sort of like shoving a shopping cart and as it begins to roll through the parking lot, turning to walk away. That cart could end up slamming into someone's car, mowing down a person, careening into a kid but if I wasn't looking at it I may never know the damage it does. I knew the vasectomy issue was there but I just couldn't deal with it right then. I wasn't ready to look at just how damaging that lie really was. I prayed for a long time and spent hours asking for guidance, for wisdom and for forgiveness from God.

"Only the wise will say God's plan is my plan". The sentence jumped out at me from an inspirational pamphlet as if it was answering a lingering question in my head. So was this baby God's plan? The leaflet was underneath the photo of me, lying at the top of a box filled with my old stuff. I was feeling nostalgic for some reason. So I started going through the box. There was that old leaflet. "Oooh, my princess bible". I thumbed through it finding passages highlighted and underlined.

"Every good and perfect gift is from above. James 1:17" I said out loud. "Certainly babies are gifts from God", I also said aloud to the open book. Oh my goodness. I came across high school love letters and my prom pictures. Now I was wearing a yellow nightgown, fluffy matching socks, a buttery soft silk scarf on my hair and a huge smile.

"Oh look how cute we are in these pictures". I came across zillions of photos of my high school besties and me wearing outfits and hairstyles that made me laugh out loud. Charla, Shelbi and Lilah were my junior high and high school partners in crime. I came across a whole photo album full of me in my hot pink prom gown and my prom date in his dapper black suit. Look how handsome he is. How did I let him get away? I'm 33, still not married and pregnant by, I don't even know who this guy is. My high school prom date was Kyle Langston. We had grown up together. He was not only respectful and raised right but also an honor student. He was so handsome, tall, kind and very funny. Kyle played high school basketball, football, ran track and he looked like it, very athletic. I was a cheerleader. So I was right there on the sidelines as he played. All the teachers loved him. His parents were always kindhearted, smiling and their home was inviting. He lived a short distance from me but in a house WITH PARENTS. That was pretty unusual in my neck of the woods. He was the youngest of five siblings or was it six? I just remember his brothers and sisters were also really good people. We would gather around the piano in their house, someone would be playing and we would all sing. They could all play the piano, including Kyle. After senior year I went one way to college, he went another. He is definitely the one who got away.

Going through the box of oldies but goodies was fun and took me back to my childhood. I was a good girl who became a fine young lady and ultimately a responsible independent woman.

"I have plenty of love to give, a great love for God, a clear sense of who I am. I could give a child direction and raise him or her to be a good and decent human being, right?" I said to myself. Before now, I had been talking to my loved ones about possibly adopting. I was getting older and had been longing to be a mom for some time. I really didn't want it to happen like this. I wanted a family, not a kid. I believe couples should be married before they have children, even before they have sex. I had given in to temptation a time or two or several. I'm not proud of that. I was beating myself up pretty good. Then I started praying again.

A few more prayers and long stares out the window and something was happening. I was actually getting excited about the whole finally becoming a mommy part but I was terrified of the circumstances and consequences that would come with being an unmarried pregnant woman. Now how do I go about going through a very public pregnancy? After all, I am on the news every day. We have to sign contracts promising to conduct ourselves in a way that doesn't shed a bad light on the news station or ourselves. I don't want anyone to think I don't take parenting seriously. I certainly don't want girls and young women looking at me and thinking this is ok. "Do as I say, not as I do?" I'm not a hypocrite. My actions have always backed up my words but this was a direct contradiction of everything I believe in. How will I get on TV and not wear shame right over top of that perfect makeup?

EIGHT

That afternoon my cousin

Max and his wife Zora were having a big party at their house to celebrate me being in town. My family is very close knit and every time I come home we get together for good food and great laughs. I was really looking forward to it.

Max's house is beautiful and even more so on a day like this when it's filled with family and laughing children. I'm the youngest of my cousins. So at this point they are all happily married with children and very well established. Most of the kids were hanging out in the basement or maybe I should say they were well entertained in the lower level of the family residence. Downstairs there was a game room, theatre room, computer room, workout room, a couple of bedrooms and bathrooms. Let's just say plenty of room to have a good time. I smiled at the thought of having my own child run around this house and at family gatherings someday. That could apparently come sooner than I had planned.

Upstairs the food was still cooking; bacon wrapped fried oysters, fish, pasta salad, BBQ ribs, macaroni and cheese, potato salad and several other things that didn't actually make it onto my plate because there wasn't enough room. I think there were even boxes of pizza. Yes, we like to eat! The meal smelled scrumptious.

"Scrumptious? Girl, we know where you come from. Don't use those big words with us Ms. TV News lady" they joked. Oh yes, did I mention the jokes? My family is full of them and wisecracks. It was more than good to be with people who knew me and loved me, who didn't lie to me and trick me. I must have given a million hugs, kisses and said a billion I love you's that day. After our last gathering a few months earlier my cousin Morris had gone to work the next day talking about how much fun we'd had. One of his coworkers said 'oh you must be hung-over' and Morris explained how we don't usually have alcohol at our family gatherings. The guy said 'and you stayed there almost all night? How did you have any fun?' That's so strange to me, how so many people equate alcohol with fun. I'm so thankful that isn't our thing.

My cousin Nora looked so pretty there at the gathering, as usual. She was more like my sister. She was my best friend. She was always rocking the best bags and boots. On this day, Nora's navy leather Prada purse and matching ankle boots looked like a million bucks. She was only wearing jeans and a sweater but she looked like she had just come from a photo shoot. Her sleeves stopped short of her stacked diamond and platinum bangles. Her large tennis bracelet made up completely of marquis diamonds matched her sixcarat wedding ring. She and her husband were high school sweethearts. I was more than excited to walk down the aisle in their wedding as a bridesmaid. I had hoped she would someday do the same for me. I'm still hoping.

"Ooooh Bubble Bath" Nora squealed referring to the color of my nail polish. "Your nails look marvelous Daf". She obviously enjoys good grooming just as much or even more than I do.

"I can't seem to stop wearing I'm Not Really A Waitress" she said.

"I can see why. That red is fabulous on you Nora. I had I'm Not Really A Waitress two manicures ago" I said excitedly.

Nora and I were doing our usual. We were talking, catching up and enjoying every second of it. Then she asked the question out of the blue.

"Daffodil are you pregnant?" she looked right into my eyes.

I had planned to tell her I thought I was pregnant but she beat me to it. I had barely only missed one menstrual cycle.

"I haven't taken a pregnancy test but yes I think I am. My body feels different Nora. I'm pretty sure I am pregnant. How in the world could you guess that?"

"Well, I know my little cousin and don't forget my husband and I have four kids".

"Oh yeah. There is that. If anyone is a pregnancy pro, it's you." We laughed. "Are you planning on spitting anymore kids out of that thing? You guys are putting buns in the oven faster than the yeast can rise".

"I don't even know what that means," she laughed. I told her all about what was going on with Oxford and me.

"Well, if he wants to get married maybe you should consider it. Why not get married before you start showing".

"That isn't even an option. Everything in me says this guy is trouble but I just didn't see it before now". I left out the part about the vasectomy. That fact was still neatly lined up and put away somewhere deep in my mind. It was too difficult, too painful, too frightening to think about. She hugged me and just like that day at the pool she held my hand in a different way this time. She was right there for me throughout my pregnancy and after. I didn't want that night or the trip to end. We all prayed together before leaving Max's house that evening and before I knew it I was high above Michigan looking down on my home state through a tiny airplane window heading back to Texas.

NINE

Back at home my well-manicured hands spent plenty of time clasped in prayer. I bought a pregnancy test but it was days before I could bring myself to take it. "Just take the test," I told myself. So I did. Nora and I were right. I was pregnant. There was no need but I checked, double and triple-checked the test. Are you sure? I wanted to ask the little, white, plastic stick.   Positive, positive, and positive it repeated.   That little plus sign seemed to be shouting at me. I caught a glimpse of myself in the mirror. Do I look different? Do I have a glow? I pulled up my shirt and I was actually a little disappointed to see my flat belly.

"Wow when did I get so much definition in my abs. Looking good girl," I told myself out loud. I was 5'10", 130 pounds. I tried to poke my stomach out to simulate a pregnant belly but my very arched back was far more curved than my tummy. So I'm nowhere near showing. That will give me a little time, for what? To pray God will help me work this out.

"Lord I need you now more than ever" I prayed more than a few times. Now I need to tell Ox. Oh my.
Oxford and I were watching television at my house and I just blurted it out.

"I'm pregnant." I sort of looked straight ahead and spoke the words into the air. I pushed each syllable right out of my lips. Rather than delivering the news to his face, it was more like I was making sure it was reaching his ear. When I turned to look at him he was smiling.

"You obviously didn't practice that delivery. Daf why did you tell me like that"? He laughed.

I really didn't know the answer. I hadn't practiced how I would tell him. I just needed him to know. So I gave him the information but it was like he already knew.

"I know why I haven't had a girl because only strong women have girls. You're carrying our little girl. You're one of the strongest women I know. Our baby is definitely a girl. Oxette Jr. You want a girl, right? Daffi what do you want to have?" he asked me as he smiled from ear to ear.

"What do I want to have? You want a girl"? I hadn't made it that far. I was still digesting having a baby in my unmarried tummy. Oh, right. I guess it will be a boy or a girl, huh? I sort of asked myself to myself while deep in thought.

"You've thought about this?" I asked him.

"Of course. This one won't be our only baby. I've thought plenty of times about having babies with you. I had a dream about it. We were shopping for baby clothes in my dream. I told you a long time ago. I love you. I'm in love with you. I want to marry you. Now you don't have a choice. You have to accept the ring," his words caught me off guard. He was still smiling. So did he seriously believe I no longer had options or was this just a light-hearted way to remind me of his marriage proposal? I hope I'm reading too much into that one sentence but the whole conversation was bothering me. I don't know how I thought the talk would go but I assumed it would be a lot different than this. I had really hoped he would be surprised by my pregnancy and tell me it was a miracle, that he must have Olympic quality little guys who could somehow swim past the whole vasectomy procedure. That didn't happen. He didn't mention the v-word and I pushed it right out of my mind, again. I had to.

I was familiar with the stereotype of women trapping men with pregnancy but I had never heard of guys trapping girls. I guess I had to come by that information the hard way. I felt that was exactly what was happening to me. Why would someone do something like that? How could I fall for something like that? I'm a smart, educated, professional woman, although I was feeling far from that at this moment. I felt naïve, embarrassed, betrayed and blindsided. Something was telling me the ambush wasn't over. How could I do this to myself? Maybe I was worrying too much. After all, he seemed excited about the baby and he has been asking me to marry him for months. Maybe he only told me he had a vasectomy to sound more responsible and not because he was trying to deceive me. Maybe I should just go to sleep because I'm sick and tired of thinking about it. No really.

Boy, am I sick. Ughhh the nausea. Yep I'm pregnant.

I was craving oranges and prime rib and I seemed to be eating both by the truckload. Anytime my pregnant belly started to feel topsy-turvy all I had to do was eat a little something or in my case I would eat a lot of something and the nausea would go away. Certain smells, that never bothered me before, suddenly were the worst ever. I still wore perfume but I would have to change scents just about every other day when a fragrance started to make me sick. Oxford's cologne made me sick and then so did Oxford. I called him one morning on my day off and his voicemail came on. I was surprised when he didn't call right back because he always wanted to spend my days off with me. He was "retired" from filmmaking so it wasn't as though he was at work and by this time he had quit his landscaping company. There was no talking him out of parking his riding mower for good after some guy told him a group of women were at a baby shower at one of the fancy houses and saw him mowing a lawn. The guy said the ladies laughed at him saying he must be broke if he was mowing lawns for a living.

"What do little boys make $10 per lawn? What a pitiful man," they supposedly said.

Landscaping was something Ox loved doing and he was great at it. Not to mention because he was so good, contracts were coming in left and right. He was making far more money in his lawn business than I was in TV news. I told him all of those things and really tried to encourage him to continue but there was no convincing him. He was done and all that new equipment sat unused as he fell back into his old, depressed slump. So the day I called and he didn't answer I was a little worried about him. He returned my call well into the evening.

"Hey! I called you earlier. What have you been up to all day?" I said excited to finally hear back from him.

"Don't grill me about what I've been doing. I know you called me earlier. I don't have to tell you what I'm doing everyday". He snapped at me? He was talking to me that way? I was stunned.

"What?" was all I could force from my lips.

"You heard me".

"Well, we're in a relationship. You're supposed to want to share your days with me and talk about what you've been up to and you certainly aren't allowed to speak to me the way you are right now." I said after a long pause. "Are you ok?" I asked him.

"You know what? I don't have to want to do anything and I can be as big of an (a-hole) as I want to be and there's nothing you can do about it. You're carrying my baby and you have to deal with me for the rest of your life. What choice do you have? I've been walking around on eggshells around you for too long thinking you might leave. It ain't sh** you can do about leaving now." He was now apparently Mr. Hyde. Dr. Jekyll was long gone and I was speechless. Yes, me Ms. Communicator who gets paid to talk for a living couldn't manage to squeeze one word from her throat, not a peep. Before I knew it there was no one on the other end of the phone so I didn't have to try anymore to make any sounds come from my mouth. Were we disconnected? I think he cussed me out and hung up on me.

"Oh gosh. This is worse than I thought." I told myself. What kind of maniac behaves this way? I don't think a guy has ever cussed at me before or hung up on me. He was downright nasty, mean and vicious. I didn't want to have to be attached to this guy for the rest of my life. That fact seemed to make him very proud. I was disgusted at the thought of him but even more so at myself for getting into such a mess.

After days of prayer for direction and guidance it was clear to me, perhaps this had previously happened to him. Maybe a baby had been used against him this way. I'm not sure why but victims have a way of going on to victimize others, doing the same wrong to someone else that was done to them. This is certainly the same disrespectful pattern of behavior Gerta displays when telling Oxford all the different names of women who are supposedly his mother. So he learned from her you don't have to be kind or respectful or even honest with people you supposedly love. If you don't learn love, respect or honesty at home is it even possible to ever ascertain those things? Meantime love, respect and honesty are so deeply engrained in me, I don't know how to behave any other way. After more prayer I sat down to talk with Oxford about it. I told him babies aren't little rolls of revenge designed to use against people. They are blessings from God.

"I'm sorry you feel that I'm now stuck with you because of the baby but that just isn't the case. I have plenty of options and putting up with someone who's going to disrespect me and use profanity against me are not included in those options. That just isn't something I'm going to deal with or tolerate".
"Don't tell me what you're not going to tolerate". He barked back.

"Hang on. This is a discussion, not an argument. Come on. We're going to be parents together. Let's decide right now to be great parents. Let's work together. We can make this whatever in the world we want to make it. Let's make it wonderful. Let's pray and fast about it. Let's be the type of parents we would have loved to have," I said smiling.

"Who the (f-word) do you think you are, Oprah? You ain't sh** but a baby mama," Ox stared me down as he delivered the sentences.

"This conversation is over. Please leave my house". I ordered. His disgusting profane vulgarity was making me sick.

"Gladly. Is this small piece of sh** even a house?" he insulted as he walked out the door.

The next morning I was making an appointment with a doctor I never thought I would see. I scheduled an abortion. On the day of the appointment I was distraught and walking around in a daze. It was so unnatural being there once I arrived in that office. I felt like I was in a place full of aliens or robots. I just felt weird. So I was supposed to walk in pregnant, with my baby in my tummy and walk out without her? I knew that would leave me empty in more than one way. God, what to do? What do I do?

Fortunately in the state of Texas you have to have two appointments before you can end your pregnancy. The night after that first appointment I was doing some heavy praying and I really wanted to go back for that second appointment. I didn't want to have to be attached to Oxford for the rest of my life and even more than that I didn't want this person who seemed so vicious and mentally unstable raising my daughter.

Then something happened that never had before. I heard the words "Oh ye of little faith". I was at home alone but I heard someone speak that sentence, that bible verse from Matthew 6:25. When I listened again, of course, nothing. Only silence filled my frilly bedroom but the words and the voice comforted me. With that one quick sentence I knew everything would be ok. I was reminded of who my Father is and the miracles that could happen as long as I am obedient to Him and as long as I have faith. I stopped crying, finished praying, went to sleep and thank God I never went back for that second appointment.

TEN

Maybe I was being dramatic, over analyzing Oxford's actions. Maybe I was wrong about everything. Maybe he really didn't try to trap me. "Lord help me please" I'm going to try one more discussion.

"Hey. Are you acting like this because you don't want another baby? I can't, I won't have an abortion. So..." I tried to continue but he flew off the handle.

"You're not killing my baby. Wait until everybody in Houston finds out. If you have an abortion I'll make sure everybody knows exactly what The News Lady did...Ms. Christian." Veins were bulging from his shaved baldhead. His voice was rough and loud. In every discussion lately he seemed more interested in outing me than in conversing with me to tackle the topic at hand. He always seemed more concerned with wanting strangers to know what was going on with me. Will he ever truly talk to me again? I'm not going to continue to put up with him raising his voice at me. For now, I ignored his ranting and his threats.

"I was saying. If you don't want the baby, I do. If you want to relinquish your rights as a parent then you just let me know what you want to do. I'm so confused by your behavior. You act like a completely different person since we found out I was pregnant. I feel like I don't know who you are." I said to him.

"Well, you're going to have a lifetime to figure it the (f-word) out because you're stuck with me now. I'm not giving up my (f-word) rights. This is my baby and I'm going to fight for custody. I'm going to make you miserable the rest of your life" his words trailing off as he left my house, slamming the door behind him. My framed picture by the front door swung side to side from the impact. What was with this whole thing about acting like the baby is some sort of a life prison sentence? Is that what babies have symbolized for him? Now he's hoping to inflict that same pain on me? Gosh where is the man I met, the man who is loving, thoughtful and kind? He seemed to be long gone. Would someone really fake being that way but why? Then just as fast as that wicked behavior showed up, it was gone. He was begging me to forgive him.

"You're so patient and nice to everybody but me. Come on Daf," he whined almost like a child. "Why can't you just be patient with me and give me another chance. I love you. Let's just get married. Let's be a family." He begged.

"What's the deal with you berating and disrespecting me recently? One day it's like you hate me, you're using profanity and today you're begging me to marry you? What's with you talking to me like that, using that language and being so doggone rude to me lately? No one has ever talked that way to me. I'm not used to anything like that and I'm not going to get used to being disrespected," I told him.

"I respect you more than any person in this world. You were talking bad to me. It was just a couple of arguments," he pleaded but we hadn't argued. I wasn't talking bad to him. After a long conversation I still didn't have any answers about his behavior.

"People argue," he reasoned. "Don't leave me Daf because we argued. Daffodil don't walk out on our family. We have a baby on the way. I'm so sorry babe I used that language when we were arguing. Let's not argue anymore". He was being so sweet I nearly got a toothache. I certainly had a headache. I truly wanted a family and not a baby so I was cautiously giving us another chance. Had a bun not already been in the oven I undoubtedly would have left this kitchen, turned off the lights and padlocked the front door of the house. In other words, I would have ended things with Oxford, for sure, and continued living my life in peace but because we were expecting a baby I truly tried to make it work.

I told my mom I was pregnant over the phone. She was in Michigan. I was in Texas. I wanted to tell her face-toface but I couldn't keep that secret from her. I knew she would want to know. I felt I had really let her down but she immediately forgave me and looked forward to loving the baby. Things were going pretty well with Ox and me. He was back to cooking fantastic meals for me, surprising me with the most awesome gifts I could imagine and making sure my pregnancy was as comfortable and as perfect as possible. I knew I needed to go to Michigan and make the announcement to my family. Of course, there were a few family members I told before I made the trip but now it was time to go home and tell everyone else.

I told Oxford my intentions and since we were making plans to eventually get married, he was going to come home with me. Bringing a man home to meet my family and telling them I was pregnant all in the same visit isn't how I imagined my loved ones would meet my husband. I still wasn't convinced he was my husband but I was hoping maybe that would change. Maybe he would somehow convince me he was my heaven sent soul mate who I want to spend the rest of my life with but that, I felt, would likely take a miracle. I still couldn't forget that behavior he had not so long ago shown me. My cousins who are more like my brothers and sisters would be hurt that I am unmarried and expecting. They certainly want better for me. We're all Christians and although they wouldn't approve, they also wouldn't condemn or berate me. I was looking forward to it but also nervous about the visit.

"I don't see the big deal. People have babies all the time" Oxford dismissed the importance of the trip.

"Well, this isn't the way we do things in my family. We have families, not babies," I answered.

"You're a grown woman. Why are you worried about what they're going to say? Why are you even telling them? Just let them find out" Ox was actually serious. I could tell right then we had very different opinions about parenting, family and about living for Christ.

"A grown woman? But I'm a child of God and I always will be. I'm not so much worried about what my loved ones will say. I just know they want better for me and for my baby, than for me to be struggling alone as a single mother. I deserve to be a wife, to have a husband and children, not just children and my family knows that. I know that," I could feel myself getting emotional. I still didn't understand how I could let this happen. How could I do this to myself? Then it hit me like it hadn't before. This man would soon have four babies by four different women and his second to the oldest child had already made him a thirty-year old grandfather. How could I get involved with these people? I wasn't normally reckless. I was usually responsible and I had spent my whole life trying to be obedient to God.

"How can you say just let my family find out. These are people I love and respect. I enjoy sharing my life with them. They gladly share their lives with me. I have waited my whole life to become a mommy and you don't think that's news I want to personally deliver to the people I love most in this world?" Tears were streaming down my cheeks, for many reasons.

ELEVEN

I caught a glimpse of my tear-filled face in the reflection outside of my Grandparents large living room picture window. The image showed a seven-year-old tomboy; only this was a sad version of myself. I had been running on rocks in the driveway, slipped and skinned my knee. My cousins all ran over to make sure their baby was ok. I was. After all the tears and dramatics, somehow I pulled through. I lived.

I found myself deep in thought about how much I loved going to my Grandparents' farm. They had pigs, cows, chickens, kitty cats roaming around and enough land to hold hundreds of homes but only one small house sat on all those acres. Then there was the chicken coop, the big red wooden barn, the storage shed, the vegetable garden, rows of corn and all the fruit trees. I must have climbed those things a hundred times. Some of the boys would get in trouble when they threw the apples at each other. I was always intrigued at how the fresh fruit just magically littered the ground around the tall trees, as if they spilled straight from the grocery store bags they were supposed to come in. On this day, which I was reliving in a very vivid memory of my childhood, I wasn't fazed by the bark digging into my hands while holding on tight to climb. No, today I was running free. I felt like a bird but only my feet were my wings. I was in and out of the tall stalks of corn and moving lightning fast up and down the rows of tomatoes, cucumbers, squash and zucchini. I also spent much of my time upside down doing cartwheels and walking on my hands. I don't know what it was about being here that made me feel like I had found my long lost friend freedom. The wind on my face felt like a million kisses from God out here.

The farm was what we called, out in the country in Milan, Michigan about forty-five minutes from where we lived in Wayne.   The trees seemed to stand taller out here. Everything from the birds to the breeze just seemed different, better somehow. Maybe I loved it so much because that was our meeting place. My whole family would gather, especially on weekends. We would all play outside together and top off the day with a wonderful meal that evening before we prayed together, then headed back to our homes. Sometimes we would enjoy our supper outside my Grandparents home, eating at picnic tables in a clearing near the garden. The snapshot in my mind includes my Grandfather's tractor parked underneath that old lamppost, both looking like antiques to me, even then. Even as he grew older my Grandfather was still meticulous about keeping the cow pasture, the hen house and even the pigpen far cleaner than some people's homes. I thought my mom was so lucky to grow up here on the farm.

My cousins and I loved feeding, petting, playing with and talking to the animals. We would also play tag and hide and seek. The absolute best was riding bikes down the dirt road my Grandparents lived on. Just getting from their house down their long, skinny driveway was a trek in itself, not to mention getting to the closest neighbor's house. Take that bike ride and you were ready for the Tour de France. Most of my grandparents' land held hundreds of trees. I loved to find rocks and see how far I could throw them. I would propel pebbles from my little fingers until my arm ached. Rock throwing is sort of a luxury not everyone has. Once I tried to throw a rock in my apartment complex and YIKES I could see it veering far from the path I had intended. Boy that thing traveled so far off course I think it packed an overnight bag. The rock slammed THUD right into a car window. The glass didn't break but of all the vehicles parked outside I hit the car of a woman who just so happened to be with her daughter, key in hand and about to unlock the car door. Oh my palms were getting sweaty.

"Why did I throw that stupid rock anyway?" I scolded myself. Maybe the woman wouldn't notice.

"That girl hit your car window with a rock," her daughter gladly pointed out. Did she really have to do that? Ahhhh SCREAM, panic. I thought to myself. Should I just haul off and run?

"Stupid rock" I thought again. I soon found out it was me, not the rock the woman thought was stupid.

"Was that what I heard, a rock hitting MY window? I know this little stupid heifer didn't hit my car," roared the lady and that was the nice part. By the time she had finished yelling at me, she needed to say, "Please excuse my French, my Japanese, my Greek, my Farsi and my Mandarin" but she didn't.

I seemed to think a lot about childhood during my pregnancy. I was also trying to gather things that were special to me that had been passed on to me so I could now pass them on to my daughter. There was that old, wooden, upright piano that I had asked my Grandmother for but she didn't give it to me. Ooooh I know, that beautiful brooch with the elegant pearl. Actually, I bought that or did I buy it for my mom and then claim it for myself? Gosh I really couldn't think of anything my Grandmother had given me. I felt sad about that for months especially because it was too late to get any gifts from her now. My Grandparents passed away two weeks apart, three years before my daughter was born. Nine months into my pregnancy I was going through the books in my home library. I call it my reading room. I found a bible addressed to me from my Grandmother. She wrote a little note inside, with a few bible verses, Matthew 8:26 "Why are ye fearful, O ye of little faith?" She paraphrased Matthew 6:31 "Do not worry about what you will eat, drink or wear" and Matthew 6:33 "Seek ye first the kingdom of God and His righteousness and all things shall be given unto you". Grandma, as I called her, had also written the date July 30, 1982, my tenth birthday. I suddenly remembered getting this gift from her. I think it was the only present she had ever given me.

"Wow this is the same bible verse I heard spoken to me early in my pregnancy," I said to myself and smiled. I called my grandmother a lot when I was away in Atlanta at college and after I started my TV news career in Kentucky. Every time I had a problem the solution she gave me was wise and always helped. Thinking back on it now, I remember she always answered the same way. She would tell me "seek ye first the kingdom of Heaven and all things will be given to you". Grandma "Why don't I have a husband yet?"

"In God's time sweetheart. Every woman is supposed to have a husband and every man a wife. Seek first, God and His kingdom and He will give you everything you need" my Grandma answered. She was a really intelligent woman who lived for Christ indeed. She certainly loved the Lord.

I remembered that conversation clearly as I held my gift from her in my hands and also in my heart. As I thumbed through the bible I started thinking about just how well everyone in my family is doing, just how close we all are. Even at our worst we are doing better than most because we still have joy, peace, loving homes, unconditional love, good sound minds and great food to eat. Although, sometimes that food may come from a loved one's table it was still a good meal prepared by loving hands in the comfort of home and we always prayed before we ate and before we left one another.

"Father we thank you for your love and protection. We thank you for our loved ones. We thank you greatly and graciously for all of the wonderful blessings you bestow upon us. We thank you for such great companionship, wonderful food, fantastic conversation and an all-around good time that you always bless us with when we are blessed enough to be in the presence of our family members once again. We love getting together with one another. For that, we thank you from the bottom of our hearts. We thank you that you make it possible for us to not only gather but to thoroughly enjoy the assembly when we unite. Lord we give you all the glory. We praise your very name and we ask you to bless our comings and our goings as we leave one another today and continue about our daily lives. We ask you to please keep us healthy, keep our love for you and for one another strong as we depart from each other on this day. Until we meet again please keep our family ties strong, our bond unbreakable, our homes happy, filled with peace and love and please keep our children and all of us wrapped in your arms and showered with your abundant blessings and miracles. Thank you for being our Father and our provider, our strength and our salvation. Please God bless our finances, our faith in you and bless us to continue to live obedient, Christ-like lives. Together we agree to have faith in these words and to continue to pray for one another. We love you Jesus. Please bless us and let us be blessings to others. Amen."

Any one of us could rattle off a heartfelt prayer at any given time, including the children. I thank my Grandparents, especially my Grandma for that. I couldn't help but think about my Grandmother's praying hands. Her bowed head, with two long pretty neat braids, had assumed that position millions of times before. She was a praying woman. When her eyes closed, knees bent, head lowered and her hands clasped, it was like picking up a telephone and dialing Him right up. She knew

God and He knew her. She loved Him and He loved her. She had been saved by God, had given her life to Him, since she was nine years old. She never uttered profanity; the taste of alcohol had never been on her lips, insults did not roll off her tongue and God's light radiated around her for everyone to see. She was kind, jovial, loving and sweeter than those buttery pound cakes that she baked better than anyone else in the world. She was also smart, an amazing speaker and a creative writer. I had found that thing I was looking for to pass on to my daughter. My Grandmother had given me an amazing gift after all. She may not have showered me with jewelry, money or even given me that old upright but she gave all of my loved ones and me something so much better. She gave us Christ.

TWELVE

Taking a peek out of the tiny airplane window became an all too familiar routine. This time I was headed to Michigan with Oxford. Things were going pretty well between us. I was hoping we were now on the right track and maybe wedding bells would be ringing in the near future. After all, we already had a baby on the way. I couldn't wait for him to meet my family, show him my grandparents' farm, which is still in the family. I wanted him to see my old schools where I was in the gifted and talented program, show him my church, and have him meet my pastor. Most of all I was really looking forward to Ox being a part of our family food fest. Every time I came to town we all gathered at someone's house with plenty of good grub and this time I would be delivering the biggest news of my life to the people who loved me most. You would think telling the news, after all these years of working as a journalist, was routine for me but not this information. I still didn't exactly know what I was going to say or how I would say it.

Oxford and I arrived at the Detroit Metropolitan Airport early on a March afternoon. It was just the first day of the month. So Old Man Winter was comfortable, settled and had no plans of leaving town any time soon. Ox was wearing short sleeves and had not even brought a coat. Maybe that was a sign that things weren't going as well as I was trying to tell myself. Remember, I still had not addressed the vasectomy issue and I purposely didn't tell him to pack warm clothes in an effort to avoid an argument. Before the trip I had tried to warn him that it was still very cold in Michigan and he interrupted.

"I've traveled all over this world. You don't have to tell me what the weather is like in Michigan," he snapped.

So there he was in 30-degree weather with his hands shoved deep in his pockets and he wasn't so much as wearing any sleeves. Nora picked us up from the airport. She was all smiles and eager to see him again. They had already met when she visited me in Texas.

"Hey Ox. You want to get your coat from your bag? It's much colder here than it is in Texas, huh?" He seemed aggravated that someone else was now also pointing out it was cold in Michigan and he didn't know it.

"We're not renting a car?" he not so quietly complained to me. That's considered kind of rude in my family. We go out of our way to do things like pick one another up from the airport, provide great hospitality when loved ones are in town, share meals, open our vehicles, homes and hearts to one another. He had always talked about how close his family was also and how they did the same thing. So although we hadn't discussed the details of this trip, from our many previous conversations I had thoroughly described my family and the things we do.

"I never rent a car when I come home. Someone's car will be available. We're only here for a weekend. I didn't think we needed to waste money on a car," I said. He seemed furious, not his words just his demeanor. I knew he was upset.

We were headed to pick up my mom at her apartment and I was pointing things out the whole way.

"Oh gosh. Look. That place might not look like much but they have the best Coney dogs in the world. We have to go there, Ox, while we're here" I told him.

"I am hungry. When are we going to eat?" he asked.

"We're going to pick up my mom and head to my Cousin Max's house. Everyone will be there and Max and his wife Zora are cooking a meal for us" I explained. Oxford didn't say a word. What's with him? I thought. Maybe he was near frozen and couldn't speak. After all, he was the only idiot in Michigan who wasn't wearing a coat. We took our bags inside my mom's and Oxford said, "We're staying here?" Of course, where else? We were only here a couple days and my mom had never even met this guy who I was now having a baby with. That just isn't the way we do things in my family. He seemed genuinely excited about meeting my mom and he told her so.

Fifteen minutes later at Max's house my Aunt Jocelyn was the first person we saw when we walked inside. Oxford seemed to get another burst of excitement. I had told him plenty about my Aunt Jocelyn. She helped spoil me rotten. She bought me my first car, a 1984 Red Ford Escort in 1987. I was 14 years old and could legally drive because my mother didn't. My driver's license was called a minor restricted license. Two years before that, my seventh grade class was traveling to Washington D.C. for a week. When I heard how much the trip would cost I thought, of course I'll go...eight years from now when I save up the $250. So what do you think Aunt Jocelyn did? She not only paid for my seventh grade school trip. She bought me a week's worth of clothes, an entire new wardrobe to visit our nation's capital. I had so much fun on that shopping spree buying my new Washington D.C. wardrobe. Nora is Aunt Jocelyn's daughter. Nora helped me pick the perfect slacks, sweaters, boots and even a couple of blazers so I could look neat and professional for my first visit to our country's capital. I was so thankful to her for that. It made me feel so special. In elementary school Aunt Jocelyn even bought me my violin that so irked my neighbors. I loved and took such great care of that violin. Oxford saw Aunt Jocelyn there as we walked into my Cousin Max's house and I saw him put his hand out. Did I ever tell him? Oh well, it isn't a big deal.

"Oh honey I don't shake hands" she said to him and Oxford stormed off. My Aunt Jocelyn is an even bigger germophobe than I am. Once the General Manager/President of my television news station and his wife invited me to have dinner at their beautiful Houston home. I took my mom and Aunt Jocelyn with me because they happened to be in town visiting. So here's the president of my news station standing in the doorway of his mansion. He's inviting us in, saying pleased to meet his guests. He extends his hand to my mom. They shake. He does the same to my aunt and here it comes.

"Oh honey I don't shake hands". Being in the news business he did what any journalist would.

"Well, why not?" He started inquisitively asking her questions about why she doesn't shake hands. "Oh so you think my hands are full of germs? Well, these hands prepared the food. Are you going to eat my food?" he smiled.

"It smells great. Let me see how it looks". She answered a quick yes after walking into the kitchen, seeing the spread and meeting his wonderful wife, who is an awesome and God-fearing woman. It was a friendly and even funny discussion complete with laughs and smiles but things had taken a different turn after Aunt Jocelyn said the same thing to Ox. He was clearly offended or upset or I don't even know what to call it. He was just being ridiculous. If we were in a cartoon we would have seen steam pouring from his ears.

I had decided earlier in the day to wait until everyone arrived and just before blessing the food I would tell my family the news. I'm pregnant. That way we could quickly move on to something else once I blurted it out. Then I could suggest "let's all thank God for the food". I could say an extra silent prayer asking God to help me get through this and we could eat. However, this grumpy goat I had brought with me wasn't making this easy for me.

"Hey. If everyone could quiet down for a second I have something to say. I'm almost three months pregnant". Family members were dropping like flies, people began fainting, chins were hitting the pretty square ceramic tile floor, blood pressure was rising or more like boiling over, cholesterol levels shooting and squirting oil from stunned onlookers, screams and gasps were filling the air. Then silence. Ok, so that's kind of how it went when I, one more time, daydreamed about telling them all at once. So after that terrifying thought I decided to just start telling people individually and before the night was over everyone there would know. Good plan? We'll see.

THIRTEEN

I was sitting on the couch nervously talking to Max.   "Max I came home to Michigan for a reason. I want you to meet Oxford because...because I'm pregnant," I revealed.   Max's face went from excitement to concern. Maybe he thought I was going to announce we were engaged but his expression clearly changed when I said 'pregnant'. This could have been July, because some fireworks were about to pop off. With my back now to Max, we were both facing Oxford. Still seated on the couch Max hugged me tight and talked to Oxford without letting me go.

"Hey man. Wow. This is our baby," he said referring to me. "What are your intentions with her? I mean what are you guys planning to do now?" Max was pleasant and kind and said what any father or loving big cousin would. Max knew I didn't have a dad who would say that for me, not a dad who was around. So Max was saying it. Max is seven years older than me and has always been a peacemaker from as far back as I can remember and we needed some peace made on this night. You will never guess how Ox responded.

"Look. I'm not about to be interrogated by you. So what she's pregnant. What's the big deal? She's grown. I didn't come here to meet y'all anyway. I only came to meet her mother," he said in the roughest, rudest, nastiest, loudest tone he possibly could. His raised voice even startled the kids in the basement. His mother, sisters and friends in Texas had asked me a number of times when I was going to marry Oxford and each time I pleasantly answered their questions and that was before I was pregnant. Now I'm sitting here a single woman, pregnant by a man my family has never even met and he can't give them or me the courtesy, the respect of telling my loved ones his plans with me? Are you kidding? I went off. I exploded with words that would make any sailor blush. I spewed language I didn't even know I knew. Cell phones were being whipped out of pockets to warn other relatives tonight's big dinner was now canceled. Don't come.

I regret allowing him to make me behave that way. Ox was smiling, "Yeah. Show them who you really are. You put on this Ms. Goodie Two Shoes front. Show them who you really are. Ms. Christian. Do they know you use words like that?" he kept taunting me. I was so aggravated that he would bring such chaos and disrespect to my family.

I'm not sure why he believes my personality is an act. Maybe my life is just so different from his he can't even believe someone would actually live the way I do, in peace. I know, sad right? My family members are the people who know me better than anyone else in the world. I'm not a phony person by any stretch of the imagination and certainly not with the people I love but he was convinced otherwise. Max and Nora finally calmed me down while other family members sat quietly, probably wishing they were anywhere but here. Needless to say, Oxford's trip was cut short. I stayed. He flew back to Texas. He immediately started calling me, first threatening to take me to court to get shared custody of a baby that had barely been growing in my tummy for two months. In many previous conversations he knew how I felt about family court. Parenting is a matter for parents, not a judge. Then he started threatening to sue me to allow him to go to my doctor's exams and my ultrasound visits.

I hadn't answered any of his calls. He was leaving all of these raging threats on my voicemail. I was still in Michigan trying to enjoy myself. He was determined not to let that happen. He called my cell phone and my Mom's home phone constantly. I finally answered and after relentless harassment about taking me to court, I told him we didn't have anything else to discuss. "I guess I'll see you in court" were my last words to him before I hung up on the lunatic still raging and yelling on the other end of the phone. The threats to sue were only meant to hurt me and to bring turmoil into my otherwise peaceful life. When I once again didn't accept his calls he left hundreds of voice and text messages apologizing profusely and professing his love for the baby and me. Would I really have to deal with someone like this the rest of my life?

After I arrived back in Houston his mother called me. Ox was also on the line. He said he thought Max was throwing low blows at him, making fun of him. Ox said he thought everyone, including Max, already knew he had been asking me to marry him and he believed Max was just trying to embarrass him because I hadn't agreed to accept the ring. He asked if he could have the phone numbers of all of my relatives who were there that day so he could apologize. My family certainly deserved it. So that's what Ox did. He called every one of my loved ones, said he was sorry and had extensive conversations about his plans with me. I do believe he was sorry but as I tried to point out to him, he has a history of going way too far and then saying he's sorry. That pattern goes as far back as the story he told me about being a jerk on the high school basketball team. He apologized for flying off the handle to his teammates but by then he had gone too far, they voted to kick him off the squad. I tried to get him to see that, to learn from this latest incident and to stop the pattern before it was too late but my words went in one ear and right out the other. I certainly was not used to having to put up with someone I didn't want to be bothered with. I was the "walk away" queen. In fact, I once broke up with a guy who lived in a beautiful penthouse apartment because he bought black out shades to cover his windows. He lived 25 stories in the air. "Who does that?" I asked my girlfriends.

"I know. You're right. Who does that? Who breaks up with a perfectly good man you've been seeing for more than a year for something that trivial? He proposed to you for goodness sake. You chose a ring. Why throw all of that away because he said he didn't always like the view?" Paige shot back at me.

"So we dated for fourteen months. It wasn't a waste. We had good times but I'd rather know he's not the one before we tie the knot. Could he not have just moved into a regular house then? Isn't part of the point of living in the penthouse enjoying the amazing view? Putting up blackout shades in the penthouse is such a turn off. It was like I instantly lost all feelings for him, all of them. Nope, still none. He is a great guy, just not my guy. It's not like we were engaged. The ring he bought was beautiful though," I rambled.

"You're a quack. When will you learn to compromise? Relationships, marriage are about sticking by someone through thick and thin," Nora scolded. Maybe that's what God was teaching me patience, compromise and commitment. I was well known for leaving this guy because he didn't have strong looking hands or that one because his eyes looked too beady or his jokes were more like stories that dragged on and on and after the punch line I found myself staring at him with disgust or the guy whose cheeks made his face look too jolly. So it's safe to say I had a track record of guys being like razors, disposable but on certain prickly legged days my pink triple blade glider meant far more than any man. Ok, that's a problem. I have long since known I have to improve in this area before God decides to bless me with my husband but boy this is one lesson I am learning the hard way. That's what happens when you ignore God, He'll keep telling you until you are forced to listen.

FOURTEEN

"Good Monday morning"

floated gracefully from my smiling lip-glossed mouth. "Hope you had a wonderful weekend. Have a great day". The words were melodic and in perfect harmony as they streamed from my lips. Is it bad to be overly kind to someone because you know it makes her mad? In my defense I don't know how to be anything else. I like being kind. Proverbs 16:24 "Pleasant words are as a honeycomb, sweet to the soul and health to the bones". How can you not love and live by that scripture? I enjoy being a nice person but my joy sure seems to make certain people angry. I knew ducking into my boss's office to say hello would, in her mind, be the same as trying to sick a hungry pit bull on her. She usually came to find me on Monday mornings to insult me. I anchored the weekend news and every Monday was the same.

"You call that anchoring? What kind of crap was that? You do such an awful job. I don't know how you ever made it into this business but I'm going to be the one to take you out. You won't be here much longer," she would routinely and gladly greet me with those words like clockwork on Mondays. On this day, I beat her to it. I came to find her for a proper

Monday morning hello. My joyous, happy greeting was met with a cold, vicious stare. Then she cut me off.

"Did you make an appointment to come into my office? I've told you don't so much as speak to me unless you make an appointment to do so," she yelled like a mad woman. I could feel the heat from her blood boiling as I walked away smiling. Her increasing anger was so intense I feared the ceiling sprinklers would start spitting water all over the newsroom. This had gone on for years, her beginning of the week verbal accosting. This little Monday morning entertainment of mine was actually very similar to the first time I met her. I had been on a one-week vacation from work when she started. When I returned I couldn't wait to introduce myself.

"Hello. I'm Daffodil. Some people call me Daf. It's so nice to have you here. How are you? I just wanted to say hello. I was on vacation. I'm back now. I'm excited to meet you. How are things so far?" I seemed to keep adding sentences because she wasn't saying anything, just staring at me like maybe I wasn't wearing any clothes or like my hair was on fire. After a quick feel in each place I realized, no I'm not nude. No, my hair isn't in flames and nope this is not going well. Why is she being so cold? Boy, if looks could kill.

"I know who you are. I know all about you. Don't ever come to my office again without an appointment," she almost whispered in the most unprofessional tone anyone has ever spoken to me. I was shocked.

"I didn't realize you were busy. I just wanted to say hello. It's nice to have met you" I smiled and walked away quite confused. My relationship with her never improved, no matter what I tried. I actually ended up buying her about a dozen bibles over the years. Thinking about that makes me laugh out loud. There was the Women's Bible, the Study Bible, the Holy Bible, King James Version, New International Version, Living Bible, Mother's Bible only to name a few.

With every Godly gift, I thought gosh she just isn't getting any nicer. I'm not sure if she was reading any of them but I sure hoped maybe if she was just around The Good Book the message would somehow seep into her pores and flush the devil right out of her. It didn't work. He must have been hanging on for dear life. I'm shocked at how long management allowed her to behave so unprofessionally and illegally. Abuse of power and harassment are against the law for a reason but I guess this company didn't get the memo. I think management's motto was "belittle" and "berate" but never "be kind". One sure sign someone shouldn't be in power is when they do things because they can and not because it's necessary or makes sense.

My own boss ambushed and sabotaged me every chance she got. For instance, I would get a special assignment in an open staff meeting. She would privately tell me there was a change in plans and my report was canceled. Then in a meeting with most of the staff present she would say with a big smile, "Hey how long is your piece that's airing tonight?" What a dirty rotten scoundrel. She actually pulled off telling me my story was canceled, not once but twice. After that, anytime she told me about an adjustment to my story I would send an email to her and several others confirming the change.

She must have threatened to fire me two hundred times and said she was writing me up even more than that. Once, she called me into her office. I went in and sat down. She promptly told me to stand up and look out into the newsroom. She pointed at the desk that was closest to her office. It had been reporter Shelley Sangler's desk. No one had seen Shelley in months. We were all wondering where she was. When my boss told me to look at Shelley's desk she grinned and said, "Shelley's stuff is gone. Your desk will soon look like that too. I'm going to do the same to you, throw you right out of here". She had such an excited look on her face. Someone walking by would have thought surely I was in the big office getting a promotion. She repeatedly told me of her plans to ruin my career. She bragged to me about how she had been successful at ruining many careers. She even named people by name. Insane right? A few times I tried to have a sane, professional conversation with her to get this madness behind us but no such luck. I went into her office (after making an appointment, of course. An appointment she canceled seven times before she allowed me to actually speak with her but who's counting!). I drew a line down a clean white sheet of paper. I wrote pros on one side and cons on the other. I asked her "What are some of the things you like about my work and the things you would like me to improve upon?" Her response?

"If you don't know the answer to that you are dumber than I think you are. If you don't know the answer that's proof you don't deserve to be here. You shouldn't have to come into my office and asked such a stupid question. You should already know," she ranted.

"We seem to have a very bad relationship and poor communication with one another. There's disrespect, disdain and dislike going on here and in my opinion those things are very unprofessional and don't belong in the workplace. There's just no room for that in a professional setting, in a place of business. We don't have to congregate after work but we are on the same employment team. We should respect and communicate with one another well enough to achieve the same professional goals," I responded. Did I just talk bad about her mother and didn't realize it? Good heavens I think this woman would hit me if she thought she could get away with it. She was furious. With hatred in her eyes and profanity spewing from her lips she informed me that would never happen. I would never be someone she would accept on her staff.

"Because you think you're better than everyone else. You think you're a superstar. You walk around here like you're a star in Hollywood. I'll make you a producer and see how much of a superstar you are then," she ranted. Was she serious? How do I even respond to that? What is this high school? No most high school kids are more mature than this. Is this middle school?

"Well, if that's the only issue then we can solve that right now because I don't believe I'm better than others and I don't believe I..." I calmly tried to explain but she cut me off with more profanity. My words seemed to infuriate her and she threw me out of her office. That went well. Not! A short time later she sent me to Dallas to cover an ice storm. She told me she chose me to go because "There have already been seven fatal wrecks in the storm. It's dangerous out there in all that ice and I just can't risk losing a good reporter". Wow, seriously? Did she just tell me my work, my life is so valueless, so worthless it doesn't matter if I live or die? Her harassment had reached new heights.

Even through it all, year after year, I remained professional and still loved the profession I had dreamed of working in since grade school, the profession God was blessing me to work in. I had been with this news station for years before she arrived and I wasn't going to run to another company just because she was unprofessional and didn't like me. I had my 401K, my pension plan, weeks of vacation built up. I knew God was protecting me and as much as she threatened to fire me, only He could take away the blessings He had given me. Although, I did have to cross every "T" and dot every "I". If I so much as sneezed she was accusing me of trying to spread viruses to kill the staff. I couldn't believe the things I was getting in trouble for. I couldn't believe she was getting away with it. When I complained to my Chief Executive Officer he would say things like "Oh you girls can never get along. What's wrong she didn't compliment your shoes? Well, there are three sides to every story. Hers, yours and the truth." I was so insulted and deeply disappointed that he didn't do anything about it but the more I prayed, the more peace God gave me. The devil or his workers couldn't steal my joy no matter how hard they tried.

FIFTEEN

The enemy seemed to be coming at me from all directions. Oxford was crying a lot. So is he the pregnant one? I had to look down at my very large tummy to confirm, yes, it's me who's expecting. Oxford and I were at Nordstrom shopping for baby clothes for our little Sweet Pea. We had already found out we were having a little girl but we started calling the baby Sweet Pea when we first discovered I was pregnant. So there we are in the middle of the store with our arms full of precious little pink dresses and super soft blankets for our baby girl and he starts balling like he is the baby.

"I had a dream about this. This is like de ja vu. I love you and Sweet Pea so much. I'm glad you guys are my family. I hope you accept the ring soon so we can get married. I love you" he barely got the words out through sobs. Tears were streaming down his cheeks as he hugged me. I was tempted to shove his thumb into his mouth and give him a blankie to cuddle but I hugged him back instead. We must have held each other there in the kids' department of Nordstrom for a good four minutes. What a sight, huh? This big bear of a man, towering over everyone else is sobbing loudly, uncontrollably saying how happy he is to be having a baby with me. Could we not have had this little exchange privately? Part of me was saying it was sweet but a larger part of me was feeling great concern. Was he emotionally unstable? He had been severely injured a number of times throughout his career as a stuntman. Oxford had suffered several concussions. Does he have a traumatic brain injury that has gone undiagnosed? His behavior was so all over the place. A brain injury just seemed logical but what do I do about it? How would you tell someone I think there's something wrong with you, something wrong with your brain? You're not right in the head. I have done stories with many brain injury patients; some of them injured riding motorcycles, a police officer shot in the head in the line of duty who survived, a 17-year-old young man shot in the head walking in his own neighborhood and a 15-year-old girl who was riding a skateboard down a concrete embankment and landed on her head. Oxford seemed to have the same symptoms as every traumatic brain injury patient I have ever interviewed, memory loss, violent outbursts and extreme mood swings from anger to sadness to uncontrollable crying. I tried to comfort him every time he cried. His happy tears about Sweet Pea's arrival could hit at any time, the mall, the restaurant, at home or in the Chinese buffet lunch line but his tears of joy just seemed to me to be emotional instability.

Being pregnant made me re-visit a lot of my happy childhood memories. I was constantly talking about when I was a kid. My pregnancy seemed to have the opposite effect on Ox. He seemed to get frustrated when he tried to remember his childhood and couldn't.

"I just don't remember Daf. Why do you remember? How can you remember back that far? Ok seriously what is the earliest memory you have?" he asked me.

"I remember being three years old and going to Niagara Falls on the Canadian side. It was beautiful. That same summer we also went to a wax museum on Mackinac Island and I was terrified when what I thought was a wax figure started moving. I ran right out the door, down the street and over railroad tracks before my mom could catch me. We were there with my Aunt Jocelyn and her two kids Nora and Josh and my Aunt Jeanette and her four boys Randall, Max, Morris and Matthew. We had all piled into my Aunt Jocelyn's large, brown Chevy station wagon and took a few road trips. We had great times," I answered. He seemed so helpless and aggravated that he couldn't remember. I tried to help him.

"Try thinking of an old snapshot and that photo might help you remember" but he couldn't even recall any old pictures. That was really odd to me. He seemed like a poster child for a brain injury patient but why was I the only one who believed that?

His memory, or lack thereof, actually scared me one time in particular. It was June 2006. I was six months pregnant and waddling like a duck for more than one reason. Yes, I was expecting and on this day it was raining cats and dogs and I was out reporting in torrential rains. I was doing live shots, giving live reports, every 30 minutes for our national newscast. So my reports were airing across the country. I was six months pregnant and standing in dirty floodwater. On top of that, school had been canceled because of the bad weather and several little boys were out in the high water with me. They were trying to catch the snakes that were swimming around in the water. I know, right? So I mentioned that on the air and one little boy came over to me during one of my live reports so I talked with him on the air. "Hey this water isn't sanitary. It isn't safe for you to play in it. It's dangerous for several reasons. You guys need to get out of it and go home," I scolded, getting in a little Mommy practice.

"We will. There are just so many snakes in this water. It's fun. We caught a water moccasin and let it go back into the water. Now we're trying to catch some more," he smiled, wading his hands through the water and looking intently into the murky floodwater as if searching for treasure. As I talked about Houston's high water the rain continued to fall. My face was getting wet but my bright blue news rain jacket and black rain pants were keeping the rest of me dry. My little black TV News baseball cap kept most of the water from my eyes. I'm not sure if that was a blessing or a curse because then I saw it. Live on the air I pointed out ripples in the water where it looked like something was swimming close to the surface. The cameraman zoomed in and you could clearly see something moving, gliding by. That made the boys very excited and they went running after it. The national news anchor then scolded me right there on the air, telling me to get out of that water.

"That's certainly no place for a pregnant woman. Surely there's another reporter who cover the flooding and you can find another assignment" he seemed genuinely worried. I thought it was strange that a complete stranger was more concerned for my safety than the newsroom full of people who I had worked with for years. Anyway, that thought quickly left my mind. Well, I am wearing tall, thigh-high rubber rain boots. The floodwater was never touching my skin. After I finished my report I made the boys get out of the water and go home and I said a little prayer as I made my way back to the news van. I'm not sure why but 1 Peter Chapter 5 verses 6-8 came to mind. "Humble yourselves under the mighty hand of God that he may exalt you in due time. Casting all your care upon Him. He cares for you. Be sober, be vigilant because the devil walks about seeking whom he may devour".

I climbed back into the news van and I had a million phone messages. My family members were less than thrilled to see pregnant me standing in dirty water surrounded by snakes. Ok so it sounds awful now but it really wasn't that bad. Leaving wasn't an option. I still had hours of live reports to deliver before I could call it quits for the day. So I just wanted to talk to someone who wasn't scolding me. I just wanted to laugh for a minute before getting back to work.

I called Oxford and said, "Bird Flu" and I broke into laughter. He didn't know what in the world I was talking about. When we first met, Ox and I had a running joke about Bird Flu.

The term was fairly new and it sounded really funny. We would talk about how the poor sick flu filled bird was probably curled up on her couch wearing fluffy, slouchy socks, a thick cozy bathrobe, wiry uncombed hair with bags under her eyes, a thermometer sticking out of her beak and sipping Theraflu or hot, honey and lemon tea. We could clearly imagine those poor little birdies that had come down with the flu. So Ox would call me or I would call him and we would say "Bird Flu" and crack up laughing or if we were with each other we would get a certain look and the other one would say "Don't even say it" and we would shout "Bird Flu". I know, it was goofy but it was really funny to us, at the time. Sometimes we would use it in a sentence "Hey Bird Flu what are you doing? What the Bird Flu was that? Oh I'm not doing much just Bird Fluing around." Apparently it was such an inside joke that Ox tucked it away deep inside and forgot about it. I tried to jog his memory but he had no clue why I was saying "Bird Flu" to him. Even when I reminded him this was a running joke between us he still didn't remember, not even a little bit.

He also forgot our B.Y.O.R. joke. Bring your own roll. When we first started dating he said he didn't know if he could afford me because "you're hard on a brother's toilet paper budget". Before my pregnancy I suffered horrible nasal congestion and allergies. I'm not sure how or why it disappeared after my pregnancy but it did. Anyway, I had to blow my nose five million times a day from the time I was a teenager until the day I gave birth. So when Oxford and I met, if we were at his house he would quickly run out of Kleenex when I was around and I would start in on his toilet paper roll. Soon he would start doing a mock pat down, pretending to search me when I arrived at his house and he would say today is B.Y.O.R., Bring Your Own Roll and I could only come in if I had done so. Then he would say, "Ok I'll let you in. It's ok if you didn't B.Y.O.R. I'm just going to have to try to get another Hollywood contract, sell another award winning screenplay to be able to buy enough tissue to keep up." He soon got Sam's

Club and Costco memberships and my nose and I had all the rolls we needed. He even forgot that. How on Earth can anyone forget something like that? He joined, not one, but two wholesale membership clubs for Pete's sake because of my nose blowing and he forgot?

Wow, frightening.

SIXTEEN

Our second visit to Michigan went much better than the first. By this time, Oxford had called and apologized to my family members individually and each accepted his apology. We went back to Michigan for the baby shower. I was seven months pregnant and enjoying every second of it. I felt so beautiful, so feminine. When we shopped for my dress for the baby shower the outing was an event in itself. Nora, Paige and I had a blast picking the perfect dress. We walked around the fancy mall admiring the amazing clothes, bags, shoes and jewelry. I found a long silk maternity maxi dress that was on sale but it made me look like a million bucks. I was so excited about becoming a Mommy and even more stoked about celebrating my pregnancy with the people I love most in the world but before we go a step further the pregnant lady has to get a bite to eat or a few bites. We talked and laughed at that restaurant over appetizers, entrees, soups and salads for hours. They ate too!

Michigan summers are so beautiful. It was July and I was in heaven being there at home with my family. Nora and Paige, had pulled off the baby shower of the century. Everything about it was perfect and I'll remember it forever. The shower was held at a restaurant that sits right on beautiful

Belleville Lake. The decorations were elegant and breathtaking. There was even a life-size maternity mural of me.

"Oh she's so beautiful," I squealed not realizing I was kind of complimenting myself by admiring the "me" mural hanging on the wall. When the event first started the sun was glowing, reflecting off the water and there was a magical breeze blowing the warm summer air around. The dining room was enclosed on three sides and the fourth glass wall was open allowing the shimmering sunshine and the soothing summer air to come in, putting them both on the guest list. The food was perfect, seafood, steaks and these cheesy potatoes I just couldn't get enough of. A marvelous meal, an amazing atmosphere and lots of loved ones surrounded me. Even the men had a great time including Oxford. At my baby shower thrown by my co-workers in Texas the guys also had a great time. Ox won all the games. He's a little bit competitive to put it mildly. That was when I was going through my Mexican food craving and the shower was held at a Mexican restaurant there in Houston. My work shower was also an absolute blast. My friends slash colleagues threw the fiesta for me in late June.

I was three and a half months pregnant when I announced my pregnancy at work. Not everyone was kind. Some people were downright mean. I was thankful for the ones who were not. I, of course, had already broken the news to management. I was right at three months along when I did that. I explained how I was getting older and decided to have a little one before my biological clock became rusty, dusty and stopped ticking. Thank God my big boss was supportive. We talked for a long time about my pregnancy in his office. He had known me for years and I was grateful to hear him say I would make a great Mom. I had waited my whole life for that title of Mommy and I was really glad when people shared in my excitement. By this time I had talked plenty with God, gotten the sad feelings about not being married behind me, I had beaten myself up plenty about that and now I was truly looking forward to my bundle of joy that God had blessed me with. I had accepted God's plan as my plan. My daughter is definitely part of God's plan. The feelings of failing as a Christian weren't completely gone but Proverbs 16:20 "He who handles a matter wisely shall find good: and whoso trusts in the Lord, happy is he" and Proverbs 17:22 would often come to mind, "A merry heart doeth good like medicine but a broken spirit dries the bones". When you have faith, whatever Satan means for bad, God will truly make it good. There at my baby shower in Michigan it was so much fun watching everyone enjoy themselves. I loved knowing we were all there on beautiful Belleville Lake to celebrate my baby girl. Before the big bash was over the moon made its appearance and its bright reflection was dancing in the water. There must have been a million singing stars glistening in the night and the party was still going strong. I stood there just outside the dining room on the wooden balcony with the waves making a melody of their own. The moon and the twinkling stars together were almost like flash bulbs sparkling from heaven; as if the celebration of my precious baby girl was so important even the angels were snapping pictures of the event. I pulled my journal from my large leather Chloe bag. I had been writing "Love Letters" to my daughter for months now. I was so anxious to meet her and chat with her so I started talking to her early on, out loud as well as in writing. Through these letters in this journal I was giving her a play by play of my thoughts, emotions and my love that was growing for her every second. On this night I described just how special the shower was and how everyone couldn't wait for her arrival. I described the delightful dinner right down to the smallest detail. Soon it was time to call it a night. It's like that with my family. We love hanging out with one another until the wee hours of the morning. That is also one of my greatest blessings. We prayed together before leaving thanking God for his many blessings including the little baby that was growing inside my tummy.

SEVENTEEN

It was Friday, my day off. I went to the hair salon where the stylist worked her magic on my hair. I also got a relaxing massage, manicure and pedicure. I was very pregnant and Sunday was my due date. My mom was in town anxiously awaiting the big day. After the soothing salon visit we went shopping until the mall closed. Then we stopped by Target for a few more items. I had been out and about all day and I wanted nothing more than to go home and devour a big bowl of Rice Chex with cold milk, bananas and honey, my latest craving. I had also been wolfing down Cheesecake Factory as if it was the last time I would ever get my hands on the stuff. We carried the shopping bags into my house and the phone was ringing. It was about 11:30 at night by this time.

"Hello," I answered. My Cousin Josh's wife Jinger (that's Ginger with a "J" she would tell people) was on the other end.

"Hey. What are you up to?" she asked. I had already washed my hands and as we spoke I was preparing my much wanted bowl of Rice Chex.

"So you did a lot of walking today, huh? Is that baby ready to come yet?" Jinger asked. I had just sat on my couch, dipped my spoon into my delectable, mouthwatering meal and scooped up a spoonful of scrumptiousness when...

"Huh (breathing in air). Gasp. Oh my gosh. My water just broke," I shouted. My eyes were wide with excitement. Right on cue after Jinger asked if the baby was ready to come the baby answered for me. All I could think about was "I finally get to meet her". I made my way to the powder room and my water broke and broke and broke and broke. I ran a shallow bubble bath and without submerging myself in the water I quickly bathed, put on a pretty dress and fixed my hair. I know, but this is a big event. I wanted to be pretty for it. Oxford arrived at my house and he drove us to the hospital. By this time Ox and I were not in a relationship together but we were going to be parents together. I had never gotten over the ugly way he behaved including that first time in Michigan disrespecting my family and me that way and he never really proved to me he was 'the one'. He had never proven to me that he was a good and decent human being. In fact, shortly after the Michigan baby shower I tried to discuss the vasectomy issue with him and he said he didn't know what I was talking about. He lied to my face saying he had never told me he had a vasectomy. Lying, being disrespectful and he had started to verbally blow up at me at any given time. He certainly wasn't the one. I no longer had a choice about Oxford being the father of my child but I did have the option to leave the relationship and I did. The final straw was when Ox came to my house and he smelled like outdoors, not musty or a bad body odor but just not a clean smell. He had been out at his friend's horse barn and I could tell. Everyone knows how sensitive a woman's sense of smell is when she's pregnant. So how could he not understand when he sprawled across my bed smelling that way and I asked him "Honey will you take a shower first please? You smell like outdoors"? I was pleasant. I could not have been any nicer but that didn't stop him from being nasty. He always seemed to make every conversation about money.

"Don't tell me not to lay on your cheap bed. I don't want to lay on these cheap sheets anyway," he barked. I don't understand people who do that. My bed and sheets are not cheap but did he think saying they were would suddenly make them poor quality and what did poor quality linens have to do with his pregnant girlfriend not liking his smell and asking him to shower? I didn't get it.

"I'm just saying the smell you have right now is making me nauseous," before I could finish he interrupted.

"You f****** b****. You think you're so much better than everybody else. You think you don't stink?" Wow the b-word and now I stink? That is certainly new. I asked him to leave my house. He grumbled and fussed all the way out the door. What a sad existence, I thought. Why would someone want to live that way? I hadn't talked much to Ox since that day but now the baby was coming.

Ox, my mom and I made it to Sugar Land Hospital around 1:30 a.m. It's just a few minutes from my house. The nurse checked me into a room. I was officially in labor. I called my doctor on his cell phone and he said he would see me in the morning because I would likely be in labor all night. That sounded more frightening than it was. I was just so excited I was finally going to meet this little person after all this time. I changed into one of my gorgeous pink gowns. I also had fluffy socks with me but for the moment I was comfortable and I enjoyed seeing my freshly painted toes. "It's A Girl" was the color I was wearing and those were the words on the sign I had hanging just inside the door. My contractions were getting closer together and when a bad one would hit I would breathe through it. The three of us, my mom, Oxford and me sat talking there in the hospital room happy the big day was finally here. Ox rubbed my back and feet slathering on lotion as he massaged and boy was that comforting. We had also learned the "labor rock" in Lamaze class. That's where we both stand up, I hold Oxford with my hands folded behind his neck and with my head and body leaned forward we rock back and forth.

That really helped soothe my tummy when the contractions hit. I was lying down on the bed again and I actually fell asleep for a few hours. I was surprised at how much sleep and rest I was getting while in labor. There was also a couch for my mom, a comfy reclining chair for Oxford to sleep on and plenty of pillows and blankets. This room had fancy dark cherry wood floors, was very comfortable, had new furniture, flat screen TV, large picture window, a breathtaking view of the city there from the eighth floor and it was beautiful. When my doctor said I would be in labor all night I imagined hours of sweaty pain and torture but it wasn't like that at all. The anesthesiologist showed up to give me an epidural around 5:00 a.m. I received the pain reliever and then I slept some more. My doctor woke me around 11:00 a.m. I awoke to a zillion voice mail messages on my cell phone. I called Nora and Paige back on conference call. I was ready to start pushing at 11:15 a.m. I calmly told them so. My two BFF's stayed on speakerphone as their voices and those in the room coached and encouraged me through my delivery. The nurse rolled a floor length mirror to the edge of the bed and I could see my daughter making her entrance into this world. I was so glad to have my smiling mom, full of love, right here by my side. God had truly blessed me with a perfect pregnancy, labor and delivery. Less than fifteen minutes after I started pushing at 11:26 a.m. my princess was born.

EIGHTEEN

I had my own personal chef.

His name was Oxford. He was awesome after the baby was born. He basically moved into my kitchen. Any meal was just a request away. I was getting plenty of great food and even more much needed sleep. I was well rested, well fed and well, I was so very smitten. My daughter was the love of my life. I was so glad to finally have her in our home. I had a "my home" for quite some time. I never, in adulthood, had an "our home". Now I do. SQUEAL. Ox and I weren't together but at least he seemed to be trying now, trying not to be a pain in my backside and succeeding at being more respectful. I so enjoyed watching him love and take care of our daughter. He didn't pop the question again but he did bring the ring to my house and leave it sitting in the opened box on my kitchen counter. He came to my bedroom before he left to go home one night and he told me he was leaving something in my kitchen that belonged to me. I nearly mistook it for a cube of ice and plopped it right into my glass to cool my sweet tea. I was really pulling for us, rooting for us, hoping by some miracle from God we would make it. I truly hoped although we started off wrong, by having a baby before marriage, we would soon make it right. However, so many things still weren't right. Ox was fine with coming to my house to cook but he was distant. He was expecting me to marry him but other than preparing my meals, I didn't see him.

I hadn't been to work since giving birth. I emailed photos of me with my beautiful bundle of joy the day she was born and watched the news that night as the snapshots covered the screen announcing my sweet pea's arrival. I took four months off work and it wasn't long before my little princess joined me in my looking-out-the-little-window ritual. She was perfect on every airplane ride. We vacationed, relaxed and of course, I took her home to Michigan to meet more people who quickly fell in love with her. The church was packed for her dedication to Christ and keeping up with our regular routine, what seemed like my whole family went back to my Uncle Garret's house eating, laughing and talking well into the night. My princess was hugged, kissed, held and loved enough to last a lifetime. The feeling of holding her tiny body in my arms and kissing her sweet face was one I never had before. I was enamored. She was truly a blessing, a gift from God. I was a mommy.

He was found dead, shot to death on his front lawn. Neighbors in the Northwest Houston community heard the gun blasts and called the cops. This upper crust neighborhood, these homes were full of residents who were not used to things like gunfire and murder. Police arrived finding the husband dead in the front yard and his wife and two kids shot to death inside. It was a murder suicide welcoming me back to work after my four-month maternity leave. Covering such a horrible story, especially on my first day back, was the last thing I wanted to do. Turns out he had been abusing her for years. She finally got the courage to leave and that monster didn't let her. He would rather see her and his own children dead than to see them at peace.   The family was new to the neighborhood. He had transferred to Houston from Denver just a few months earlier. The Aeronautics Engineer had the respect of some of the nation's finest. It was respect he didn't deserve. This green-eyed, olive skinned, dark haired poor excuse for a human being had the look of an actor and the heart and soul of a vicious demon. A neighbor who was framing a portrait for the family showed me the photo, which clearly captured a seemingly happier time. The woman had beautiful brunette locks that draped across her shoulders and fell nearly to her belly button. The kids were each little spitting images of their parents. Looking at the picture made me even sadder. On this day I was particularly emotional. I was having a tough time leaving my baby. I missed her so much it brought me to tears and now I was standing in front of a home where two babies were inside dead at the hands of their own father. By the time my daughter was born I had been a TV News Anchor and Reporter for eleven years and although I've heard plenty of journalists say you get used to things like this, I never will. Someone's tragedy will never become routine to me but I am professional. So, of course, when it came time to go "on" the viewers had no idea I had been crying all-day and praying for this lady, her babies and their mourning loved ones. I don't like covering crime stories.   Don't get me wrong the community needs to know when something bad happens. It reminds us to be careful, that there are crazies among us and alerts us when and where we need to be extra cautious but news stations also have an obligation and a responsibility to give good news. I had spent my entire TV news career fighting for good stories, to cover the accomplishments, the good things people are doing. I love, as a viewer, watching and as a journalist covering stories that encourage and inspire. I think it's the absolute best to do stories that help people.

Think of it this way. If you could stand on a perch in your community and everyone in town could hear what you are saying, what would you say? Would you only announce bad news or would you have an obligation and an appreciation to also give good news? Of course you would invest just as much time in giving good news. After years of being praised by other bosses for the types of stories I cover, I was now dealing with someone who was attacking me professionally for personal reasons. My boss just didn't like me. So with every story I pitched she quickly shot the idea down. I was getting written up for "not pitching stories". She said as long as I pitched doing an encouraging story she would consider that "not pitching a story at all" but doing inspirational stories was bigger than me. I was doing good things for the entire community. I was doing God's work. I would receive letters and voice messages by the busload when I did encouraging stories.

"Watching your story was like hearing a message from God," one woman wrote in response to a story I did about World War Two veterans and how their stories are dying with them. The woman told me her dad was a WWII vet and she had never spoken with him about his experience in the war. She told me after watching my story she took vacation from work, packed an overnight bag and stayed a week at her parents' home. They spent days talking, laughing and enjoying one another. They hadn't done that in years. She had been wrapped up in her career for decades and hadn't spent much time with her parents. She told me she was grateful God had used me to re-connect her with them. For the first time she heard all about her dad's time in combat. Telling the stories made him feel appreciated and respected. Hearing the stories made her feel special and proud of her father. That quality time they spent was something no one could ever take away.

Another viewer, a man, wrote to me that I changed his grandson's life. My story was about a young man who went to a bar, got drunk and then attempted to drive home on his beautiful bright red motorcycle. At 130 miles an hour the 26year-old lost control of the bike. His body went flying into the cement highway divider. He was moving so fast his leg was sliced off by the concrete median and it was left lying there on the highway.   His body banged, slammed, rolled and repeatedly hit the pavement and he finally landed far off the road in a wooded area. The motorcycle was travelling so fast it continued on without him for more than a mile down the highway. He lay there bleeding and in the worst pain of his life for nearly three hours. Emergency officials finally found him. His life was saved but he would never be the same. After watching this story, the man wrote to me that his grandson had been drinking heavily on weekends and even driving and the grandson wasn't ashamed of it either. After watching my story the man said his grandson had vowed never to take another drink. His grandson had even started going to church with him.

"It just isn't worth it," he told his grandfather but the lives I was impacting, all the letters that were being written to me didn't seem to matter. It seemed the more people liked me, the more my boss couldn't stand the very thought of me. Once I pitched a story about a domestic abuse victim. She lived with her boyfriend in an apartment and one afternoon he shot her in the head. She survived. She actually stayed conscious the whole time. This 22-year-old young woman was miraculously still alive. Her boyfriend, until now had been mild mannered and had never even raised his voice to anyone, let alone his hand or a gun.

"I can't believe you did this to me. Where did you even get a gun? Hand me your cell phone so I can call 911," she yelled.

"I've just been so depressed. I thought you were going to leave me. So I was going to shoot you then myself," the 23year-old softly confessed as he dialed 911 and handed his girlfriend the phone. In the taped 911 call I obtained later you could hear the young lady calmly telling the dispatcher she had been shot in the head by her boyfriend. It was a miracle she lived but then after a long stay in the intensive care unit, after several surgeries and after finally being released from the hospital she went home to an eviction notice. Apartment management was throwing her out because according to the paperwork "we have a zero tolerance policy on violence". Are you kidding? She's the victim of violence you idiots and now she's being victimized again by being thrown out. After her boyfriend shot her in the head she was able to call for help. Paramedics and doctors, through God's grace, had saved her. Police arrested him. He pleaded guilty and was thrown in prison for decades.

With her hair shaved from such a severe head wound and with years of rehabilitation ahead of her, she finally got out of the hospital and went home to an eviction notice? She called me for help. I couldn't believe she was being forced from her home because she was a victim of violence. I pitched that story in the meeting and I was written up for not having an adequate story pitch. My boss could play games all she wanted but I wasn't going to let this one go. I pitched this story every day for three weeks and I was written up every day for three weeks. God, apparently stepped in and the day before this young lady's belongings were to be sat out on the curb, I was finally able to do the story. Thanks to the TV coverage she was able to stay in her apartment. Property management apologized "for any inconvenience we caused". I received so many compliments on that story and a sea of letters from domestic abuse victims and other members of the community thanking me for helping. After that, I was taken off the air as a reporter for more than a year. My boss didn't put anything in writing. She didn't tell me she was taking me off the air. She just made sure I never received a story. I wasn't allowed to cover the stories I pitched because my boss would say my pitch was a "weak, non-story" and I wasn't assigned a "news of the day" story. I would come into work and the three days a week that I was supposed to be reporting I was basically riding along with a photographer, shooting video for stories the anchors would read. Then I would anchor the newscast on Saturday and Sunday, come in on Monday to insults and threats of taking me off the anchor desk by my boss. After one morning meeting where I was, again, not assigned a story I had to have a more in depth chat, no a pow wow, with the big guy. I went to the bathroom and there on that disgusting public restroom floor I bent before God.

"What are you doing to me? You blessed me with this job, blessed me to work in a career I dreamed of for years. You told me not to leave this news station even in the midst of all this madness. I'm doing everything you've told me to do. I've been obedient. I'm speaking for you just like you asked me to. Why have you left me?" Tears streamed down my face. Fortunately this was a one-toilet restroom and not a row of stalls. So there I was alone with God talking to Him in the bathroom at work as if He was there and He was. Deuteronomy chapter 31, verse 6 covered me like a blanket. Each letter of every word wrapped around me. "Be strong and have courage. Fear not, nor be afraid of them. For the Lord thy God He is with you. He will not fail nor forsake you".

I not only felt the words, I heard the bible verse loud and clear. Maybe it was a co-worker pulling a practical joke on me. Maybe someone was standing outside the bathroom door reading Deuteronomy out loud for fun but whatever the case; those five sentences were exactly what I needed. I washed my face, dusted myself off and left to do my usual, ride along with the photographer while he shot video. Then just before news time there was breaking news. Thank you God. All the other crews were too far away and I was the only option. One of the world's largest energy companies was crumbling. After days of rumors that Enron was falling and days of the Enron bigwigs ensuring everyone everything was fine, now employees were filing out of the towering downtown Houston building like ants. The workers were carrying all of their belongings in cardboard boxes. This first round of Enron layoffs turned out to be only the tip of the iceberg, which is an ironic analogy because in many ways Enron is exactly like the Titanic. Both were huge, unstoppable, and unsinkable or so everyone thought. Titanic, Enron fail? No one thought it could happen but to the shock and horror of people all over the world, it did. The next morning in our newsroom meeting where we discuss what stories we'll cover for that day, the producer of the newscast complimented me on the breaking news coverage and many in the room chimed in in agreement.

"You kicked butt. Every other station's stories merely glazed over the fall of the company. Blah blah blah multibillion dollar company going under. You got personal with employees and told some heartfelt stories. Viewers could relate to these people who were losing so much. Our hearts went out to those workers who thought they had job security then suddenly found themselves unemployed," he paused. "Boy it seems like you haven't been reporting much lately. That was the first report I've seen from you in a while. What, has anchoring just been keeping you busy?" the producer added. I couldn't believe, day after day he couldn't see her tricks and ambushes to keep me off the air or maybe he did and this was his way of bringing attention to it. After all, we had already watched her harass and fire several others simply because she didn't like them. No one wanted to be next. I couldn't believe this was allowed to go on but it did year after year. When the station was starting a 5pm newscast she called me into her office and told me so. She told me "If it's the last thing I do I'm going to keep you from anchoring the 5pm news. It won't be easy. After all, you're charming. The viewers love you. You have just about the best personality of anyone I've ever met. You are the obvious choice. Sure it won't be easy but I'm always up for a challenge". Once the decision was made I was called into my News Director's office for a meeting with her and my CEO. My CEO told me I wasn't getting the 5pm because I didn't dress appropriately, that I dress too fancy. I couldn't believe my ears. Style is something I've always had plenty of. If there is one thing I do know, it's fashion. In an open meeting in the conference room a few days later my News Director laughed out loud and said to me "It was easier than I thought". She was holding her belly and laughing so hard she could barely get the words out. I knew exactly what she was talking about. She was taunting me because she was successful in keeping me from getting the promotion to 5pm Anchor.

She was finally fired after seven years. She was hired at a couple of other stations and fired within months for doing the same things she had gotten away with for far too long at my station. I had expected an, 'I'm sorry' from my CEO who had insisted for years that 'girls just can't get along and there are three sides to every story' as if I was part of the problem but nope, he never did apologize for allowing her to harass my colleagues and me for so long. After my big, emotional, bathroom prayer to God He blessed me to start reporting again. Every time my boss tried to sabotage me being assigned to a story, God protected me. I covered a story about a recent high school graduate who was making a public pledge to remain alcohol free in college. A teen drunk driver had actually killed her dad years earlier and it became a cause she fought against. I so enjoyed interviewing her. She was challenging other youngsters to join her and pledge to party without drugs or alcohol. She said she had watched far too many lives ruined in drunk driving accidents and she was doing something about it. I still keep her in my prayers. She was such an intelligent young lady, so well-spoken and passionate about her beliefs. Of all the politicians and community leaders and "important people" I have interviewed, this teenager was at the top of my list of favorite interviewees. She was clearly making a positive difference in this world and her message was coming from somewhere much higher than her. She sort of reminded me of me. Her story made me think of a time when I was a senior in high school. All week I had been anxiously awaiting Sunday's arrival. I wasn't really sure why I was so excited about the upcoming church service but I was. I have always enjoyed church but something about this feeling was different. During this time I was going to church on Sunday's with my Aunt Jeanette. We loved Sunday's. We enjoyed and looked forward to our morning church services as if they were extravagant trips abroad. Aunt Jeanette would arrive to pick me up. Every week I was stunned at her beauty as if I was seeing her for the very first time. Her skin was as smooth and about the same color as creamed butter. Her long brown hair dangled down her back and was curled to perfection. Aunt Jeanette's skirt suits and dresses could compare and dare I say put to shame the wardrobe of even a first lady of the United States of America. So with my very limited apparel I tried to mirror my elegant aunt. On this Sunday I wore a long pink sweater that fell to my thighs, a sheer white skirt, white tights, white ballerina flat shoes and a white bow in my tightly pulled back ponytail. I was wearing all of this white and a paper-thin skirt in the dead of winter in Michigan. Hey, I did the best I could with what I had. I felt really pretty but I was really cold. We had a great time in church, as usual, but on this day at the end of service the pastor said if anyone wanted prayer to come forward and he would pray with him or her. My Aunt Jeanette and I went up. We never miss a chance to pray. That would be like choosing not to go to a dine-all-day for free at Morton's Steakhouse. Who would do that? It was my turn for the pastor to pray with me. He had been just grabbing the hand of the next person in line and without looking up he was saying a quick but loud, sweaty and heartfelt prayer with his eyes closed then he breathed an "Amen". When I stepped forward the pastor held my hand and shook, then quickly let go as if he had just grabbed a hot panhandle. We sort of looked up at one another at the same time. With brows frowning our eyes met. We both had confused looks on our faces. His eyes squinted as if he knew something about me but couldn't tell me.

"What?" I thought but didn't say out loud. However he answered my question anyway.

"You don't need prayer," he whispered as if doubting his own words. Of course I need prayer, for goodness sake. I'm a teenager for starters. Shall I go on? There's a whole list of reasons I need prayer and while we're at it a few choice blessings that I can use come to mind, as well. Have you seen where my mom and I live? Have you seen my closet? I'm wearing white after Labor Day. Certainly I need prayer. Then I saw the pastor grin. What, did he like the Labor Day joke I made in my head? Was he reading my mind? What the heck is going on here? The pastor smiled. I glanced behind me to the row of people waiting for prayer. I could see heads leaning out of the single file line. The frowns told me they were wondering why my prayer was taking so long or maybe they were trying to listen for words coming from the pastor but there were none. He seemed to be listening intently.

    Through a smile he finally spoke. "God wants you to speak for Him". Ahhhh God told you that? While God is speaking to you will you ask Him for six lucky numbers, please? I could sure use a lottery jackpot. I was only a little cynical about the pastor's dramatic message to me but of course I didn't let him know that. I'm not sure when it happened but my sarcasm started subsiding. I tried not to think about it but I couldn't stop hearing him say those words. Maybe he says that to everyone. I asked my Aunt Jeanette if he ever said that to her. She was surprised at the message the pastor gave me and she said he had never said that to her or to anyone as far as she knew.

    "Oh, maybe that's something he says to the youngsters to encourage us," I said. The next week at church I started asking some of the other teenagers if the pastor had ever told them God wants them to speak for Him. Each teen answered, no. What does that mean? Anything? Nothing? Why did the pastor say that to me? I gathered my mom, Aunt Jocelyn and Aunt Jeanette to sit down and talk about it. They told me to take it seriously. They instructed me to decide if my answer is yes or no.

    "What?" I was confused.

    "God is asking you. He gives us free will. You have to tell him yes or no and you can say no. This is very serious. If you answer yes, you have to be prepared to do just that. Pray about it." They were very helpful and pray I did. A short time later I gave Him my answer.

"Yes God I will speak for you." I didn't know what in the world I was supposed to say, who in the world I was supposed to say it to or who in the world would listen to me but I, a little girl from low-income apartment housing in Wayne, Michigan, accepted and waited for further instructions. A few years later when I was in college I visited my cousin Nora and her husband Grayson's church. There was a visiting pastor from Africa. He had a thick accent. He left the pulpit and was walking in the aisle. He was delivering his sermon and suddenly asked a woman if he could pray for her. Tears streamed from her face. She stood and in front of the congregation they prayed. He did the same with a man in the audience. Only the man didn't stand. He sat in his seat weeping from a place deep inside. After the emotional prayer, the pastor stopped in the aisle by my pew and smiled at me.

"You don't need prayer," with his accent the words sounded different from my pastor a few years earlier but it was the same sentence. Different church. Different pastor. Same message. I couldn't believe my ears.

"Jesus Christ is in you. His light shines so bright in you. He has blessed you with an abundance of peace and joy. It's almost pouring off of you. I have never seen anything like it. You live for Him. You speak for Him," he said to me in his African accent. I smiled back at him and tears filled my eyes.

"Yes, God" I told Him again. "I will speak for you. My answer is yes".

NINETEEN

"*Bleep, bleep, bleeping,* four letter word, bleep," was sort of how the sentence went. You might call that language many things but it certainly isn't speaking for God. I was sure of that. As much as I loathe profanity and anything that sounds like yelling, Oxford had a way of getting me to speak that way and he loved every minute of it.

"Yeah Ms. Christian. I'm recording our conversation so everyone can hear how you talk Ms. Fake Christian. If you apologize I'll stop recording right now," he taunted. He had left our baby girl in the car alone for the third time that I know of. Once I drove up to the gas station and there she was inside the car by herself and he was inside the convenience store. The second time, same thing, I actually had my daughter out of his car, in mine and in her car seat in my SUV before he even came out and realized she was gone. He visibly jumped when he saw his empty seats and realized she was no longer in his car. Then he looked around the parking lot and spotted me. The third time I went to the car dealership where we bought our vehicles and there was my daughter in his Range Rover by herself and he was inside the building. The door to his SUV was unlocked each time. I couldn't believe he would do that. Was she really that unimportant to him? Would he leave his wallet full of money sitting on the seat with the door unlocked? Then why would he leave his daughter? How could he be so irresponsible but after each time I simply asked him not to leave her in the car alone and I explained to him how dangerous it is. Each time he was actually offended that I would attempt to tell him what he can and can't do with his daughter. Was he kidding? After the third time I caught him leaving our daughter alone in his car I again simply tried to have a discussion about it. He had the nerve to start yelling at me. I couldn't believe my ears. How could he scream at me when he had done something so awful? Then, I lost my temper and possibly my mind (just temporarily though but I certainly got my point across). I figured I was either going to lose my mind now and nip this behavior in the bud or I was going to lose my mind after something awful happened as a result of him leaving her by herself in the car. So I chose to lose it right then.

His answer was "Well, I just won't pick her up anymore". What kind of parent would say or even think such a thing? He really didn't pick her up for some time. He didn't even so much as call her on Christmas. He was choosing not see his daughter if he didn't have permission to leave her in the car alone? Really? I was really ashamed at the way I spoke and even more ashamed that I would get involved with such a lousy human being. I was mostly upset with myself because I know how much he enjoys it when he's able to push me to my breaking point. The day of that big argument he sent me several text messages and called me on the phone a number of times. He kept saying things like "If you apologize to me, if you tell me you're sorry I'll consider picking up our daughter again". What a low life for saying such a thing.

"You know I recorded our conversation, Ms. Christian Lady. If you apologize maybe I won't put it on-line for all of

Houston to hear it. Maybe you need to take medication for that, Ms. Christian Lady. You know there are pills you can take for those outbursts and that crazy, fickle behavior of yours Ms. Proper News Lady," he let out a wicked, sinister laugh.

I always think it's ridiculous to hear people say someone makes them behave a certain way but I definitely understand that claim now. Hear me out. Say you arrive at the grocery store and you park your car. As soon as you get out there's a man at your door yelling, "You took my parking spot. You so and so, no good for nothing piece of crap". Then you reply, "Oh gosh. I had no idea. I didn't see anyone waiting for this spot. Boy, I'm so sorry. I didn't even see you" but no matter how much you apologize he continues to scream and swear at you.

"Hey I'll move my car and you can park here," you offer but he talks over you.

"Bleep, bleep, bleep," he responds. So you apologize again and decide to just go on inside the store because you realize attempting a rational conversation with this irrational person is going nowhere. You grab a shopping cart. He's still cussing. You pick up items in aisle one. He's following you and screaming to the top of his lungs. You continue on. Aisles 3, 8, 22, 25 and still the same thing. He's right there calling you names and cursing like a sailor. So a conversation with this person didn't work. Ignoring him didn't work. Apologizing didn't work. By aisle thirty-five you are now screaming like a mad person and telling him off in Grecian (those are the really bad words) because you just want him to stop and that appears to be the only language he understands. That's how it is dealing with Ox. He verbally taunts and mocks me until I'm behaving exactly the way he is but the devil is a liar. I will not let Ox's behavior change me. He may have won at his little getting-me-angry-game a couple of times but I will not begin to behave this way. 1 John chapter 4 verses 4, 5 and 6 came to mind. "Ye are of God, little children and have overcome them because greater is He who is in you, than he who is in the world.

e of the world. Therefore speak they of the world and rld hears them. We are of God. He who knows God hears us. He who is not of God hears us not". That bible verse explains so much. It certainly clarifies why a simple conversation seems so tough and communication seems so difficult with certain people. It didn't matter what I said to Oxford. As long as he was letting the devil take over his life, he wouldn't hear me anyway. I just had to make sure God was at the head of my life and that I was being obedient to Him. I knew talking and yelling that way was letting the devil guide my tongue, my life. It was not what I was supposed to do. That was far from speaking for God. I would simply pray for Oxford and pray that God would bless me with the wisdom and the strength to keep me from such ugly and devilish behavior.

"Greater is He who is in me, than he who is in the world," I repeated out loud. No more blow-ups and certainly no more using that disgusting language. I scolded myself. I don't like speaking that way. It's wicked. It isn't of God. It's nasty, dreadful and disgusting and I won't allow someone else's evilness to push me into doing something I don't want to do. God is my Father and the head of my life, not Satan.

TWENTY

I was laughing, dancing non-stop and having a ball. My best friends Nora and Paige had come to Houston to visit. My mom was also in town. My besties convinced me to go out and listen to a live band once my little princess had fallen asleep. My mom was happy to babysit for me. Paige had a friend who recently moved to Houston. So she also met us at the event. The music was wonderful. I even danced until my feet hurt. I hadn't been out in ages.

"I've had far too much to drink," I laughed with a cup in my hand after I made my way back to the table where the three gals were now sitting. Nora and Paige knew exactly what I meant. Paige's friend Gabrielle slurred "Me too" as she sipped a strong smelling concoction.

"You drink alcohol?" I said with surprise.

"Don't you? You said you've had too much to drink," snapped Gabrielle.

"I'm drinking Sprite. The cool, crisp, lemon lime taste makes me feel young and free," I shouted ending the sentence with a schoolgirl smile.

"Is June Cleaver kidding?" Gabrielle turned to ask Paige.

"She's very serious," laughed Paige.

"Alcohol is such a scam," I screamed to Gabrielle as the music got louder. "You're not only a college graduate, you're a lawyer, a partner at the firm in fact. Certainly you are smart enough to know how stupid getting drunk is. Do you know how many people ruin their lives by drinking this crap? The next thing you're going to tell me is you've tried drugs," I said sarcastically.

"Who hasn't?" she shot back. "I'm a party girl. I like to party". She waved one arm in the air, moving her neck, dancing in her seat.

"No one enjoys a good get together more than me but what does taking poison have to do with partying," I waved my arm in the air mimicking her then continued my sentence "or having a good time? Nothing. That's what. I have a good time," she rolled her eyes at me but I knew she was still listening. I tried to stop myself but blame it on the "heavy drinking" I was doing that night. Sure, the Sprite made me just keep on going.

"If I tell you I have some poison in my purse and you should take it. It won't kill you immediately but you will likely become addicted. It will slowly drive you crazy. Getting the poison will become more important to you than eating, drinking water and even more of a priority than your own children. You will likely eventually lose everything because of the poison, all of your money, your job, your beautiful looks, your mind, your loved ones, your dignity and your life. However, ingest this poison into your body anyway. If I told you that then I tried to actually have you spend money and buy this poison from me would you think I was an absolute crazy person nut case but oh let me add this, the poison will help you party better. Want it now? Does it sound appealing?

Something you want to try? So you would actually take the poison? Then why would you take the crap if someone calls it drugs instead of poison? That just doesn't make sense to me. That is the devil conducting some of his finest work, using confusing tricks and his most convincing lies, anytime he can coax people into not only spending their hard earned money to buy poison but then he makes them believe they should put it in their body and slowly kill themselves." I preached and Gabrielle certainly wasn't the choir. She may have been book smart when it came to academics but she had plenty to learn about the Good Book.

"Well, I'm going to die somehow. I might as well enjoy my life before that happens," she smiled as she attempted to light up a small pole of poison, which some people call a cigarette.

"I'll take that," as I broke the cigarette in half. "I know you're not expecting me to inhale poison just because you decide to kill yourself with this crap. Anyway," I pointed to the sign. "There's no smoking in here," I smiled at her almost laughing. I felt like I was on candid camera. I had heard so much about Gabrielle and she wasn't living up to the picture I had of her in my mind. Sure physically she was everything I imagined. She was beautiful and so was her long light brown hair and matching eyes. Her resume was majorly impressive but behind those alluring eyes and in her spirit she seemed dead. You ever met anyone like that? There was definitely something missing in her. I think it was Jesus Christ. "You really don't care that the ingredients listed on the pack include poison? It doesn't faze you that there's a deadly warning right there in black and white? It isn't a big deal to you that millions of people have become addicted to these things and died of cancer and other horrible illnesses because of them? Trying cigarettes in my 20's was the dumbest thing I ever did. They stole my beauty, gave me wrinkles under my eyes. Therefore I feel quite comfortable telling you how foolish, downright dumb and irresponsible you're being and how much of a puppet I think you're being for the devil. I've been there, cigarettes not only rob you of your health and beauty but also of your hard earned money and they stink like the trash they are," I said to her.

"Look. You telling me not to smoke just might be hazardous to your health. I'm trying to be nice but how do you think you can preach to anyone? You have a lot of nerve. The last time I checked you have a new birth certificate to file at your house but where's the marriage certificate? There isn't one, right? I may not know much about that bible you claim to read so much but I'm pretty sure there's a line in there about not fornicating, not sleeping with a man you're not married to. Have you read that somewhere? I'm certain that means you too, honey. The rules also apply to you Ms. I'll Preach To Everyone Else But Make Up My Own Rules," said Gabrielle with quite a bit of sister girl sass.

"I guess you told me. Gabrielle, we're all sinners only saved by God's sweet grace. Just because we slip in sin doesn't mean we should lie there and wallow in it. We're supposed to get right back up and live the life God intends for us. When we let the devil tempt us we're not supposed to just continue to live in darkness and live for Satan allowing him to control our lives. I'm not trying to tell you off or preach to you. I'm certainly not trying to tell you I can walk on water. I'm just trying to say some things that maybe you haven't thought of. If you think it's bad for me to try to get you to think differently about things I believe will cause you to self-destruct, then I'm guilty as charged," I gave her a big hug. "You should really come to church with me. Actually, come on. We're calling it a night. We're all headed to my church in the morning," I commanded and everyone, even Gabrielle, complied. I can be pretty persuasive.

"Don't forget to take a good look in the mirror the next time you point out someone else needs a change." The pastor's words and voice filled the sanctuary like only a minister's massive tone can. It's funny how it seems to work out. Every Sunday, like clockwork or calendar-work in this case, the pastor's sermon seems to confirm a conversation I have already had with God. All morning I had been praying about my actions the night before, going out dancing and being in a nightclub. I hadn't been in a place like that in years and it just didn't feel right being there. Maybe I felt so weird about it because now I was a mommy or maybe it was the fact that I had grown so much as a Christian and now I knew better. If God had come at that very moment and found me there while my daughter was at home, I would have been really embarrassed. He gave me such an awesome gift, my daughter, and that's what I chose to do leave my perfect present from God to go hang out in a place where people are drinking, possibly drugging, getting drunk, dirty dancing and probably far worse? So that morning I had taken a close look in the mirror and realized the awesome lady I was looking at was not a "fence-straddler". I laughed out loud at the term but I knew what I meant. I didn't want to straddle the fence, saying I'm a Christian and wearing my church shoe on one foot and my worldly shoe on the other. After all, it was God who put those Louboutins on my feet. He deserves to have them dance for only Him. It was just one night out listening to a live band but as a Christian I know there are certain situations you shouldn't put yourself in. Sure a different location, different atmosphere for listening to music would have been fine. I certainly don't want to be associated with an event where people are getting drunk, high and God knows what else. Dancing with the devil even a little bit is still a few steps too many. It can lead to a full on waltz. So I was glad to hear the pastor's sermon. It was confirmation for what God was already telling me.

"When you have been blessed with wisdom, you need to know it's just that a blessing from God. When you have wise words, a life changing message to deliver to someone, they are words from God. Like Joseph interpreting the dreams or Moses leading the Israelites out of Egypt. They were smart

enough to know their guidance, their gifts were from God."
The pastor preached as "Amen and Hallelujah" were shouted
to him from the pews. I always feel as though the pastor is
talking right to me. The message always feels so personal. I
took a deep look at myself and fell into a sort of daydream,
which tends to happen when I realize why I should do things
differently. Mid-way through the sermon the picture was
clear. Although it was just a dance club, I know there were
things going on there that I should not be anywhere near. It
sends a message of acceptance for those in observance and it
puts me in a position where I can be tempted. So there are
certain things you just shouldn't do.

The pastor wrapped up his sermon saying how the
world would be a much better place if we loved our neighbor
like we love ourselves.

"Don't be apathetic. When your neighbor is doing
something they shouldn't do don't turn a blind eye. Just like
an out of body experience, sometimes it's easier to see
somebody else's mess. When you see it call them out on it.
Love them enough to do that. I'm not telling you to name call
and start mess and pretend to do it in God's name. You know
the difference. I'm saying do for someone else exactly what
you would want someone to do for you. Love your neighbor
enough to give them support, strength and encouragement
when they need it". Hundreds of heads in the sanctuary
nodded in agreement, hands clapped, and tears fell. Some
people shouted then the choir fired everyone up even more.
Their beautiful voices belted out the best rendition of "Trouble
Don't Last Always" I have ever heard. Then after singing "I
Love The Lord" (no one can do it quite like Whitney Houston
but the choir gave it a beautiful shot) the pastor asked if
anyone wanted prayer to come forward. To my surprise
Gabrielle was out of her seat and at the front of the church.
The large, astounding stained glass window behind the pulpit
now framed her, the pastor and his wife perfectly. The brilliant
colors were glowing around them from the sun shining in.

Several others left their seats and joined them at the head of the sanctuary. After minutes of private prayers I could see Gabrielle fall into the pastor's wife's arms crying, more like sobbing. They hugged and prayed for quite some time. Gabrielle's sobs were like a child's and she realized she is a child, of God. Something she hadn't felt for a very long time. Her motto for herself for years had been 'grown, sexy and up for anything'. It's a term coined by the devil to trick people into believing once they turn a certain age they are free to sin. Gabrielle felt freedom, happiness, peace and protection from God just by now calling herself 'a child of God'.

We went to brunch after church. The five of us looked as if we had just left the runway. The pastor's wife and Gabrielle were wearing spectacular skirt suits. Gabrielle's was tweed pencil, Claret in color with a portrait collar on the three-button jacket, three quarter French cuff sleeves and she wore simple diamond studs and matching bracelet. The pastor's wife's skirt was wool A-Line charcoal with a puff sleeve peplum five-button jacket and she was wearing stunning elegant vintage Valentino jewelry. Nora, Paige and I all were cloaked in classic couture dresses. Nora was covered in Ginger colored cashmere and Yurman everywhere you looked. Paige's pleated Cerulean silk with long sleeves was topped off with a diamond by the yard Tiffany necklace and beautiful platinum and ice bangle bracelets that sounded like angelic wind chimes when she moved. My dress was straight, tailored to perfection; flesh-tone neutral buttercream hued mohair with princess sleeves, tie neck with a massive cashmere bow that kissed my left collarbone and peeked over my shoulder and a vintage pearl and diamond brooch adorned the center of the bow. The dress fell just below my knee. Must have been Dior day and we all got the memo. Pearls decorated my neck, wrist and ears. We could have been mistaken for supermodels or basketball players because of our height but do you think that stopped us from wearing stilettos? It didn't and we had the bags to match. I have always had a passion for fashion. In five seconds flat I will have already admired your shoes, seen myself in your outfit and made a mental note that I must find and buy your bag. After thirty minutes of heartfelt fashion fodder about Chloe, Chanel, Prada and several other women who were not eating with us but were very dear to us nonetheless, it was then time for most of us to listen.

It was now Gabrielle's turn to speak. She told us about how she was raised in a Pentecostal church. In college she started drifting away from God. She called it still being spiritual but not being very religious. Apparently that's something new, there's a new age religion-is-bad fad but being spiritual is in. "Whatever I tried to call it, I somehow lost my relationship with God and Jesus Christ," Gabrielle explained. Alcohol and drugs were always available at parties and became something "fun to do". Fun? Ingesting this stuff until you're stumbling, sick, throwing up on yourself, unable to walk or drive and until you have to have it no matter what? Does any addict ever plan to ruin their life with this stuff? She told us she had convinced herself that everyone does it. Doing it once in a while wasn't a big deal, right? After all, she was a successful attorney with a massive house, luxury cars parked in the garage, a big bank account, her last name was on the beautiful brick downtown building "Hoskins, Wallace and Webb". Gabrielle Claire Webb could be called many things. Now she was ready to admit drug addict was on that list. Paige was shocked. She had been friends with Gabrielle for years and had no idea. Gabrielle checked herself into rehab. Our Sunday church service followed by brunch became routine. Isn't it funny how our friendship came to be? She just so happened to end up as a partner in a law firm in Houston where I had lived for years. I was dragged kicking and screaming by my two best friends out of my house and away from my daughter as they forced me to go out for a rare night out on the town and there in that noisy nightclub God had a message for Gabrielle. I could have chosen to ignore God and remain silent. After all, whom do I think I am lecturing to this prominent attorney, trying to tell this woman whom I don't even know what to do? I could have chosen to disobey God but thankfully I didn't and fortunately Gabrielle was smart enough to open her heart and hear what God was saying to her. I knew that message I was delivering to her was coming from a good place. I wasn't trying to embarrass or belittle Gabrielle. Even when I was saying the words I felt strongly they were coming from God. Gabrielle was even more certain it was God who spoke to her saving her life. She felt sure she was headed for sudden death, maybe an accidental overdose if she had continued because she was using more and more. She thanked me with the sincerest gratitude that has ever been spoken but I told her there was no need for that. I was simply, loving my neighbor as I love myself. I was doing for her what I hope someone would do for me if they see me in trouble. In Mark 12:30, 31 the bible says "Thou shalt love the Lord thy God with all thy heart and with all thy soul and with all thy mind and with all thy strength: this is the first commandment. And the second is, thou shalt love thy neighbor as thyself. There is none other commandment greater than these". If you see your neighbor about to unknowingly step off a 100-foot cliff do you stop him or do you say to yourself 'well it was his choice to get that close'? Of course you stop him. In life we may make mistakes and we may not always make the right decisions. I just hope when I'm there someone loves me enough to extend their hand and I better be smart enough to accept it.

TWENTY-ONE

It felt as though an elephant was sitting on my chest. I can't breathe no matter how hard I try. What's happening to me? I was flailing my arms and I could feel a pillow over my face. Oh dear God someone broke in. Someone's actually in my house and now they're trying to smother me. I couldn't call out. I couldn't get any air. Out of the corner of my eye I barely made out a shadowy figure in the corner of my bedroom and then the flicker of light across a metal object. Oh no. Did this burglar have a knife? I was soaked with what I hoped was sweat. What if it's blood, my blood? Did he already stab me? Then I felt it. Air was moving into my lungs. I gasped taking one deep breath, then another. I sat straight up in bed panting trying to catch my breath. Confused, disoriented, breathing heavily and panicked I took another look at the guy in the corner dressed in black that had broken into my house and was trying to kill me. The dark object didn't move. As my eyes focused I saw I was looking at my chest of drawers. The light from the television that had been left on when I fell asleep was flashing on the shiny, fancy drawer pulls. There was no intruder, no knife. There was just me now dripping in sweat waking up from a nightmare. In my sleep I could apparently hear the TV that was still on as I slept. There was breaking news. Ten coal miners were trapped miles underground in a mineshaft in Brazil. The news anchor was interviewing experts about the risk of the men running out of air and suffocating, which explains why I then started dreaming about not being able to breathe. As I struggled to wake up I must have knocked one of the eight million pillows on my bed onto my face. My heart ached for the trapped miners and their families. How would it be possible to get them out alive? Before I could finish the thought another one popped into my mind. Don't focus on the problem. Focus on the promise, God's promise. "Ask and it shall be given". I immediately dropped to my knees and started praying for them. I knew I wasn't alone. I thought of the bible verse Matthew 18:20 "Where two or three are gathered in my name, there I am in the midst of them".

Days, weeks and months went by. Emergency officials had come up with a way to drop food to the men and get air into their chamber but how much longer could these trapped miners survive this way? I couldn't see any way out. One night I was praying for the ten men. "God please bless those ten miners. They were simply doing their job and now they are at risk of losing their lives simply for being gainfully employed? Please get those ten men out of there alive". The television was on in the background. A report was being given about the miners. "This just turned into an even tighter situation for one of the ten miners. His wife just found out her husband has been cheating on her. His mistress showed up here and is awaiting his rescue from the mineshaft" the TV told me. "Dirty rotten scoundrel" I said out loud then continued my prayer. "God please get nine of those men out of there alive". What? Do I really have to pray for this scumbag adulterer? Then I got my answer. God will deal with each of us for the choices we make. Hate the sin, not the sinner. It wasn't the answer I wanted. I had hoped God would join in with me and call the jerk a few names too but no such luck. So I finished my prayer the right way. I didn't know this story would become personal for me. I would soon be face to face with someone who was there. His corporate office was in Houston with a branch of his heavy equipment company there in Brazil. Samuel Hunter had been taking theological classes. He was now scheduled to graduate and become a deacon. Turns out Sam had been doing an awful lot of praying too. Soon after all other options were exhausted the Brazilian government called Sam's company asking if they had any tools to assist in the rescue. Sam hopped on a plane leaving his home in Houston and he spent countless nights there praying at the site in Brazil where the men were trapped miles underneath his feet. He kept coming up with the same solution.

"There is no way to make a hole large enough to get the men out without causing the earth to collapse in on them. You just couldn't disturb the ground that much without making the dirt and rock cave in". Some of the best and brightest engineers and excavators in the world had worked on this for months and everyone came up with the same answer. The men were probably living out their last days inside the grave that had already been dug for them. They would likely die there but Sam wasn't giving up. What Sam did next there in Brazil changed everything. It turns out that moment was also significant a world away in Belleville, Michigan. I was at home for a ten-day vacation. We did our usual. We gathered at my Aunt Jocelyn's house for food, fun, laughing and lots of talking. I had been fasting once a week for years and this get together happened to fall on my fast day. I was tempted to break my fast every time someone handed me a plate or said things like "girl why aren't you eating? You young people and these diets. What's wrong with you? Why don't you have a plate?" but I stuck to my fast. I prayed more every time someone tried to shove vittles into my pie hole.

I talked to God a lot that day. Certainly putting off my fast to eat with my family wouldn't be a big deal but I couldn't do it. I could just feel I needed to stick to my fast, I needed to pray but I didn't know why. As the day went on I got my answer. I was thumbing through one of Aunt Jocelyn's books and I read the line "You believe in Him for little things. You have faith, you fast, you believe prayer changes things but do you know how powerful God really is? Do you believe in Him for miracles?" For some reason the word miracles and that sentence stood out. I hadn't thought much about God working miracles when it came to my life or even when it came to present day. I know He performed many miracles documented in the bible and I'm sure He's still performing them all the time but I didn't know why I was supposed to suddenly pray for a miracle but I did. I prayed a prayer that came from deep within me. There, sitting in the family room I was admiring Aunt Jocelyn's large six-foot tall fireplace enclosed by dark brown brick topped by an elaborate mantle. You could walk inside the thing it was so big. It was beautiful. Her custom built home was full of special touches like that, oversized bed and bathrooms, beautiful chandeliers, fancy fixtures and an intercom system that I enjoyed playing with as a child. Her huge home sat on a quiet country dirt road nestled in the woods. We were all there in the family room when I barely heard Nora's cell phone ringing inside her purse. It was about 10:00 at night and it wouldn't have been unusual for her to ignore the call. After all, anyone who needed to reach her knew she was at her mom's house and could call her on the landline but instead she turned to her oldest daughter.

"Hand Mommy my cell phone please, there in my purse," she said. Like a well-run assembly line Abrielle didn't fumble around in the large purse. She reached her hand in, came out with the phone in her fingers, passed it to her sister Amalie, Amalie handed off the phone to her Grandmother who then placed the ringing cell in Nora's hand. "Hello," she barely got the two syllables out before she jumped up and with the phone still held to her ear she bolted from the house. Nora's husband Grayson jumped over the couch like a hurdle. He grabbed the keys to their SUV and he went running right behind his wife. Neither was wearing shoes or socks.

I didn't know what was going on but if it was serious enough to send her shooting out of the front door without any time to say a word about what was going on, it must have been grave. Whatever she was told on that phone had to have something to do with their two sons, Gabriel and Gavin. The boys and their friend had just left the house an hour and a half earlier. They were now nineteen and twenty years old. The college freshman and sophomore were home for a visit and headed to a special twenty and younger party at a local dance hall. I was their Godmother. I was there in the delivery room with Nora and Grayson when Gavin was born and I wasn't about to sit there consumed with worry about what was going on. I grabbed the keys to my rental. My mom, Aunt Jocelyn, Abrielle and Amalie were right behind me. I ordered the girls to go back into the house and we would be right back. I didn't know what we were headed into. I didn't know what we would see. I wanted to protect the girls but the fifteen and sixteen year olds wouldn't even consider it. "Those are our brothers. We love them too," Abrielle cried. I guess everyone knew the phone call had to be about Gabriel and Gavin. I let them stay in the car and I prayed as I raced to catch up to Nora and Grayson who were speeding toward their youngest son. He was on his mom's phone begging for help. As we drove Aunt Jocelyn called everyone in the family telling them to pray. Turns out when Nora answered her ringing telephone she heard her youngest son gasping for air. He was saying, "They're shooting at us. I'm not sure if Gabriel is still alive". Those words into a mother's ear must have been like large daggers shooting from the tiny mobile device. It was surreal and strange and incomprehensible. We didn't live that way with violence, guns and fighting. Her kids had grown up in the suburbs, raised by her and her husband. They spoke very proper English and were much more likely to encounter guns and a shootout in the pages of a mystery novel than they were in real life but somehow this was real. Nora didn't know how she was going to do it but she was headed to rescue her sons. She, Grayson and Gavin who was still on the phone prayed as the roar of the panicked parents' SUV's engine was clearly telling anyone within earshot it was being pushed to its limit. I never did catch up to Nora and Grayson but I knew the dancehall was somewhere in the area. My experience as a journalist told me I would recognize the scene when I saw it and I did.

We must be close to the dance hall now because there were swarms of teenagers running for their lives on the normally quiet streets of downtown Belleville. We had arrived in about three minutes flat. I skidded to a stop right behind five police cars. The officers were just arriving as we were. About midway down the block I saw it. The boys had been driving their Uncle Josh's Acura Legend. The black coupe was sitting there in the street with both doors flung open, the trunk was partially raised and I saw a body slumped out of the passenger floorboard and lying partly on the street. Tears started to well in my eyes and I again prayed for that miracle. I could see something rising from the car disappearing into the sky. Was the dust still settling? What was that? I wiped my tears and looked closer. The dust, or whatever it was, was gone and now something else was clear. The large men's hooded sweatshirt that was hanging out of the passenger side of the car was just clothing. At first glance it looked like a person but it was only a shirt.

"Thank you God. It's just a shirt but where are the boys?" I almost pleaded to God. Every window in the car had been shattered or shot out and large bullet holes covered the car. The bullets had clearly sliced right through the thick metal doors and the body of the vehicle. It was such an ominous, menacing sight. I couldn't believe my eyes. I thought Gavin must have called his parents before he took his last breath because there was no way anyone in that car could have survived. As a Reporter I had covered drive by shootings where cars suffered much less damage than this and everyone inside had died. In fact, I reported on one story where only one bullet fired into a car killed both the driver and passenger but now I wouldn't allow myself to stop expecting a miracle. "I pray and fast on this day dear Lord asking you to please perform a miracle. Please God bless those boys to be just fine," I never stopped praying and believing in God for a miracle. Officers were putting up crime scene tape now and I couldn't get to the car. Nora and Grayson arrived and I saw them get out of their SUV. I hadn't pointed out the car to anyone. I just couldn't. What was I supposed to say? It was chaos. Screaming kids were everywhere but that black car seemed to be shouting louder than anyone here. The story it was telling was dark and painful. Then "thank you God" I spotted Gavin and his friend seated on the curb being questioned by police but where was Gabriel.

"Oh God you are so good. Thank you Jesus for your miracle tonight. I give you all the glory. Thank you Father for sparing these boys' lives. I praise your very name". There Gabriel was, his frightened eyes looked right into mine, he was in the backseat of a police car. I think my years of experience as a journalist responding to scenes like this allowed me to process everything so quickly and locate the boys. As I turned to go and give everyone the good news I heard the sting of a mother's pain.

"My baby," Nora moaned as I saw her eyes fixed on that oversized hooded shirt that was dangling from the car onto the ground. She tried to break through the line of officers and the crime scene tape.

"Nora it's just a shirt. It's just a sweatshirt. Look there's Gabriel, Gavin and their friend. The boys are all safe. God held them in his arms and protected them," I told her as I pointed out the boys to her. I quickly gave her my shoes. I was at least wearing socks. Then I also had to calm Grayson down. He wanted to immediately get to his sons and take them home but police officers wouldn't let anyone anywhere near them. How weird was this? If it was hurtful for me to be separated from the boys by crime scene tape of all things, I knew it had to be extremely difficult for their parents and their Grandmother (who was my Aunt Jocelyn). It broke my heart to see this 6'10" 240 pound man standing there sobbing, aching to hug and kiss his sons. He couldn't understand how someone could try to keep him from his babies especially at a time like this. He just wanted to hold them in his arms. He finally lost it, walked right up to the officer and demanded, "I'm going to my sons". It wasn't a question but an announcement. This was after he was told several times to "stay back, or else". As Grayson tried to reach his sons the officer put his hand on his holster and yelled for assistance from other cops at the scene. I quickly had to help Grayson regain his composure. He was charging like a bull and repeating over and over "I'm going to my sons". With every step officers were shouting commands of their own, moving toward Grayson and ready to take him down. I couldn't let this evening get any worse.

"Grayson, detectives will soon be finished with their questions and your boys will be in your arms before you know it. I promise," I tried to reassure the sobbing father. He wasn't hearing me. I jumped in front of him put my arms straight out, planted my feet into the ground and I pushed against him with all my might to stop him from moving another step. "Look at my face. Listen to me," I explained this is routine. It will only be a little longer and investigators will be wrapped up. His whole body sobbed with anguish. Then I saw Grayson's bare feet standing in a puddle of blood.

He and Nora first stopped at another area where kids were gathered and they jumped from their SUV looking for their babies. Grayson was literally running the streets of Belleville calling his sons' names trying to find them as rocks, glass and whatever else dug into his feet. I sat him inside the car with his legs swung out of the vehicle and I cleaned the debris from his open wounds. I washed his feet with hand sanitizer and wrapped them in paper towel. I convinced him to stay put, telling him again officers had to conduct an investigation to figure out what happened. I quickly started an investigation of my own. I had been to plenty of scenes before and I knew what to look for. I approached the witnesses.

"Hey are you all ok?" they looked at me dazed and confused and slowly shook their heads yes.

"What happened?" I asked. One girl said she was the passenger in a car right behind my Godsons. A minivan with its lights out turned from a small road, drove in the wrong lane of traffic alongside Gabriel and Gavin's car and opened fire at point blank range. "It could have been our car they were shooting at. It could have been us. They were just waiting for the first car to come along to ambush and that's what they did. The van was packed with people who all seemed to have a gun. There were just hands and guns hanging out all of the windows and I could see flashes of fire and flying glass with every shot. I thought the guys in that black car were dead for sure. It's a miracle". There was that word again, miracle. She spoke to me as she stared at the black coupe full of bullet holes as if it was a UFO spaceship. It was strange looking at that car knowing everyone inside lived. The witness told me the van full of gunmen kept firing until Gabriel and Gavin's car slammed into another vehicle, continued a few more feet, then their black car slowly rolled to a stop.

"I saw the whole thing. As the black car hit the curb and then stopped moving the van pulled up, put on brakes and fired more shots before speeding off. It was so evil, such a wicked thing for someone to do. When I saw the car roll to a stop I thought I had just watched someone being murdered. I'm sure the gunmen thought the same thing." The girl was traumatized. I hugged her as tears rolled from her eyes. There was no reasonable explanation for how all of those bullets completely missed three very large young men. They were all athletes, basketball and football players. Gabriel, Gavin and their friend Shane were all around 6'9" tall. Shane, stuck in that small backseat, didn't have much room to duck. They were basically crammed in a tin can that was sitting on top of a barrel with hunters firing at the can from pointblank range. The trunk, the doors and the car were full of bullet holes and the boys were not. I had truly witnessed a miracle. After giving statements we were free to take the boys home.

Police believe gang members from the inner city targeted this suburban dance hall and randomly chose their victims, possibly as a gang initiation. Detectives said there were so many bullet holes in the car they lost count. Gavin, it turns out, in the darkness was able to get out and run when his brother told him to. He scaled a fence and called his mom as he ran for his life praying to God the whole time to keep him, his brother and his friend safe. He wasn't sure if the shooters saw him jump from the car and if they would come after him and shoot him in the back. Thank God that didn't happen. As Gabriel was trying to steer the car to safety he instructed his brother and their friend to run. He thought both boys did. Then Gabriel, too, scrambled to get to safety and away from that car. He had no idea his friend, who was in the backseat of the two door car, couldn't find the latch to flip the seat up and jump from the vehicle. So there in the back of the bullet riddled car, with crazed lunatics on the loose shooting at them, Shane actually had to take the time to feel around the side of the front passenger seat for the electronic power button that slowly moves the seat forward. He was too afraid to call out to Gabriel for help. He didn't want the shooters to hear him. So as he sat in the darkness terrified the gunmen would return, he held the tiny switch that sluggishly slid the seat forward. All he could do was wait for it to leisurely move up until there was enough space to squeeze through so he too could escape the car. That must have been agonizing. We all stayed up that whole night praying with the boys who were still trembling and in disbelief. The next day, we went to the tow yard to get Josh's things from the once luxury vehicle. It was now not much more than a heap of junk. It was destroyed, ripped apart by gunfire. This car that seemed dark, gloomy and almost haunted the night before still invoked emotion in me but now I had such a feeling of peace. Instead of seeing the devil's work when I looked at it, I saw God's work. If the cops had dusted for fingerprints I felt they would have only found His, God's prints all over the place. I began to cry when my eyes slowly started examining all the bullet holes. The car was no longer covered by darkness. In the daylight you could clearly see the damage and God's miracle. The windows were, every one of them, shattered or shot out. The front of the car was smashed. We could see holes from bullets that traveled through the trunk and ripped straight through the backseat.

I was again silently praying and thanking God for His protection, for His miracle. I knew we were all doing the same thing. Josh tried to pull the already partially opened trunk up even higher to remove whatever was inside. It rose a little and then he said "Hey. Look at this". He started to read from a sheet of paper he pulled from the bullet-riddled trunk. "He who dwells in the shelter of the most High shall rest in the shadow of the Almighty. I will say of the Lord He is my refuge and my fortress. My God in Him I will trust. Surely He shall deliver me from the snare of the enemy and from the deadly pestilence. He shall cover me with His feathers and under his wings shall I find protection. His truth will be my shield and armor. I will not be afraid of the terror by night, nor the arrow that flies by day...No evil shall befall me. He will command His angels to guard me in every way". It was a copy of a bible verse there in the trunk. Aunt Jocelyn, at Aunt Jeanette's, request had made copies for all of us to keep in our cars and in our homes. Psalm 91. A prayer of protection had been riding along with the boys. I had truly witnessed a miracle performed by God.

TWENTY-TWO

There in the black of night thunder roared, lightning seemed to burn like flames flaring up and going down but never really going away. Everything was coming from the sky but an answer. With everyone moving around him Samuel Hunter stood perfectly still. There at the site where the miners were trapped miles underground in Brazil, the rescue crews were scrambling to pack up everything and get the heck out of there before the storm rolled in. As the last of the work trucks rumbled away Sam didn't move. An enormous tremble churned from the sky and seemed to shake Sam's soul. Then the drops started hitting his head, shoulders, hands, face, shoes and soaking his shirt. There he stood alone in the darkness in the middle of a nasty rainstorm. He started to feel like an idiot but he felt somehow God was telling him to be still.

"You mean like this? Am I just supposed to stand here and what get struck by lightning? What are you trying to show me? I'm nuts and drenched and talking to myself in my Texas accent here in the middle of nowhere in Brazil," Sam mumbled and rolled his eyes. Every inch of his 6'6" frame was saturated. Even his pale face didn't glow out here in this blackness except of course when the lightning struck. Despite it all, he was obedient, stood still and silently prayed.

"If these men will be saved, it will be a miracle from you God. There is no other way." Lightning lit the area again and Sam saw a pile of trash in the distance. One of the large excavation drills had been delivered to the area wrapped in a stiff, heavy cotton material. The sky glowed again. What was once a small pile of rubble had grown considerably. The cotton had swelled significantly once it was rain soaked. It looked like a massive, soggy, 70's Afro. Sam started to laugh at that thought, and then it hit him. Sam knew what he needed to do to get the miners out alive. Now if he could just make it to his house in this rainstorm alive. He hopped in his truck and started trying to make calls but cell phone reception in the storm was horrible. He feared he would have a wreck, the plan would go with him to his grave and the miners would also soon die. He made it closer to town dodging downed trees and high water. The rain was hitting his windshield in waves. BEEP. He had cell phone service. He phoned every engineer, every heavy equipment owner and every excavator he knew, asking for input on how to perfect the plan. Sam's idea was to drill a small hole to the men, disturbing the Earth as little as possible so the dirt wouldn't cave in on the trapped miners. Then they would place expanders in that hole to slowly make it just wide enough for the miners to be able to squeeze through. The special expanders were brought in from Chicago and put in place. It took about a month for the hole to grow to the appropriate size, just as the cotton had in the rain. Then the world watched as the men were brought up one at a time. We all breathed a sigh of relief and many of us thanked God but not many knew they were witnessing a miracle.

The next morning after the miners were rescued I received an email at work telling me a Houston man who has a business in Brazil was instrumental in the rescue of the ten men. I called Sam Hunter's heavy equipment company and they invited me to the business. That night on the news I profiled the company. Sam was on his way home from Brazil. So I interviewed his wife and his sons. It was a small family business and they had no idea they would ever be involved in an international story like this. The next morning I arrived at work again. Sam Hunter himself called me.

"Hey. I hear you're looking for me," he said with a Texas twang.

"Yes. I'd like to come by and chat with you about your experience in Brazil. What an amazing and unbelievable rescue, huh?"

"You have no idea," he told me. When he filled me in on the specifics about the rescue being a miracle from God I couldn't believe my ears and even better? He was willing to talk about it on camera. Now one small hurdle, would I get approval to do the story? Just a mention of the name God and I knew many of my colleagues in the conference room would simply tune out. In the morning meeting where we gather every day to discuss the stories we're going to cover I pitched the story and said Sam was back and available for an interview. They were very interested until I mentioned Sam's faith. Just as I thought, they balked at "the whole God did it thing". "You know. I feel we already covered the story yesterday" said a couple of voices in the room.

"Well, we spoke with his wife and sons about the family business yesterday but today we get to hear a firsthand account of what it was like being there. Come on. This has been one of the biggest stories in the world. We have a Houston connection and we don't want to do the story?"

"Ok. So...since you've already been to the business and we have footage there you're going to, what, interview him at his house?" asked one of my supervisors. Uh oh. Here it comes.

"Actually. I think it might be better to do the story at his church. We're set up to meet him there at 10:00 a.m." I said nonchalantly.

"His church? Why church?"

"Well, he's been studying theology and just graduated all of his classes. A ceremony is going to be held there at his church to make him a deacon. He said he prayed extensively and specifically for the miners there at this church before he left to go assist in the rescue. He believes it was prayer and divine intervention that ultimately freed the trapped miners and that's what he's planning to say on camera," I explained.

"God? God did it? God freed the men? I watched it on TV and I didn't see God anywhere near there. Why do you have to try to inject your God into every story?" some in the room laughed.

"This doesn't have anything to do with me. Those are his words, not mine. You may not like that he believes God helped in the rescue but he does. I'm a journalist. I deal with facts. He's credible. He holds an Engineering degree and a Master's in business from a couple of the best universities in Texas. He runs a legitimate and prosperous international company. Like it or not, he was there for one of the biggest stories in the world to assist in the rescue of the trapped miners and he happens to believe those men are only free because of not only God but because of Jesus Christ and this man who was in the midst of this major international rescue is from none other than Houston. Are we in the business of reporting local news or not?" the room was quiet. "And let's be perfectly clear. I never inject my opinion or my religion into any of my stories. I'm a professional and we should all behave that way, professionally". I was off to interview Sam.

He was a kind and gentle soul. Have you ever encountered someone and it just felt like such a pleasure to meet him or her? That's how it was to shake hands with Sam for the first time. I was really impressed and thankful he was a highly educated, hugely successful businessman who was willing to say, on camera for the world to see, "those men have God alone to thank for freeing them from that collapsed mineshaft. The humans who helped were simply that, helpers of God to get those men out alive".

It reminded me of a man I heard on the radio recently who said when he was a boy his dad told him "Son, you have to be a leader for Christ. We live in a post-Christian society. It won't be the popular thing to do but it will be the right thing to do," said the voice in the radio. The man went on to explain how he now teaches his sons "Son, you have to be a leader for Christ. We live in an "anti"-Christian society. It won't be the popular thing to do but it will be the right thing to do". Openly believing in God and Jesus Christ isn't always popular but Sam could care less. There in the sanctuary of his church he told me the story of how things seemed hopeless there in Brazil. He prayed for a miracle and God delivered. His only request was that I leave out the part about him standing there in the rainstorm. That was something private between him and God that Sam would only choose to share with a select few. I honored his request. The story aired with video of the church's breathtaking architecture and immaculate stained glass windows. Sam and I walked through the sanctuary as he told me the story. The report ended with his words "There was no humanly way to get those men out alive. Think about it. How do you drill a hole miles deep, on top of 10 men, wide enough for them to fit through without causing a cave in? You can't. We have all witnessed a modern day miracle".

TWENTY-THREE

Watching 155 people levitate on water certainly has to be a miracle of its own. Well, it sure looked like the passengers and crew on the wings of that crashed plane on the river were actually standing on water. We came to know it as "The Miracle on the Hudson". It could not have been anything but. That sensational survivor story on the water happened first.   Then God saved my godsons. Now there was the miracle with the miners. I had been thinking more about miracles lately than I had my whole life. I think it was safe to say God was trying to tell me something. I was deep in thought, lost in my daydream, when I heard panic blaring from the police scanner here in the newsroom.

"A   shooting   at   Houston   Police   Department Headquarters. All units respond". I jumped from my seat with my cell phone in hand and stood by the assignment desk for a closer listen but there was nothing else said on the scanner. It now sat quiet. A news crew was scrambled out the door headed to police headquarters and I started dialing. The whole newsroom it seemed was gathered there waiting for more to come from the little electric box that now sat silent. Every Reporter was doing what I was. We were all calling our sources in the police department to find out what in the world was going on. I was calling Lt. Brad Schultz. I had just completed a story with him two weeks earlier when he solved a major cold case. He had been on the force just six years when two little girls went missing back in the 1970's. The bodies of the little girls, both only 15 years old, were found a day later in a ditch. They had been raped, beaten, brutally murdered and dumped. He vowed then to find the monster responsible. A full thirty years later Lt. Schultz followed up on a tip, he made an arrest and DNA testing proved the homicide detective finally had the vicious animal he had been hunting all those years. I had just spoken with the lieutenant a couple of days ago. He was giving me an exclusive interview on another case he was working on. He left a funny message on my cell phone.

"Hey. It's Schultz. Hit me up on my cell when you get this message". When I called him back I teased him about that for a good fifteen minutes. "Hit me up? What are you a rapper now? Are you trying to talk like the kids? What's with the slang?" We had a good laugh over that one. Lt. Schultz's choice of words was even funnier when you consider he was a 60-year old gray haired grandfather with glasses. His pale face only turned red in the sun and had never tanned in his life. He looked and talked more like a librarian than a police officer. He was a soft-spoken, gentle man. His voice and demeanor had a way of calming you. I always wondered if the criminals felt the same soothing comfort as I did when they talked to Lt. Schultz. Probably not, huh? Gosh, why isn't Schultz answering? He always answers. I left another message. "Hey. Scanner traffic says there was a shooting there at headquarters. What's going on over there?" Schultz wasn't calling back so I dialed another police friend.

"Suicide? Who?" I almost screamed the questions at him. No one seemed to know. Some of the other reporters were hearing the same thing. There was one intentional shot fired at Houston police headquarters by a veteran officer who killed himself at work. As tragic and awful as that is, maybe it was better than the alternative, having some crazed gunman on the loose inside the cop shop. Then all at once with every ringtone under the sun, our phones were vibrating, singing and ringing.

"The shooting happened in homicide." The voices, the sources reported to the Reporters but who? What detective would do such a thing? Ten minutes later we got our answer.

"Lt. Brad Schultz" I didn't hear anything else coming from my cell phone. I was shocked and tremendously saddened. Tears streamed from my eyes. Near the end of the workday Lt. Schultz sat at his desk, pulled out his service weapon, put it to his head and ended his life. I prayed for his family and his soul. I was really disturbed and confused by this. He seemed like such a peaceful person, more like a person at peace. How is it possible he was so tormented, so tortured that he would be driven to something like this? Then I was embarrassed that I was calling him to find out about the shooting at police headquarters. I hoped the four missed calls from my phone and the two voice messages I left on his phone wouldn't bring his wife, daughter or whoever would be checking his cell phone more pain. Knowing what I know now, my calls and my voicemail messages would seem incredibly insensitive. His loved one listening to the messages would hear me, the nosy uncaring reporter, asking, not "are you ok?" or "how are you?" but "what's going on?" I felt so ashamed, so guilty. So I said another prayer. Then I cried there at my desk in the newsroom.

I pulled myself together to deliver my report for the 5 o'clock news. The story I had been working on all day was on two twelve year old best friends who had raised $107,000 for charity. They shared the same birth date and instead of asking for presents they had a birthday party and asked for canned goods for the hungry and donations for "Make A Wish Foundation". These two little girls had raised in one day what many adults would take years to earn. I loved this story. It was encouraging. It was proof that there were not only bad things but also good things happening in the world. These little girls reminded me why I still love my job. I believed I was making a difference. I understood that even on a day when some felt hopeless like they couldn't go on others were here to inspire and remind us why we should press on and not only face but look forward to another day. These two kids were smart enough to know we're all in it together. One day you'll need a hand, the next you'll lend one. When one feels lost others have to be a beacon of light. Today, I was helping provide that light in our newscast. People all over Houston would be encouraged and inspired after watching my report and they told me so with an inundation of emails after the story aired. I was extremely proud of that.

I had to stop reading emails and get to rehearsal. Tomorrow is the big charity fashion-show I'm in to benefit the homeless and tonight is our practice run. I so love this event. I get a chance to see so many of my media friends that I don't often get to bump into. I had been doing this show eight years. It made me feel like a kid again. It was like playing dress up then prancing along that beautiful stage so everyone could see. Only now I wasn't sliding into my mom's hard earned apparel. The three fancy outfits I was "modeling" in the fashion show were the best of the best. Saks Fifth Avenue was our sponsor store providing the clothing. Need I say more? I walked into the River Oaks Country Club and the smell from the fresh flowers was heavenly but it wasn't only the scent. The place was full of marble floors, elegant tables, marvelous mirrors, sophisticated sofas and it was decorated beautifully. I guessed this must be what heaven was like. I made my way to the back and in the dressing area there it was, a large rolling rack full of visions of beauty. There was a pale pink tweed Chanel suit, a long chiffon crimson Cavalli gown and an angelic knee length ivory silk Vanessa Bruno number that floated around me when I walked. The three divine ensembles were hanging together and had my name written on a large card that was attached above the first hangar indicating this was what I would be wearing. I slid out of my hot pink Butter by Nadia wrap dress and prepared to play dress up.

It is a five thousand dollar per table event. The mellow music playing was inviting as visitors found their seats. Then the lights went down. The stage lit up and the music got faster. Guests were given a fashion show where members of the local news media were the models. We streamed out one by one strutting to the music in articles of clothing with price tags that made many mortgage payments seem like a drop in the bucket. Even so, these guests would simply pull out their checkbooks and buy as many items that were modeled in the show as they pleased. This was Houston after all. The crowd and the city were full of old "oil" money. After the fashion show everyone was treated to a magnificent four-course meal. The dining hall was full of chandeliers and all things elegant. With every article of clothing purchased by guests or by us, the media models, Saks donated a large portion of the proceeds to the Star of Hope homeless shelter. We had raised millions over the years. I was very thankful for that but I wish I could change one thing. I believe some of the families the shelter helps should be allowed to attend and maybe even model in the event. Especially the women and the children, men don't necessarily get into that kind of thing but organizers told me if they take away tables to give to the Star Of Hope clients that would mean less money raised because less tables would be sold. I was determined to change that.

"As soon as I financially can I'm buying two tables for some of the women and their children who are living in the homeless shelter" I promised myself out loud. Not only do we need God, shelter, food and love in this life it's always a treat for me to enjoy beautiful surroundings such as this fashion show and the meal that comes with it. Those ladies and their kids would love it. I'm also going to add a raffle. The guests filling the tables will buy raffle tickets. Each client in attendance from the shelter will have her name written on a ticket. If her name is chosen she will win one of the dresses modeled in the show and the attendee who bought the winning raffle ticket will receive a discount off of her clothing purchase.

"Well, maybe the clothing article given to the shelter client won't be a gown. I guess that would be weird for someone to lug around a $10,000 Oscar de la Renta if they are in a shelter trying to find a home. So in the raffle the woman would win one of the casual outfits modeled in the show," I smiled and promised myself I would make it happen.

TWENTY-FOUR

I was in desperate need of holy water. Who says that? I know. I realize this isn't your average everyday essential item you find on your "things to get" list but trust me it's necessary. By this time I had a new boss who may have moonlighted as Dracula sucking the blood and the life right out of unsuspecting victims at night. Actually, he did that in the daytime too, minus the slurping your blood part. He just drained you in every other way. I have never been one to say bad things about bosses or have bad experiences with them but, wow, now this made the second bad boss in a row. I wasn't exactly batting a thousand, more like striking out, throwing gutter balls or to use a tennis term, I was getting love, zero, from the person who sat in the big office. I was getting about as much love professionally as I was personally. Pretty sad, huh? I had worked in four different newsrooms, seven if you include my campus TV station in college and my two internships at CNN and Headline News, and I had never had a bad understanding with a supervisor or any of my coworkers for that matter. In fact, I have been in the workforce since I was fourteen years old. Shortly after my fourteenth birthday I got a summer job cleaning up the junior high school. Then I worked at the neighborhood pizza parlor "Pepperoni Pete's" it was called. I learned to make dough and pizza from scratch and yes I can still spin the dough in the air and flip it on my fingertips. I recently did a story on a pizza parlor making heart shaped pies for Valentine's Day, one of my favorite holidays, and as part of the story I washed up, put on an apron and got to work. It was like riding a bike. I was impressed to see I still have it. Also, from age fifteen to twenty-one years old I worked at Parkside Credit Union there in my hometown Wayne, Michigan. During my college years I only worked at the credit union in the summer but my point is, in all that time at all those companies with all those different people I had never had an issue with any of my bosses or supervisors. Maybe I should re-phrase that. Not one of my bosses had ever had an issue with me until my last two. I was always openly praised and one of the best and most valued employees everywhere I worked. If I thought bibles would work for my last boss, now I was guessing holy water would do the trick on this one and I'm not talking about just a spritz. Oh no.

I had convinced myself if I could just figure out a way to douse my boss with holy water things would work out just fine. Here's the problem. I'm not talking a vial of the stuff. Oh no, no, no. For him? My instincts tell me I should go with a bucket, not a small child's beach pail but a car wash sized container or better yet the big metal washbasins like my grandparents had on their farm. If I could only come up with a sneaky way to saturate my boss with the holy water, without him knowing I did it. Maybe I could carry the basin full of holy water into the building, do a ninja roll pass the studio without spilling a drop, Tom & Jerry cartoon tippy toe through the newsroom (complete with sound effects), MC Hammer can't touch-this spider step to the side, then SPLASH it's-holy-water-time right over the top of my boss's head. I could quickly kneel and freeze into a seated position only moving my eyes back and forth and in true Scooby Doo style my boss would think I was a chair. Nah that wouldn't work, he might decide to sit down and dry off. Ooooh I know. I could catch him in the parking lot on a day that it's raining, come up behind him, drench him with the holy water, run off and disappear into the building while he's wiping the water from his eyes but what if the holy water doesn't work as well diluted with rain water? So there's only one way to do it. I would jump up from my desk, start shouting, "We did it. We are number one," dump the tub of holy water over my boss's head then yell, "I'm going to Disney World". I could tell him I was having flashbacks of my old NFL days and tell him I thought we had just won the Super Bowl. Could work, except I don't think women are allowed to play in the NFL. I wonder if my boss knows that. I don't think he's much of a sports fan. Well, the holy water idea is still a work in progress. In the meantime, he told me, "I don't want you on my team. You have a bad attitude. I know you still want to work here but oooh it's not looking good for you".

"Wow, seriously?" was the best I could come back with. In that same meeting he told me he didn't like my voice. He said it wasn't hard enough. You'll never guess what he told me after that.

"You know, some of the women in the business with the best voices get their sound from years of smoking cigarettes and drinking whiskey and vodka. It's true. One of my best friends, a woman I worked with at my last station has an amazing news delivery voice. That's exactly how she got her voice, cigarettes and heavy alcohol," he told me. Then he gave me a 'you-might-want-to-try-it' look as he nodded his head and stared his beady, piercing, unblinking eyes right through me. I couldn't believe this idiot. Did he really think I was desperate enough to give that nonsense a try? Whoa, he was even more wicked than I thought. I left his office deflated, not knowing how I would win or even fight this battle. My ratings were always excellent for the newscasts I anchored. I have plenty of viewers and fortunately the viewers love me but that doesn't seem to matter. How is that possible? That told me this didn't have anything to do with my professional performance. No, this criticism certainly wasn't professional. This was personal. Then different thoughts entered my mind. These two bosses from 'you know where' (from h-e-double hockey stick) weren't a coincidence. I've spent my whole life working hard, doing a good job and being a valued team member. Now two bosses back to back want me fired? God was trying to get my attention.

"Ok. I'm listening God," I mumbled but only a depressing silence filled my ears as I walked back to my desk from my boss's office. I started to feel discouraged and began to doubt myself. Maybe all these years I wasn't doing a good job. I was willing to make changes, improve but that's how I know these aren't professional critiques but personal insults. He said I have a bad attitude? No one on Earth can with any honesty say I have a bad attitude. His suggestion for me to improve, start smoking and drinking? What kind of sense does that make? It didn't but I still started feeling overcome with hurt and sadness that my boss would say he doesn't "want me on his team". I knew he would soon make moves to make that happen.

"You don't have to be sad," the voice told me. I jumped and looked around but no one was there.

"Don't have to be sad? Did you hear what he just said to me?" my voice got Chris Tucker higher with each word, although I wasn't actually saying them out loud. Then, it was more like I heard these words with my heart.

"But did you hear what I said?" and the answer was yes. I heard, what I know was God, telling me I would be just fine and just like that the sadness was washed away.

That's one reason I value having peace at home so much. I may not be able to control how I'm treated or disrespected outside the walls of my house but I'm certainly not going to stand for that nonsense then go home only to be mistreated inside my own home or in my personal life. Apparently Oxford hadn't gotten the memo. In just a few hours I was about to find out just how true that was. Ox was about to go far beyond simply disrespecting me but as I sat in the parking lot at work I had no idea. I didn't have a clue my day was about to go from bad to a living nightmare. After my shift, after such an awful day at work, all I wanted to do was go home and see my four-month-old little princess. I had spent the last few hours at work thinking about how she would so excitedly smile and laugh when I walked in the door. I couldn't wait to hold her in my arms, talk to her, kiss her sweet face and hear her precious voice as she, in her baby talk, gabbed right along with me. As I sat there in the car, before pulling out of the parking space at work, I prayed for my boss. I was asking God to deliver him from the evil that was clearly guiding him to behave the way he did with me, to soften his heart toward me. I haven't always been such an assiduous, obedient Christian who would pray for my enemies. That comes with growth and maturity. There was a time when my holy conversation with the big guy upstairs would have gone more like this.

"Like, God do I have to pray like for my boss of all people?" I would ask in the best child's high-pitched valley girl voice as possible. That one sentence would drag out for a good two and a half minutes as I whined the words. "That guy is a jerk. He's mean. God here's how I see it. I'm only trying to do what you say in the bible. You say, 'many will be called but few will enter the gates of Heaven'. I'm simply trying to help you out, help keep that number down, help keep the riffraff out. We don't want it too crowded in Heaven, right? I don't like crowds. In fact, I think I might be allergic to standing in line and waiting, and itchy rashes are not in this season. Anyhow, the less people who make it into Heaven the better it will be for, well, me. I would have a large stretch of that big beach in Heaven all to myself most of the time. Talk about paradise.

The beachside chef would have plenty of time to prepare shrimp, scallops, fluffy homemade rolls, cheese grits and fresh squeezed orange juice just for me. So if my boss wants to be ugly now. He'll be swimming in fire and brimstone later while I'm kicked back on my eternal vacation in ecstasy". Wow, my prayers and I have come a long way.

I finished my prayer, started my car and headed home. I smiled as I thought of the baby Christian I used to be and the God's girl I turned into. "When you know better, you do better". I said out loud. My two best friends have teased me for years saying life is always so easy for me.

"You never have any serious issues to deal with. How do you make it well into your thirties without facing a single real problem?" They would ask. Well, I had quite a few now. I'm a single mom and my boss wants to throw me out on my backside. I like what I do. Plus, I kind of like the whole having food, water, shelter, clothing and being able to take care of my daughter- thing that a paycheck provides. Not to mention the health care. My best friends had given me a plaque one Christmas. It reads "La La Land". You know, Elvis lived in Graceland. Michael Jackson lived in NeverLand and I live in "La La Land", according to them. That's the name of my house and apparently the name of the place I often dwell. So I happily hung my plaque in the home the sign was named after. I secured it right next to the framed decorative panel that reads "Hey I know I live in my own world but they know me here". I do kind of like the idea of living in my own little private, happy, peaceful, whimsical world. So what I sometimes skip through my house. Doesn't everyone?

So here's the running joke in my circle. My friends will put on this little skit saying while other people sit around with real issues on their mind, my thoughts, well, are on burdens of a lesser kind. One of my friends will start by saying, "Here's what's on my mind. I just can't stop thinking about it. I'm not sure if my marriage is as strong as it used to be". Another will add, "Yes, I need to talk about my marriage issues too". Then someone will say, "I'm not sure I can pay my mortgage this month and I'm really worried my kid is heading down the wrong path". Then one of my friends will pretend she's me and say, "Yeah I know what you mean. Times are tough. I haven't found a single pair of dark denim jeans that I really love in at least three months and I'm not sure if my legs look as great as they possibly can in the jeans I'm wearing now. I was just sitting here asking myself I wonder if my waist looks small and cute in these jeans or just cute?" Then they all die laughing. Sometimes my painful problem, according to my besties, is "Can you tell I have a perfect backside in this skirt? I mean what's the use in being perfect if you cover it all up and no one can tell or even worse? Do you know what I did? I think I really made a big mistake this time. I had my new silk, tulip sleeve sea foam shift dress hemmed and it may be a half-inch too short. What am I to do? It's not as though I can magically make the material re-appear. There's a huge difference between showing a little leg sexiness and downright vulgar. Skank is never in season. Now what am I supposed to do with an unwearable next season Marc Jacobs? I can't very well give it away and be responsible for someone else's fashion nightmare. This is an absolute disaster just like the time I scratched my brand new Tom Ford sunnies the same day I bought them". Then they all fall on the floor laughing. Come on now. I'm not that bad. Anymore!

Thinking about my best friends and the relentless teasing, which was all in fun, put a big smile on my face as I fought rush hour and made my way home. That must have been an odd sight, huh? Can you imagine being the driver next to me, glancing in my window and seeing a strange woman with a weird ear-to-ear smile plastered on her face as she's stuck in traffic on a highway that looks more like a parking lot? Just as I glanced at the guy in the black Hummer stuck next to me in traffic, my grin turned giggle grew into a full-fledged I-can't-breathe laugh. I was thinking about how my 65-year old mother literally dances in her seat in the passenger side of my car when a good song comes on. I'm talking getting down, grooving like she's 22 and on a dance floor. So Gladys Knight or Al Green will be blaring from the radio and out of nowhere she'll start snapping her fingers and bobbing her head back and forth to the beat. No, you don't get it. When she does this her neck is like a spring flinging her head back and forth like the dudes in the head bobbing skit on Saturday Night Live, only this is an elderly woman in the car next to you nodding her noggin as if she was a teenage boy listening to rap music.

"I don't get it, Mom. Why do you do that?"

"Do what?" she always answers as if surprised by my question. Is she kidding? I'm not sure why my mom's head bobbing to the beat was so humorous to me right now but it was. I seemed to be jumping from one funny thought to another. Now tears were rolling from my eyes and my side started to hurt I was laughing so hard. I seriously couldn't catch my breath as I thought about Nora, also known as the black Lucille Ball. If there was a situation that was goofy, outlandish, bizarre and ridiculous Nora was going to be caught right in the middle of it. For instance, she and her high school sweetheart husband have been married since the day after Jesus' last supper and she's so careful about not wearing clothes that are too revealing, I don't even think her husband has ever seen the woman naked. Ok, so I exaggerate but honestly Nora never wears short skirts or shows her arms or wears tight fitting clothing.

"It's tacky," she says and no one is ever going to catch her putting her body on display for all to see. Well, there was that one-day. I was in town for the weekend, staying at my BFF's Atlanta home with her, her husband and their four beautiful babies. I love staying at their house. I always feel like I'm on vacation in a palace or a castle. Nora's house is one of the most beautiful homes, inside and out, I have ever seen. First of all, her community is a neighborhood of mansions. Outside, her 10,000 square foot three-story home always looks as though it's prepared to be photographed and featured on the cover of a magazine. Inside her house is like a museum but a comfortable, homey museum. You see some of the most gorgeous, unique items you ever want to lay eyes on.

She, on a weekly basis, has the house completely torn down and re-built. Ok, so I exaggerate again but workers are at her house so much I'm pretty sure at least three of them have their own bedrooms there. I'm only partially kidding. I know her handy man and his team by name. Ray is almost part of the family now. So one day Ray and his crew are doing the usual, collecting really nice checks for doing I'm not sure what at Nora's already beautiful home. Perhaps they were washing the windows, again. All 600 of them were on ladders looking in through uncovered glass, the curtains were pulled back to let the sunlight in. It was broad daylight after all. Nora and I were headed out for a little lunch and some shopping. So, what did she decide to do? Of course, change clothes. The 1,200 (give or take a few) workers at her house were so routine she completely forgot they were there. She went into her bedroom, closed the door (God forbid if I or the kids or her husband happen to see the junk in her trunk), and she took off her clothes preparing to put on her shopping ensemble and did I mention she doesn't wear underwear? So here she is in her best birthday suit standing there and her huge bedroom has at least eight gigantic windows. On the other side of each stood some very red-faced workers who by now were banging on the windows to get her attention, trying to remind her they were there. She had nowhere to run. The nearly glass enclosed bedroom which sat high on the third floor had eyes peering in from every direction. The woman who wouldn't dare let anyone see her in even a pair of jeans without a long jacket to cover her bottom, was now praying those jeans, a mini skirt, a half shirt, a handkerchief could somehow magically appear and cover her goodies but no such luck. Call me cruel but, oh my gosh, it has been so much fun teasing her about this one.

"What, you needed a little extra shopping money? How much did you make in tips? If you thought these guys were at your house a lot before this, you'll never get them to leave now. The good news is you'll no longer have to pay them to be here. They're going to be hanging around whether you fork over cash or not. Heck they'll probably start paying you to allow them to be here," I earned the right to clown her about that. You should have heard the things she said to me a year ago after her husband walked in on me while I was in their shower after he returned from work, heard the water and thought it was Nora in there. Their bathroom is just so awesome with all the latest gadgets. Nora told me to give it a try. So I did and I wish I hadn't. I was majorly embarrassed when he walked in and only water covered my body. We both screamed like we were being attacked by wolves. Then everyone in the house came running into the bathroom. Great! As if I wasn't embarrassed enough.

Why was I thinking of all these goofy stories? I didn't know the answer but I was certainly enjoying it. I had a complete comedy show going on in my head while trapped in traffic. After the day I had, I was truly appreciating, more like relishing my long joyful laughs no matter how insane I must have appeared to the other drivers.

"When is this freeway congestion going to clear"? I threw the question out to my empty SUV. "I need to get home and kiss my princess," I continued conversing with my invisible occupants.

"Boy today has been a strange day but it'll be better when I get home to my sweet baby." I had no idea I was rushing home to what may become my last day alive.

TWENTY-FIVE

SMACK! I saw it coming before I
heard the impact but there was nothing I could do to stop it. It
happened so fast. In bumper-to-bumper, stop and go traffic,
the car on the side of me slammed into the van in front of it.
Fortunately no one was hurt but the car was crunched up
pretty good and I continued trying to make it home in rush
hour traffic. Just then my cell phone started to ring. Caller ID
told me it was "home" calling. When I became a Mommy I
would always get excited and a little nervous when I received a
call from "home". I could never say hello fast enough. I always
wanted to feel that relief of knowing the phone call was not
because something was wrong with the baby and this time was
no different.

"Hey there," I answered the phone. "Is everything ok?"

"Yes. Everything's fine," my mom answered and my
heart started beating normally again.

"What's up?" I smiled.

"Daffi your power just went out," my Mom informed
me and my smile was wiped from my face. "I was sitting here

with the baby watching TV and everything just went black. The A/C stopped. All the electricity just went out," my mom explained.

"You're kidding? Let me call the company and see why there's an outage in the neighborhood. Hopefully the electricity won't be out long. I'll call you right back". I couldn't believe what the lady at the electricity company was telling me. My power was out "for non-payment". Ok, so I know what those words mean but it took me a while to comprehend. "Non-payment? My electric bill hasn't been paid?" I asked the lady as if she was the one who was supposed to have paid it.

"Oh gosh. Can I pay it now with my debit card over the phone?" I blurted out as if the faster I asked the question the faster the power would be turned back on at my house.

"Of course," she answered.

"Oh thank God." I gave her my debit card number. She said she just needed to wait for the card to be accepted and she would give me my confirmation code. As I held the line I was so disturbed by how I could do something so irresponsible. Well, I had been really stressed at work. The whole having bosses who want you fired thing can take a toll. I was also suffering separation anxiety now that I was back at work and leaving my brand new baby for someone else to take care of because my maternity leave was over. My cousin Nora warned me I might suffer what she calls "Baby Blues, postpartum depression" where you seem to be sad for no reason and or experience "Mommy Memory". She says new mommies can become so consumed with making sure the immediate needs of the baby are met that you just "plum forget even things that used to be routine. That's mommy memory". I was keeping a daily diary of my feelings because postpartum can be serious and Nora cautioned me at the first sign of Baby Blues I should immediately talk with my doctor. Fortunately, I never did experience that. I was deep in thought when the lady at the power company shocked me. It was as though she shot me with a stun gun straight through the phone.

"Great. Ma'am your payment is processed. We should be able to get a technician out tomorrow night or the following morning to get your power back on".

"So I can't just make the payment and the lights pop back on automatically?"

"No ma'am. It doesn't work that way. Our technician shut your electricity off and a tech will have to turn it back on," she laughed. She actually chuckled while delivering the sentences. What was funny?

"But the power just went out. Surely the technician is still there by my house. Certainly it took him a few minutes to pack up his tools and equipment. On top of that, I live in a cul-de-sac at the back of my sub-division. It takes nine minutes to drive pass the playground, the tennis courts, the duck pond, over the bridge, pass the clearing where you can see the cows on a good day and then you finally come to the exit gate where the smiling guard always nods at you as you drive by. Will you at least give it a try and call the tech to see if he is still in my neigh..." She cut me off.

"Ma'am. You didn't pay your bill. This is what happens when you don't pay. Now that you have paid, we have to follow policy to get your power turned back on. Our technician is still in your neighborhood. I just spoke with him. He radioed in to say he would be back at the office shortly. He was stopped at the duck pond in your sub-division organizing his tools and equipment but we have rules ma'am. The priority for you should be keeping the power on, ma'am, not begging to get it turned back on once it's shut off. That's why we have notices with dates and amounts to give you a courtesy reminder and you ignored that. Have a good night ma'am". She scolded me in her southern drawl and hung up on me.

"Thank you for your kindness and consideration ma'am. I have been a loyal customer for nearly 10-years and you are clearly considering that, correct? I hope when you need someone to put "people" before "policy" that person is as understanding as you are," I said to the dial tone and I headed home to my house to tell my mom the power was out because I didn't pay my bill. I was constantly making someone else's crisis my emergency. Why didn't anyone ever seem to give me the same courtesy? Just the other day I received a call from a woman who lived in an all-inclusive apartment complex. Residents pay their rent and the utilities are included. Well, the tenants lived up to their end of the bargain but the slumlord had not. In the Houston heat the residents had been without power for a week and seven days without air conditioning in Houston can be a death sentence. So I pitched the story. I wasn't approved to do it because we needed someone to cover a 'news of the day' story but that didn't stop me. The story I was assigned was important but so was this one. If I worked fast I could still get help for those residents before I started working on the case of a business executive who was kidnapping prostitutes, blindfolding them, taking them to his suburban home while his wife was at work and kids were at school and he was raping and beating them. Well, he was finally caught and his trial was starting today. I still needed to secure a legal analyst and try to track down victims and relatives of the suspect, especially the wife.

First, through property tax records I tracked down the owner of the "powerless" apartment complex, Mr. George Clements (I use the term "Mr." lightly). Through one of my trusted sources I learned Mr. and Mrs. Clements had regular routines they followed. So I called and told good old George I knew where he played golf and the country club he and his wife belonged to, where she had lunch every Tuesday before enjoying an afternoon of spa treatments there. I informed Mr. Clements I, a photographer and a large news camera would be happy to meet him and his wife at their fancy pastime places if the tenants at his apartment complex didn't have power before noon. As added incentive, the photographer and I even jumped in the news van and headed to the Clements' estate. As we drove I made calls to set up the news story I was actually covering. The Clements' ritzy neighborhood was less than excited to see a news crew coming. I saw someone peek from the Clements' window as I knocked on the door but no one answered. I made sure to call out announcing "Mr. and Mrs. Clements I'm here to speak with you about your rental property in Southeast Houston. The residents haven't had electricity all week." Then I asked if they would please open the door to talk with me. That didn't happen. I left my business card wedged in the elaborate, thick wooden front door. The residents had their power restored in less than an hour. I just couldn't leave those people without lights, air conditioning and without a way to cook, any longer. That was just inhumane. I didn't get anything out of it other than great relief knowing I could help right a wrong for all those people. I loathe tension and confrontations. I didn't look forward to confronting the Clements but some people could care less about doing bad things to others as long as they believe no one will find out. They have a way of doing the right thing if they believe everyone will know about what they are doing. So I clearly made those residents' crisis my emergency. I knew if this guy thought he was going to be embarrassed on the news he would get the electricity bill paid and the power restored. If I hadn't stepped in there's no telling how long this creep would have left those people that way. I made it right on time to the courthouse where a different creep was about to come face to face with yet another blindfolded female. Only this time lady justice, hopefully, would not become one of his victims.

I arrived at my house and, yep, the power was off. I pulled into my driveway and, out of habit, pressed the garage door opener and I was mildly surprised when nothing happened. It was a good thing my mother was in my house. I didn't carry my door key with me, ever. I always go in and out of my house through the garage but no electricity means the power garage door opener was useless. So had my mother not been inside I would have been in big trouble, locked out for sure. Boy, it felt weird to park outside. I got out of my shiny SUV, walked to the back of it and just stood there. My high-heeled nude colored patent leather Prada's were planted in one spot on the cement and my head slowly swiveled looking around at our pretty homes in our neat little cul-de-sac.

"Wow has Dean and Katy always had those magenta flowers and yard lights?" I asked myself. "They look good. Are those solar?" With my arm bent to keep my mocha Chloe bag dangling on my wrist, I could feel the handles of the large and lovely leather satchel starting to dig into my skin but I still didn't move. I had that fish out of water feeling but my rust colored high-waist tweed pencil skirt and matching silk bell sleeve tie-neck blouse wouldn't be without water for long. "Whew". The hot January day was turning into a very warm January night. I finally forced my feet to start walking before I began to glow with great intensity. In other words, I was trying to avoid turning into a big glob of sweat. I could already feel my perfumed lotion starting to melt on my thighs and shoulders. Perspiration and Dior just don't go together, I don't care what season it is. My steps were slowly taking me closer to the entrance of my house. The green lawn and plants were vibrant and so were my yellow, pink and orange flowers. Oh my beautiful red and hybrid pinky orange rose bushes were standing, no more like posing there in front of my large octagon shaped window. I need to give Jose a raise. He's really doing a fantastic job. When I zip right into my garage I guess I just don't notice these things. The colors were as inviting as the thick floral welcome mat that seemed to smile in front of the heavy beveled glass and mahogany wood front door. I could sort of make out my reflection in the glass. How could someone who looked so put together be so irresponsible and forget to pay her electric bill? Not to mention, this woman I was staring at was a new mother. How could she effectively care for a baby if she couldn't even be dependable enough to pay her bills on time? I felt ashamed and I didn't look forward to telling my mother. She was an awesome mom who always paid her bills on time. We didn't have much money but I never had to worry the power, water or gas would be shut off. In fact, my mom made sure to teach me the importance of being responsible and paying bills, not on time, but early. Now, after years of setting a good example and all of her hard work that went into teaching me to budget and pay my bills, I was letting her down. I was essentially saying 'Mom, I don't care how you do things, could care less what you tried to teach me. I'm going to ignore how important you say it is to be reliable. I choose to be immature and undependable. You wasted your time trying to teach me otherwise.' There I was standing, staring at my front door. I was frozen with the glow of the doorbell on my hand but I hadn't pressed it yet. I wonder how this little light is still shining. Maybe it's wired through the back-up battery for the alarm system? The thought left my mind as quickly as it had entered. Ding Dong. I finally did it. Through the glass door I could see it was dark in my house, only the glow of candles and my mom moving closer to the door. She opened it with a smile.

"Hey Daf did the electricity company say when the power would be turned back on? I wonder what happened?" she asked. Instead of standing tall, like I normally do, my shoulders were slumped. I was donning droopy Dior and my face matched my eyes. Both were somber. She immediately changed her facial expression when she saw mine. "What's wrong, honey," she asked without saying a word.

"Mom, I didn't pay my power bill. That's why it's out. I don't know how I could forget to do something so important but I did," I revealed with embarrassment. She saw how upset I was. She knew I had learned my lesson and nothing she could say would make me feel any worse than I already did.
So in typical, "my Mom" fashion she started.

"Don't beat yourself up. You know, you now have two people to be responsible for. You understand that and I know you will likely never do anything like this again. You work hard. You are a great mother. I'm so proud of you. You've had a lot on your mind lately and it's ok. The electricity will soon be restored and so should your faith in yourself. You are one of the hardest workers and most reliable people I know," my Mom reassured me and gave me a loving, much needed hug. She had done her job raising me and now as an adult it didn't take arguing, fussing or fighting for me to remember what she had taught me. She was still my number one fan and the loudest on the squad in my cheering section. What in the world would I do without my mom? I hope I don't have to find out any time soon. Tears were starting to well in my eyes as I thought about how much I love her and how I appreciate all the support and everything she had so lovingly done for me. The truth is I think I was still very emotional from my pregnancy. My body and emotions were not quite back to normal and I was still adjusting to my new job as "Mommy". For the first time in my life I was holding that title and I took the new challenge very seriously. I was enjoying every second of motherhood but I still took the responsibility as just that, one heck of a task. My mom and I stopped hugging when I heard a beautiful sound. My little one was awake and calling out from her bed. I quickly washed my hands and walked into her soft pink and yellow room.

"Hellooooo Sweet Pea," I sang to her smiling face. I reached for her and she almost leapt into my arms. Her giggle was like music and seeing her little face every day after work was like laying eyes on a masterpiece. Having her was better than winning the lottery. She was just such a treat. It was a blessing to be able to squeeze her tight and call her, my own. She started looking around and I'm telling you I thought any second she was going to ask me why we were chatting by candlelight. She was big and very alert to be just four months old. On my mom's quest to find candles and flashlights she came across something else. Pictures. She had only been back in Houston at my house for less than two weeks. So she hadn't seen all the photos of the engagement ring Oxford left all around my house but she discovered some of the ones I hadn't yet found. She laughed.

"What are these?" She was grinning as she held up the snapshots of the beautiful, brilliant diamond ring.

"Oh gosh. Oxford hid a million and one pictures of the engagement ring he bought for me all over my house. He's trying to leave subtle hints to try to get me to marry him. So, pack a little bag. I guess we're staying at a hotel tonight," I said changing the subject and it didn't go unnoticed but my Mom didn't push. She had that I-would-love-to-know-why-you-won't-marry-Oxford look on her face but the question never left her lips. You know, it wasn't that I didn't want to give her the information. I just didn't know what info to give. I didn't really have an answer for why I wasn't saying yes to Oxford. I just felt I didn't know him and the longer I knew him, I still didn't know him. Confusing? I know. That was sort of how it was trying to get to know Oxford. He would say we were best friends and that I knew him better than anyone else in the world but I always thought 'how could that be so?' He could be as kind and as sweet as pie and super pleasant to be around but then there were those times he disrespected me to the fullest. Sure, he always apologized after but these were incidents that shouldn't have happened in the first place. A large part of him was a stranger to me every time I saw him. It was weird and I didn't know how to explain that to my mother. It was almost as if he couldn't decide exactly who he wanted to be and so he was sort of all over the place. That was sometimes my perception but I didn't know if it was fact. So I thought maybe this is a good time for my mom to get to know Oxford a little better. No time like the present. I picked up my home phone and started making melodies with the keypad. Area code and phone number, ten digits later and "Hey beautiful," Ox answered.

"Hey my power's out. Can the baby, my mom and I stay at your house tonight?" It's funny how I didn't feel embarrassed telling anyone else my electricity was off but somehow revealing that to my mom was the worst. I knew she taught me better and I felt it was a slap in her face for me to disregard everything she had shown me. She truly led by example.

"Are you kidding?' Oxford shot back. "You don't have to ask me that. You guys are always welcome at my house. You never have to leave if you don't want to. I'll be glad to get home and see my favorite girls. I cooked earlier. Help yourself. My mom is there at my house. Go on in and I'll be there in a couple of hours," he told me.

TWENTY-SIX

I loaded our bags into my SUV and just as I closed the back hatch the January breeze across my cheeks stopped me in my tracks. I could see her large, beautiful mocha colored natural curls blowing across her face. It was a face that looked very much like mine. She was just eight years old and didn't notice the boy that seemed to be staring at every inch of her until he had it all memorized. I had heard the story before but now it seemed to be playing before me like a feature film on a silver screen. I was frozen solid in this daydream that felt more like I was witnessing the events firsthand. It was like I was there. I could smell the morning dew and the dust from the road in this small farming community. The boy's hands were shoved deep into his pockets on purpose as he stood there on that dirt road watching the 8-year-old girl. He was hiding his fingers, which had become severely disfigured. At just eleven years old Rheumatoid Arthritis had caused his hands to close. His fingers had been bent and curled tight into his palms for years. His toes, hidden in his thick white tube socks and high top red canvas Converse gym shoes were the same way. Alexander had been the neighborhood paperboy for months. He knew this family was new to the area. It was a community of black farmers in 1952 in what was then rural Inkster, Michigan. There were just a handful of homes on each small winding road in the area. Alexander was on his paper route when he saw the Keigh family outside doing yard work and tending to the animals. The four girls in the family, my mom and her three sisters, were working the vegetable garden. The oldest girl especially, was so beautiful even as a baby, everyone who came across her said the brown haired girl looked like a sweet, perfect, gorgeous little flower. So her nickname was born Dahlia. As my Aunt Dahlia picked tomatoes Alexander stood, staring, mesmerized at the very sight of this eight-year-old living doll. My grandfather locked in on the little boy's unblinking eyes.

"May I help you, son?" Grandpa called out to Alexander. Another big breeze came blowing by, which wasn't necessarily unusual for an early Michigan morning but something about this day felt different. The dew was in the grass. The sun was just beginning to peak out from the clouds to welcome the new day and the cocks crowed just after the question, giving Alexander time to think of what he would say.

"Looks like we might get rain, sir" Alexander called out to the Keigh property. Then he ran off. A half-mile down the rugged road Alexander burst through the door of his family's home. His chest was rising and falling and he was out of breath. His dark chocolaty plum colored face, white button up shirt and blue trousers were full of sweat. He was breathing heavy and stopped to catch his breath when he saw his mother in the kitchen preparing breakfast. She looked at him as he stretched his arms out in front of him. Tears began to fill her eyes and soon started rolling down her cheeks. Alexander's mother let out the longest and loudest scream of her life.

"What happened to you? How did this happen?" His mom finally formed the words but they came out through deep sobs and the sentences were barely comprehensible. She was looking at her son's hands. His fingers were straightened out for the first time in years and they were not bent, stiff, crooked and curled by the arthritis that had afflicted his tiny hands for so long.

"Thank you God," Alexander's mother whispered.

"She did it. She made me better. I could feel my hands and my feet uncrippling as I looked at her. She makes me better. Mom, I'm going to marry her," the eleven year old told his mother about Dahlia the oldest of the Keigh girls who lived down the road. His mother smiled with a little confusion and a lot of joy at seeing the miracle before her eyes but soon Alexander Benjamin's feet and hands were bowed and barely usable again. Just a few months after the paperboy first laid eyes on the pretty girl, the Benjamin family moved away from Inkster to Milan, Michigan forty miles away.

Ten years later Alexander heard rumors in their Milan neighborhood that a new family had moved in, with daughters. He and his buddy walked a quarter mile down the dirt road to check out the new girls in town. At 21 years old Alexander was a tall, strong, masculine man with a dark black mustache and goatee and shoulders the size of an ox. His skin was juicy and beautiful like a basket full of black and blueberries. Many girls dreamed of eating him up by the handful. Most had no idea Rheumatoid Arthritis had left his hands and feet bent and curled since he was a child. Doctors had already warned him to expect the same thing to start happening to his arms and legs. Alexander was expected to have disfigured extremities by age 25 and to be completely disabled and unable to walk by 30. He lived with severe pain in his joints and throughout his body but he never complained and never let the illness stop him from working and playing hard. The strong strapping young man was also deeply religious and raised in the church. When he showed up at that new family's home in his neighborhood Alexander knew it was divine intervention when he saw the Keigh's there in the yard. The once eight-year-old girl that he fell in love with so long ago was now eighteen years old and even more stunning. Her brown eyes squinted in the sun as it shined on her smooth sand-colored skin. Her large, springy, bouncy curls cascaded over her shoulders and down her back. This time Dahlia did take notice of Alexander. She whispered something to her sister Jeanette as she looked at Alexander and he got really excited.

"Hey look man," he elbowed his friend and grinned larger than the Cheshire cat "she's looking at me." "No, man. She's frowning at you," the friend said.

"No. She's squinting. The sun is in her eyes," Alexander smiled. As he thought "I've got to get to know her. This time I'm not letting her get away".

Unfortunately for him she looked at him saying, "Ewwww he's sweaty. Looks like he needs to bathe". It happened again, like magic. Standing, staring at Dahlia Alexander's feet and hands started to straighten. He said a silent prayer asking God to bless him with Dahlia as his wife. He immediately got his answer. As clear as day, God told Alexander Benjamin "Together you and Bella "Dahlia" Keigh can do great work for me. If you agree to be obedient and speak for me I will give you Dahlia to be your wife". The two married two short years later and my Uncle Alexander swears the story is true, right down to hearing God's voice. He loves to paraphrase Deuteronomy 28:1, 2 saying 'when you are obedient to God nothing is impossible, your miracles will be plenty and blessings will find you and be yours even when you don't seek them out, even when you think you don't have room for anymore'. He says God gives everyone that offer and many decline. They would rather suffer and work for the devil than to be healed and work for God. His hands and feet never bent again and although his body ached from time to time Uncle Alexander's ability to walk was never taken away. In fact, I had no idea my uncle's hands and feet were ever disabled or even that he had Rheumatoid Arthritis until he told me the story well into my adulthood. He became a minister shortly after he and my Aunt Dahlia married. He was the head pastor at Daily Deliverance Church in Milan, Michigan for decades. As much as I love hearing love stories, theirs is truly miraculous, special and I never get tired of hearing it. Although I wasn't sure why it was playing out in front of me now. I thought of my Uncle

Alexander's large strong hands as he held my daughter just a couple months earlier.

"Your hands are looking good. How are you and Aunt Dahlia doing?" I asked him. He always had a sweet story to tell about my aunt.

"We're great. Your aunt is still as smart and beautiful as ever," he smiled. "God has been good to Bella and me. I would be really sick without your aunt. She makes me a better person, a better Christian, a better human being. I'm still in love with her, you know." I thought about how great it would be to have love like that. To have a husband who was my best friend who felt I was not only a huge blessing in his life but a miracle sent to him by God and even after decades of marriage he was still in love with me. Nora and Grayson have that kind of love. I wondered if Oxford was going to be that man for me. There standing at the door of my SUV in front of my pitch black house I asked God to please shed light on what decision I should make concerning a future with Ox. I asked Him to please give me my answer about Oxford tonight.

TWENTY-SEVEN

I guess this day was pretty weird. My house was dark and "powerless" after having the electricity turned off "for non-payment ma'am". I had just watched my Aunt and Uncle's love story play out before my eyes like a movie and I didn't know why. Now we were arriving at Oxford's house and the gate was already open, just waiting for us. Normally I was on the phone with him as I drove up the dark, private road. As Ox saw my headlights the gate would slowly, gracefully reveal access to the exquisite estate, inviting me in. I would always jokingly sing "haaaaaaaaa", the sound of angels as the heavy wrought-iron entryway swung open. On this night it felt odd, as though there was something there in the darkness lying in wait for us but I hesitantly drove in anyway. I shrugged off the odd feeling.

We parked in the area behind the house, just outside the four-car garage, beside the tennis court and just beyond the full basketball court. On this warm January night the swimming pool looked fantastic. Colorful lights in the heated water revealed what looked like a pool at one of the finest resorts. I was tempted to take a swim. We'd had plenty of late night swims before but on this night I was ready to just wash the day away and settle in for the evening. We were all tired, even my little Princess. I kissed her chubby smiling cheeks as I carried her into her dad's house. She was such a happy baby, always talking, smiling and laughing. Her laugh was more than music to my ears.

Oxford wasn't there yet. So I lugged our bags inside. My Mom and I sat in the family room talking with Gerta for a bit before we excused ourselves to get cleaned up. After taking baths and I bathed my Sweet Pea, the four of us met in the breakfast area. We were in clean jammies, smelling and feeling fresh and refreshed. I was feeding my daughter and like any good slumber party we were all snacking on the steak and crab dinner Oxford cooked earlier. Then he walked through the backdoor. He was perkier than any cheerleader and I know cheerleaders. I was one until senior year in high school. A few sentences from "Spunky Ox" and I was immediately taken back down memory lane. In an instant and in my mind, I was dressed in a short pleated skirt, a tight blue and gold sweater with a big "W" on the front, my first boyfriend's varsity jacket and shaking pompoms to melodic words. I was two seconds from jumping out of my seat and yelling "S-C-O-R-E lead us to victory" but a massive kiss on my forehead from Ox smashed me back into the kitchen chair and back to reality. Then "smack" he gave my daughter a wet one on the head and with lips still puckered he was aiming for my mother's eyebrows. Three smooches to the forehead and then he blew a kiss to his mother. He was smiling and talking non-stop.

"How are my favorite girls in the whole wide world? It's nice to have so many lovely ladies here. I should always be this lucky. My house should always be this blessed to have my favorite girls here," Oxford sang with spirit. He was quite lively at eleven o'clock at night.

"Who are you Marsha Brady?" I asked and I'm telling you I could almost see long straight blonde hair on his normally baldhead.

"What? I can't be happy to see you guys?" he laughed. "Wait, Ms. Keigh," he said to my Mom. "I've got something to show you". He almost skipped out of the room. He quickly re-appeared with a Pinocchio like presence but he stopped short of saying "I'm a real boy now". Ox held a small box in his hand. He was grinning from ear to ear as he slowly opened the tiny-hinged square that held a not-so-tiny diamond engagement ring. It was shiny and beautiful and BIG. The four-carat princess cut diamond was surrounded by what seemed like one million sparkling smaller diamonds covering the platinum band.

"Boy, it sure looks beautiful. Might look even more beautiful on my finger," I thought but didn't dare say it out loud.

"I'm gonna' marry your daughter, Ms. Keigh. I gave her this ring and proposed but she hasn't accepted yet," he looked at me and smiled. I could tell my mom was excited. She was a single mom and she wanted better for me. I knew that. She didn't want me to experience the same struggle. Parenting is hard work and even more so when you have to go-it-alone. She wanted her granddaughter to have a full time father, unlike the part-time, sometimes dad I had. My mom grew up with both of her parents on that farm in Milan, Michigan. Her parents were married for seventy-one years, and they died two weeks apart right around age 90. My grandmother passed first, then my grandfather died of a broken heart. He missed my grandmother so much it killed him. Oxford's touch interrupted my daydream. He took my hand in his and I could see a tiny circle headed straight for my ring finger. I panicked. I quickly curled my fingers and slid my hand back into my lap as if I was yanking away from a snapping turtle or even a hungry Rottweiler. I didn't really understand the reason behind my reaction. I felt if that ring slid onto my finger it would grab me and set a series of booby traps into motion that would keep me imprisoned forever. I was pretty sure that reaction was a little more than cold feet.

"The ring is beautiful," my Mom said. "Tell me about yourself. Why do you want to marry my daughter?" my mom smiled at Oxford as she tried to get to know him better but his reaction was strange. He just kept rattling off a string of words that seemed to never stop.

"Your daughter is so beautiful. I've never loved anybody like I love her. I'm just a big softy, a teddy bear. You think I should have bought a bigger ring, a bigger diamond? It's so good to see y'all. I'm so glad you all are here tonight. You are welcome in my house anytime. You don't have to wait for your daughter to come. You like to swim? I have a pool. You can come by and swim if you want," my mom grinned and tried to get a few words in as Oxford rambled. I could tell she thought it was nervous chatter. She looked at him as if she thought 'How sweet. He's nervous to get to know me' but I didn't believe that was the case. I thought Ox was high on drugs. I had never seen him like this before. In fact, I don't have much experience dealing with people under the influence that I know of but I was almost certain. He wasn't slurring his words or anything like that but he just wasn't quite right. If eyes are the windows to the soul, either his windows or his soul was glassy, glazed over and in what seemed to be a drug-induced stare. It was as if someone wound him up and I was afraid to see what would happen once he started coming down. Well, it was late. Maybe he could sleep it off and I could have a talk with him about it in the morning when he wasn't intoxicated.

"Alright good and fine people that's enough talk of nuptials this evening. I'm exhausted and it's time for all of us to turn in," I said standing with my daughter in my arms. "Where are we sleeping, Oxford?" I asked. He smiled. "I'm not kidding. Come on. Tell me so I can show my mom to her room and I need to know where the princess and I should crash," I said.

"Maybe Oxford will show me to my room," my mom said as she started asking him more questions. I could tell she was excited and wanted to get to know him better. She was also glad to hear he wanted to marry me. I hugged and kissed her. She did the same to the baby.

"I love you. Sleep well and say your prayers," I called out to her.

"I love you too Daf," she said back. Ox held up one finger.

"Stay right there. Don't move," he said to me. "I'll be right back." He left to show my mom to her room upstairs. I told Gerta goodnight, changed the baby's diaper and grabbed a bottle of ice-cold water. Oxford came back a short time later.

"Come on let's go in my bedroom," I gave him a true evil eye. "I'm not going to try to touch you. I promise. Let's just talk until we fall asleep. I hardly ever get to see you and the princess. I'm excited about having you guys here," I was too tired to argue. Then I started thinking maybe I'm wrong and Ox isn't under the influence. As far as I know Oxford doesn't do drugs. He despises them. He previously told me he hates drugs because someone close to him had been addicted. Maybe he was behaving this way because he was glad to have us here. This is the first time he's spending quality time with my mom. He had been asking me to marry him and now maybe we're closer to that actually happening.
Heck, I don't know. I need some sleep.

"Oxford please! Just stop talking," I said. Oxford was yapping non-stop like one of those tiny aggravating dogs that can be heard by everyone in the neighborhood but can barely be seen by anyone even if the little runt is standing on your foot. Ox was talking so much our daughter started giggling.

"She, unlike me, thinks your babbling is hilarious," I pointed out and that egged him on even more. He started playing with her, talking to her and making her laugh even more.

"Where's Daddy's princess? I see her. I see her. Peek-A-Boo. Sweet Pea needs sugar right here," he kept kissing her and making noises on her neck and she loved it. His loud voice was echoing through the house. I saw a dark figure in the bedroom entryway.

"Hey," my mom smiled. "You guys still awake, I hear. What's so funny?" she asked.

"Oxford, apparently," I answered giving a small smile in the direction of Ox chomping on Sweet Pea's neck.

"Oh Oxford she loves that. She's going to have you doing that all night," my mom laughed. Mom was still on cloud nine about being here with Oxford and about the thought of us righting the wrong we were currently in. She was thinking perhaps we would get married and have a proper family. My mom climbed onto the foot of the huge California King bed and started talking to Oxford. It was almost like someone flipped a switch. He shut completely down when mom sat on the bed as if she had sat on his face or something. He was cold, staring at her with disgust, clearly telling her, without saying a word, she didn't have a right to be here and he threw her out of the room. I couldn't believe it. He held her arm, helped her up off of the bed, led her to the bedroom door and he said, "It's late. Do I need to show you to your room again? We're about to go to sleep now".

"Oh. I'm sorry. It sounded like you guys were wide awake. So I was just going to enjoy you all for a little..." my mom was saying but I have no idea if she was finished.

"Good night," Oxford interrupted as he closed the door in her face. Ok, now he has gone way too far. Who does that? In my family hanging out together is what we do. While most of my family is still in Michigan, I have relatives who live all over the country. So we often visit and, of course, we stay at each other's homes. Typically, we all hang out in the same room until we just completely fall out and can no longer keep our eyes open. Even if most of the people in the house go to bed for the night it isn't unusual for a small group to gather in someone's bedroom talking and watching TV until we pass out. I've been the third wheel and crashed many times at the foot of a loved one's bed and talked with them and their spouse until we all fall asleep. My family is just really close like that. We enjoy one another and there has always been an open door policy. No matter what time of night, I have never felt as though I couldn't go into a loved one's room and talk. Apparently Oxford's family was not the same but I had to find out the hard way.

"Oxford that was pretty rude. Why did you throw my mom out of the bedroom like that?" I sort of whispered to make sure my mom didn't hear.

"Why would she come in here like that, sitting all on my bed and stuff? Nobody invited her in here. Nobody asked her to come in here. She can't just come walking in here," he ranted loudly, enraged. I was shocked. Then there was a knock at the bedroom door. Oxford snatched it open but used his body to block the doorway.

"Look. Don't come back to this room tonight. Get upstairs to the room I showed you and don't come back down here," he actually yelled those words to my mother and he closed the bedroom door in her face. I actually laughed a little.

"You can't be serious. Oxford do you really think that was acceptable?" I got up to open the bedroom door. I turned the doorknob and the door barely swung open. Then I saw Ox's large hand go pass my head. He smashed his fist into the door and slammed it shut.

"That's enough Oxford," I calmly said to him.

"You're right that's enough. I've had about enough of this crap. Get back in the bed. You and your mother need to stop playing these games," he screamed like a madman.

"Ox no one's playing any games." He and the situation were already way out of control. I had earlier had the suspicion that he was high on drugs. Now I was sure of it. All I wanted to do at this moment was deescalate the situation and discuss it with him the next day when he was no longer under the influence. I'm not sure how she did it but my little princess managed to fall asleep there on the bed. She looked so peaceful in the middle of this madness. I felt completely disrespected and I was more than upset and outraged that he would be so insulting, rude and disrespectful to my mother. That was a no-no but my plan was to have him sleep it off and have a VERY LARGE discussion about it in the morning. For now, I would remain civil, go check on my mom and everyone could get some sleep.

"Why would she come barging in here like that if she's not playing games?" Oxford yelled.

"Ox, you know, I think my mom came to the room because she's excited about getting to know you. You showed her the ring and went on about wanting to marry me. She's excited. In my family..."

"I don't give a (f-word) what she is. I don't give a (f-word) about your family. She better take her a** back upstairs and not come back in here."

"Oxford please move your hand from the door so I can go and see why my mom knocked and so I can apologize that the door was slammed in her face."

"Get the (f-word) back in bed."

"Ox! Are you kidding? You can't order my mother away from your room like that. You certainly can't speak to her or me the way you're speaking right now and you can't command us to do anything." By this time he was talking over me, more like yelling and cursing over me like a madman.

"Get the (f-word) back in bed." I just couldn't believe his behavior.

"Hey Ox. I really appreciate you agreeing to let us stay the night but we're going to get going," I said to him and that made him even angrier.

"Get back in the (f-word) bed. I'm not going to say it again," he yelled. I couldn't believe he really thought he could speak to me or to anyone this way. It was almost comical.

"We both know that's not going to happen. I'm not getting back in your bed. You know I don't deal with people who speak to me this way," I picked up my daughter and our overnight bag. "You have lost your patience and now I'm losing mine. Get out of my way and let me out of your room."

"You (f-word) (b-word). Who do you think you are? Who do you think you're talking to?"

"Look. I'm not going to argue with you and now I'm no longer going to have a conversation with your disrespectful, ignorant behind. Move out of my way." I could hear a voice in the hall.

"Suck 'em? Open your bedroom door." Thank God. It was Gerta.

"Go back to bed mama. Everything is fine," he said in a sweet-as-sugar voice.

"Open the door Suck 'em," she nicely asked again. My heart was racing and I was actually terrified trapped in that room with him. He stood now not saying anything, just staring a hole right through me. He was breathing heavy. I watched his chest rise and fall as if he was contemplating his next move. His eyes were sort of squinted and one twitched but he never blinked. He looked at me with hate in his eyes. Just minutes earlier he was bouncing off the walls with excitement saying how much he loved me, showing off the ring and bragging to my mom that we were going to get married. This guy is nuts. His behavior is all over the place. This was serious. This was dangerous. 'What in the world am I supposed to do?' I thought to myself as I also said a silent prayer or two. How did I get mixed up with this nut? How did I get myself into this? How do I get myself out?

TWENTY-EIGHT

Thank God Gerta was insistent. "Suck 'em? Open the door," she called again and this time he did. He flung it open so hard; it slammed into the wall making a loud noise that echoed all over the house and I walked out of his bedroom carrying my daughter and our bag.

"What happened?" Gerta asked. I could see my mother with her overnight bag on her shoulder standing near Oxford's mother. They could both apparently hear every word being said inside the bedroom. So my mom knew we would need to be leaving in a hurry.

"What happened?" Ox's mom asked again.

"We're going to go," I said as I tried to make my way to the backdoor as fast as I possibly could. My mom was right behind me. Eyes reveal a lot about a person and that was the first time I saw that look in Oxford's eyes. It was pure evil. Gerta asked me another question. I'm not even sure what it was. I was focusing on getting the heck out of there. I thought it was safer for me to save my words for later, walk fast and go. If, at that moment, I told his mom what happened, what Oxford had done, that would have infuriated him, it would have opened the door for dialogue and the madness would have started again. I was certainly trying to avoid that. I didn't want to argue and I didn't want to attempt to have a conversation with Gerta when Oxford seemed so out of control. Now, just wasn't the time. It wasn't safe. I would just call her once we made it to safety. The longer I spent in that house, the more I felt my life was in real danger. Gosh, was the backdoor running from us? We seemed to be walking to that door for five minutes and we still weren't there yet. God please get us out of this house, fast, please. I could feel it deep inside. I needed to pray harder. Something was really wrong here. Then I felt it, a hit or more like a pounding at the back of my head as Oxford grabbed my hair and then my throat.

"You just gonna ignore my mother? You (b-word). You don't disrespect my mother," Ox growled. Of course, by behaving this way and completely disregarding his mother and mine, he was disrespecting his mother and mine to the fullest. Even these actions in his mom's absence should make him feel he's bringing shame and disrespect to her. So I knew his attack on me had nothing to do with him believing I wasn't respecting Gerta but she seemed to believe it or maybe she was using a tactic to get him to stop. I don't know.

"It doesn't matter if she's disrespectful to me. She doesn't have to answer me. I'm fine with that," Gerta told him as I struggled, without success, to get out of his grips. Was she serious? She had known me for some time. She knew I wasn't a disrespectful person and I felt she must have known if I wasn't answering right then there was a reason for it and I would explain later. Ox used me not answering Gerta as an excuse to do what must have been a normal way for him to resolve issues and her sentence seemed to fuel him.

I thought a much better thing for her to say would have been "Hey, Nutcase are you crazy? What are you doing? You don't treat anyone like this. Don't you ever grab her or any other woman by her hair and you certainly don't choke a woman or anyone else for that matter. Now remove your hands from her throat or we're going to have some real problems up in here. I raised you better than this. This is not how I brought you up. You're talking about she's disrespecting me. You are my son. You are disrespecting me, embarrassing me and ticking me off. I brought you into this world and I'll take you out. Don't you ever pull any crap like this again". Well, that was what I thought she should say but she didn't and the attack continued. I was horrified and so was my mother who was begging Oxford to let me go and pleading with his mom to please do something. How did I get here? How in the world did I get involved with someone who would behave this way? I couldn't believe I would put my mom in such an awful situation. She had worked hard since I was born to give me nothing but the best she could, which included a constant peaceful and joy-filled environment, and this was the best I could do in return? I was ashamed and embarrassed and I almost had to remind myself 'and you're being assaulted'. Really? Oh gosh, I am. That was just so shocking to me and it actually took me a bit to grasp, to really wrap my mind around, what was going on. 'He's beating me up' I finally concluded. How did I get involved with such a monster? How do I get out of this? I soon found out you don't get out of being attacked by asking the person to stop, at least not in this case. He seemed so focused, so driven to hurt me. My words, my pleas for him to stop, seemed to disappear into thin air before reaching his ears. I pleaded, I commanded, I asked, I prayed. I did everything but break out into song and dance and sing the sentences, putting on a performance full of pleas and prayers for Oxford to stop.

"Oxford. It's me. What are you doing? I do NOT behave this way. You let go of me right now and allow me to leave your home. Don't you ever attack me again. Don't ever disrespect your daughter, my mother, your mother or me like this again. Oxford! Stop right now. God please help me. We may not be together but we are parents together. God please don't let this evil stranger be my daughter's dad. Please God bring back the man I know. Ox, you're scaring the baby. Stop," but he further disrespected me as I tried to speak. He spoke right over me, yelling at me and calling me names.

He wasn't hitting or throwing punches. He was manhandling me. He was throwing me around like a ragdoll. Was he toying with me? He kept pushing me. He was nearly shoving me to the ground and I would go flailing backwards and finally catch my balance at the last second before I hit the ground, before I tumbled onto the beautiful but hard slate. Maybe he was trying to push me to the floor where he would better be able to get the best of me. Good heavens. If he succeeds in getting me to the ground it's over. I found out I was kind of athletic on my feet. Although I was as tired as all get out, this big guy wasn't getting the best of me. I thought 'Oh gosh. If he punches me he can really knock my block off,' but he kept alternating between choking me and when I would break free he would either grab me to pull me back to him or Ox would shove me so hard I would go flying with my hands flapping in the wind. It was the kind of off-balance hobbling you see put to funny music in a slapstick comedy, clown skit or cartoon after the character slips on a banana peel or trips on a not-so-obvious obstacle. Who knew it was so much work to stay on your feet when you're shoved off balance? I was getting exhausted. I was winded and he showed no signs of tiring. I knew this was too much for me. My small "help Lord" prayers turned into big, full on conversations with my Savior. I needed him to save me now because there was clearly nothing I could do.

"Help Lord," I said aloud. Ox grinned at the words, looked around his house then back at me and raised his eyebrows as if asking 'Oh where is He'? He was choking the life out of me. My hands were sticky with his blood and I tried again clawing his face so he would let me go. Ox ignored the open wounds on his face but as I clawed I accidentally poked him in the eye and out of reflex his hands left my throat and he grabbed his watering eye. That was my chance. I bolted for the back door and out of the corner of my eye I could see my mom carrying my baby right behind me. Just as I turned the knob, flung open the heavy wooden door and felt the warm January night air on my face I heard "Oxford. Please. No," my mother cried out in the most desperate voice I've ever heard. My heart started pounding even faster. Certainly he wasn't attacking my mom. I quickly turned around to see Ox had grabbed my daughter from my Mom's arms. You've got to be kidding me and things were about to get even worse. It almost seemed as if the world was moving in slow motion as I saw my daughter's own father raise his tiny baby over his head. His arms snapped back, and then lurched forward. My heart dropped. My eyes and my body zipped in the direction it looked like the tiny baby might be going but I didn't see her sailing through the air. A fake throw? I was only partially relieved. Would the next throw be real? Not who, but what was I dealing with here? What would make someone behave this way? I didn't have the answer. I had no idea how this ordeal would end. Would I ever hold my baby in my arms again? She was crying with such sadness it broke my heart. I was right there and couldn't comfort her. How could he do this to her? Her screams were so painful to listen to. My mother started to cry. I started praying even harder.

"Oxford give me the baby. Hand me the baby please," but he ignored me, still holding my daughter over his head. I felt like I was starting to lose my mind. I was hearing her somber sobs, weeping and wailing and seeing her high in the air like that, unsteady and in the hands of someone who was clearly unstable. I couldn't take seeing my baby girl in the grips of what was clearly a madman. It was like a switch in me clicked and in a split second I visualized myself attacking Ox with everything in me because I couldn't take one more second of my baby's heartbreaking pleas for help. After I envisioned it, then I made up my mind I was about to do it. I was about to attack him, punch him, kick him and go wild on him and rescue my baby. Seeing her in trouble was beginning to be more than I could handle. Just then I thought of 1 Corinthians chapter 10, verse 13, which basically says God will not allow us to be tempted more than we can handle. Then by some miracle I saw my daughter in Ox's mom's arms and she was handing her over to me. I then made a mad dash, right on my mother's heels, out the back door but my freedom didn't last long. My Land Rover was right there but not close enough. Ox was attacking me again. He snatched a fist full of my hair from my scalp and he was yanking over and over trying to do it again. My head was snapping back like a Pez dispenser. I couldn't believe he was still this angry. I tried to remember what we had argued about but couldn't. He was yelling and cursing and calling me horrible names. Why was he so angry? His mom, mine and I kept trying to reason with him and we were begging him to stop but he didn't even seem to hear us. Since Oxford wasn't listening I was hoping his neighbors were. Over the top of his ranting and the baby's cries I began yelling for help at the top of my lungs.

I screamed for help over and over until my throat started to hurt in more than one way. Oxford's hands were squeezing my neck. It was so painful. Someone had already taken my daughter from me. I think she was with my mom. I was exhausted. I couldn't fight anymore and I could barely breathe. No matter how hard I tried to suck air into my chest I just couldn't do it. As my body started to go limp I could feel Oxford dragging me away from my SUV and toward the swimming pool. "If he gets me into that water it's over," I thought but I couldn't stop him. I couldn't even get air into my body. His hands were pinching my windpipe. He was apparently playing for keeps. He clearly wasn't going to stop until... There was only one thing I could do. Pray. And pray I did. The last thing I remember was Psalm 91 popping into my mind. 'Whoever dwells in the shelter of the Most High will rest in the shadow of the Almighty'. Then in a flash everything went black dark, then bright white. In the light I could see Oxford and I weren't the only ones in this sinister struggle. What in the world? The whole backyard at this enormous estate was full of people fighting. I could see great, strong and brave warriors battling ugly, slimy and creepy villains. Were these angels and demons? Then I could see Oxford's body limp like mine and almost in a trancelike state but it wasn't so much his body as it was his soul. His body was completely taken over by a growling, foaming at the mouth demon but how could I see this? Why could I see Ox's soul? Was I hallucinating or even worse? Was I dead? I wasn't going to accept that. As long as I could pray I was going to. I kept asking God for help. I said the prayer of protection from the bible verse Psalm 91 over and over. The praying was all in my mind, of course. I wasn't saying anything aloud. I was watching all of this fighting taking place there in the backyard and I wasn't even sure if I was insane or if I was even still alive.

I kept praying. Psalm 91:1 "He who dwells in the secret place of the most High shall find protection under the shadow of the Almighty. I will say of the LORD, He is my refuge and my fortress. My God, in Him I trust." The words were playing in my mind as if they were scrolling on a TV news studio teleprompter. I knew this prayer but from where? It was familiar, more than just a bible verse. Which book in the bible does this come from again? It came to me. Psalm, of course. How could I not recall that? This was my "in case of emergency break glass. My prayer of protection, Psalm 91". "Surely He shall deliver me from the snare of the enemy and from the noisome pestilence. He shall cover me with his feathers and under his wings shalt I trust: His truth shall be my shield and armor. I will not be afraid of the terror by night; nor the arrow that flies by day; nor the perilous pestilence that walks in darkness; nor the destruction that wastes at noon. A thousand will fall at my side, and ten thousand at my right hand; but it shall not come near me." My body felt cold. I could smell chlorine. I could hear the water in the pool playfully slapping the sides of the swimming pool wall. Was I cold because I was in the water? I wasn't sure but the words of that prayer continued to flow, continued to tumble through my head.

"Only with my eyes will I see the wicked punished. Because I have made the LORD, which is my refuge, even the most High, my habitation; therefore shall no evil befall me, neither shall any plague come nigh thy dwelling. For He shall give His angels charge over me to keep me in every way. They shall take me up in their hands, so that I will not even dash my foot against a stone. I shall tread upon the lion and the reptile: the young lion and the dragon shall I trample. Because she hath set her love upon me, therefore will I deliver her: I will set her on high, because she hath known my name. She shall call upon me, and I will answer her: I will be with her in trouble; I will deliver her, and honor her. With long life will I satisfy her, and give her my salvation."

I finished the prayer, the bible verse Psalm 91. I was substituting 'she' and 'her' everywhere the verse said things like "I will be with him in trouble". I always do that when I read the bible. That gave me comfort. If I can remember that, maybe I am still alive. I could feel myself breathing. In fact, immediately after I finished the prayer, the next breath I took was a long, slow sort of sigh of relief. A peace came over me that could only come from one place. God. He was surely with me.

By this time we were now right there at the edge of the pool. Instead of jumping in from the ledge, Oxford was making his way to the swimming pool steps. At this point, Oxford was the only one struggling. He sort of looked like a person straining to carry an armful and handfuls of heavy grocery bags. Only he wasn't lugging and dragging items but a person. It was me. He had me by my throat. My dangling legs were like the rest of my body, limp. So the next thing that happened was truly a miracle. I immediately thought of the pastor's sermon last Sunday. In his strong and powerful voice he declared, "Do what you can. God will do what you can't. When you do your best God will always do the rest" the pastor proclaimed. That's what was happening to me right now. I had nearly no breath left in my body but before I knew it, just like that, one quick spin and I was out of Oxford's grip. I could barely breathe. It was all I could do to get air into my lungs. I certainly couldn't take the credit for that NBA style fancy footwork, impulsive impressive pivot special spin miracle move that got me away from Oxford. There was a path of light leading straight to my SUV. I saw my mom get into my Land Rover with my daughter on her lap and slam the passenger side door.   Suddenly that bright light was gone and there was darkness ahead of me. I could see fighting again. I knew this was much larger than just Ox and me. It was truly a battle of good versus evil. Ox grabbed me again but this time I had no fear. Instead I recited Psalm 23. "The Lord is my shepherd. I shall not want. He maketh me to lie down in green pastures. He leads me beside the still waters. He restores my soul. He leads me in the paths of righteousness for His names sake. Ye as I walk through the valley of shadow of death I will fear no evil. For thou art with me. Thy rod and thy staff they comfort me. Thou prepareth a table before me in the presence of mine enemies. My cup runneth over. Surely goodness and mercy shall follow me all the days of my life and I will dwell in the house of the Lord forever".

God was with me. He had sent his angels to protect me and I knew it. I could see them fighting the evil for me. I looked Oxford in the face. "I'll do what I can. God will do what I can't". No matter how he tried to grab me, Ox just couldn't do it. I was quickly moving to get inside my SUV and it was like suddenly he just couldn't keep up. I yelled to Gerta to go inside and get the gate opener. "No really. It's ok. Please, open the gate," I hollered as I jumped into my driver's seat but as I pulled the door to close it there was Ox. His hands were around my throat but as I leaned inside my SUV he jumped back as if an electric shock had jolted him. He stood there blocking me from closing my door but every time he tried to reach in to grab me he couldn't.   He was looking me right in the eye calling me names and telling me how I wasn't leaving his house but there was an invisible shield that kept him from getting to me. I could see a sheet of paper peeking from underneath the seat but I wasn't sure why it was catching my eye. I kept glancing at it and repeating the Psalm 91 prayer of protection. Staring right at one another, Ox yelled, "You are f-ing crazy. I can't wait to tell everybody how f-ing crazy you are," spit was flying from his mouth into my face.

"Look at what you did to my face. You are psychotic. I'm going to ruin you. Everybody in Houston is going to know what you did Ms. Phony News Lady. Ms. Fake Christian," and he slammed my door. I quickly hit the automatic door lock button, in a quick glance I saw the key shining there in the middle console, jabbed the key into the ignition, started the SUV, jerked the gear into reverse and sped toward the gate after getting my SUV turned around. It seemed like this was taking forever. As I hastily made my way down the long driveway I could see the gate was still closed and I was terrified that Ox was inside his house getting his gun and he would soon be back outside coming after me. Why isn't the gate opening? I decided to speed up and drive right through it. Just then I saw it. The large wrought iron bars started swinging open. "Thank you God". Was I driving that fast? Was that dust floating around my SUV into the sky? Certainly I was hauling backside to get out of there but the floating dust clouds seemed to be glowing. I didn't have time to stare. As I drove through the open gates and made a sharp turn out onto the road that dust somehow gave me peace and comfort. The white, wispy slivers of light almost looked like God's angels returning to heaven after he sent them to help me survive a battle for my very life. I shrugged off that thought and locked far away even the notion that I might have seen glowing fighting warriors battling dark evil bad guys. I must have blacked out and because I was praying I likely visualized what I was saying, seeing God sending me help, sending his angels to help me. The devil had his hands around my throat and God delivered me. He saved me.

My Mom sat there without saying a word. My daughter was wide eyed but quiet and clearly comfortable in Grandma's arms. We were headed to a hotel where we could get a goodnight's sleep. I was thankful Ox didn't know where we would be. Then I wouldn't have to worry all night whether he was coming after us. I looked down at my dress and it was nearly ripped off my body. My long sleeve knit DKNY button up collared shirtdress was barely hanging across one shoulder. Nothing else was covered. My whole left side and my belly were completely exposed. I glanced in my rearview mirror and I looked like a madwoman. My hair was all over the place and my hairline was wet with sweat after that intense struggle for my life. I still had Ox's blood on my hands and in my nails. I will certainly be quite a sight walking into a hotel lobby like this.

Something was tickling my ankle. It was that paper that kept getting my attention moments earlier as Oxford blocked me from shutting my SUV door. As I sped down the road I reached for the paper. Glancing at the words and into my rearview, to make sure Ox wasn't coming after us. I was overwhelmed at what was there on the paper. It was the prayer of protection, Psalm 91. My Aunts Jeanette and Jocelyn made plenty of copies and mailed the printed bible verses to everyone they love. They asked us to place the papers throughout our homes and vehicles and that's what we did. I'd had this Land Rover more than a year. So I had completely forgotten about the prayers under each mat and in the back trunk area. It was that prayer that seemed to keep Oxford and his evil out, even as they so desperately tried to get in. This is the same prayer that, two years after protecting me from Ox's attacks, also safeguarded my godsons as someone opened fire on the car they were driving in. That was also the only other time I saw those dust clouds that seemed to glow and rise into the sky after evil was defeated and good was protected, safe and sound. I was thankful to God for His protection and at the same time fearful that Ox had started something that he was determined to finish.

TWENTY-NINE

My front door swung open with a thud and he walked into my house. My alarm was blaring, seeming to yell to the entire neighborhood trouble was brewing. Fortunately, it was only a test. The alarm-installer-guy was upgrading my home alarm and showing me how the system works. I didn't feel comfortable going back home until this mission impossible style home alarm system was up, running and every door and window were monitored. When the alarm was armed my house was like a James Bond laser light filled top-secret spy room. The pinpoint red beam would pick up the slightest movement. The motion detector would catch whoever was there and the alarm would start screaming as loud as it could. A distress call would then go out immediately and help would be on the way. Well, help is already as close as a prayer but it never hurts to have reinforcement, right? While, some people have 9-1-1, I have GO-D, my 9-1-1 Psalm 91 and I have faith that through that alarm system He will get assistance to me as soon as I need it.

"If you have any questions, here's my card. Just call me or press this button and we'll be on your line faster than you can," he interrupted himself, "What's your favorite thing to do?" the installer asked me.

"Ummm shop, vacation, eat good food. Oooh eating cherry cheesecake is my favorite thing to do on a cool crisp February afternoon like this," I smiled as I dreamed of the sweet treat in front of me.

"Ok, so press this button right here and we will respond faster than you can order a big fat scrumptious piece of cherry cheesecake with extra cherries," he smiled back. My five-month-old daughter giggled at the funny man. He was a character, in a good way. I thought to myself he should do stand-up comedy. He would be good at it. He was sort of a skinny, tall, lanky mix between a white Chris Rock and Linguini from Ratatouille but only the alarm installer guy had a hilariously deep Barry White voice, if you can imagine that. I glanced into the family room and caught eyes with my mom as I opened the front door. I was thanking and saying goodbye to the nice man. I felt so ashamed that I was paying for this expensive system, not to keep me safe from strangers but to protect me from a man I knew very well, or once thought I knew. A man I had previously welcomed into and opened my home and my life to, in a very intimate and special way, a way not many people knew me. I was embarrassed. Certainly my mom had taught me better. She raised me to make good choices, to be selective about who I make friends with. I thought I was a good judge of character. All these years I thought I was being so careful. I was college educated, a career woman and quite good at my job. I thought I was intelligent, much too smart to choose a man who would beat me up. The alarm installer was long gone and I was still frozen there deep in thought, feeling really upset with myself for failing to avoid getting into such an awful situation.

Just three hours before this I was here at the door letting out Lt. Peter Parkee. I had worked professionally with Lt. Parkee with the Sugar Land Police Department for more than a decade but this morning was different. I called and told him what happened. It was so degrading saying I had been a victim of domestic abuse. I told the lieutenant I wanted the incident documented, my injuries photographed and I wanted him to hang on to the information and only use it in a future case if Ox came back and attacked me again. I was too ashamed to move forward with formal charges. Lieutenant Parkee tried to convince me otherwise and although he didn't agree with my decision, he still went along with my wishes. I let the towering detective, who looked like a cross between a blond surfer dude and a broad shouldered Brad Pitt, into my house and he immediately smiled at the shrine of family portraits of my daughter and me framed and decorating the foyer.

"You do love the camera don't you?" he laughed and his face turned even redder with every chuckle.

"Yeah but not like this," I pointed to the camera in his hand and then gestured to the clear as day choke marks still covering my neck.

"It isn't your fault. Why are you embarrassed? He should be ashamed for assaulting you, for committing a crime against you. I would be happy to go myself and put handcuffs on this monster and let's see if he's in the mood for hitting someone then. I guarantee you this coward won't raise a hand to me," Lt. Parkee looked right into my eyes and I dropped my head feeling even more shame that someone would have to have this talk with ME.

"Let's get it over with and then I'm waking your baby girl before I leave. My wife and I haven't had a little one around the house in about five years," the lieutenant smiled. Lt. Parkee was wearing his baseball uniform. He played on the police department league and today the officers were taking on the local firefighters. I was still standing as stiff as a board and trapped in thought when my ringing cell phone forced me to move. As I ran to grab it I realized how great my house smelled.

"Those cupcake-vanilla-pumpkin-lavender plug in thingies are scrumptious, aren't they? What scent is that again? Do you remember, mom? Doesn't my house smell delightful?" I asked my mom.

"Your house is delightful. It's beautiful. You always keep it so neat and clean. I'm so proud of you. I love your house," my mom smiled as I answered my phone. She always knew how to make me feel better. She knew I was beating myself up and nothing she could say could make me feel any worse than I already did. She had offered to pray with me more in the last few days than she had in the last few years and I appreciated our prayers together. My mom knew praying with me could help me and get me through this much better than any scolding words she could say.

"No. Oh no. Please tell me that didn't happen," I whined into the phone. My special projects manager was on the other end of the telephone telling me my story, which was scheduled to air today in the 5pm newscast, had been accidentally erased. My knees almost buckled when I heard the word 'erased'. The station was hosting a phone bank for domestic violence awareness. My story was supposed to air informing abuse victims that help is available. Then we would have volunteers set up at the station standing by to answer calls from women needing answers about getting assistance to escape potentially deadly situations. It's funny how God works. Had I not become a victim of domestic abuse maybe I never would have pushed for this story or made the decision that we had to air this story.

"Yes. All the video associated with your story was somehow deleted. I'm so sorry. I don't know how it happened. It's just all gone. It isn't in the system anymore. I just wanted to let you know so you wouldn't be expecting to see it this evening," said April Marx who had been my friend and colleague for years.

"No, April, I'm coming in. This story has to air. I'm telling you this story is going to save someone's life. I know it. I have five hours before airtime. I have to shoot the story again. Is a photographer available? Actually, April please make sure a photog is ready to go with me. I'll be there in 20 minutes.

Thank you so much April. See you soon," April is awesome. I knew she would help me make it happen. I rushed off the phone and out the door right after kissing my princess and showing my mom how to arm the alarm. Lillian Walenski was at work. I dialed her cell phone number five times before she answered.

"Lillian, I apologize, may I please come by and talk with you again? Our last interview somehow disappeared," I explained.

"Maybe that means no one wants to hear from me. Maybe it's a sign. You guys are doing the phone bank right? That should be enough. Just put the number on the screen. I'm sure women will call," she said.

"No, your story has to air," I answered.

"What do you mean it has to air?" Lillian was sort of defensive and I didn't blame her. She had poured her heart out to me on camera. Now I was telling her 'ooops' it's all gone. You weren't important enough for us to take care of the first interview. So now let's slap something together, at the last minute. That's what I felt like she thought I was saying to her but it wasn't. Her story was so important, so necessary. People needed to hear it.

"You mean your TV station has to have something, anything to fill that time? It must be a slow news day. You guys are always after what you think will make for good ratings, huh? Well, it's not just a story to fill time for me. This is my life, you do know that right?" she asked.

"Yes believe me I do. This doesn't have anything to do with needing to fill time. It has to air because it will make a difference. Your story is going to help rescue others and help save someone's life. I just know it," the words reluctantly left my lips. I got the feeling she thought I was a reporter feeding her a bunch of bologna just to get a story but that wasn't, at all, the case. After a long pause I heard these words.

"Come on by, since it 'has to air'. If it's deleted again I'm not doing this again. I barely made it through that first interview. Through tears and pain I gave you every detail, blow by blow. I thought you were sincere when you cried too as you listened. I'll make sure a conference room is available and I'll bring in a couple boxes of tissue. It's a touching story. You might cry. Oh but you've heard it before," Lillian said with the sort of sarcasm that would have made me feel small if I wasn't being genuine. She knew her story would help others but she didn't believe I felt the same way. She thought if my station was reckless with losing the story the first time, we couldn't have cared about getting the message out there but I certainly did care, especially now. It's funny how God works things out that way. Maybe if I hadn't experienced domestic violence, maybe I wouldn't have realized the urgency, the need to air this story but believe me I knew it now. I knew this story had to air.

Lillian was the president of a Houston oil and gas company. Her title was just as impressive as her looks. She was a tall, pretty, intelligent woman with a commanding presence. She was a domestic abuse survivor. Lillian met her husband in bible study, believe it or not. They lived in a neighborhood, in a house, that many people would pay to tour. In their 12 years of marriage Lillian's husband repeatedly accused her of cheating, even though she wasn't. "Because he's just a little jealous," she told herself. He also seemed to get upset whenever she wanted to talk on the phone or go see friends and loved ones. So, calls and visits to her also became few and far between. "Because my husband loves me and wants to be around me and spend time with me," she convinced herself. She was also forbidden from wearing anything her husband thought was sexy. So tailored clothes stayed in her closet and she only wore baggy, illfitting outfits. "Because my husband only wants me to be sexy at home for him," Lillian thought but after years of this behavior she couldn't ignore it any longer. Lillian was an abused woman and for years she didn't even know it. She would soon clearly know just how abusive her husband is. All these years she convinced herself it was something else but her husband was controlling, right down to what she could and couldn't wear. He isolated her from everyone she loved and he became insulting. "You look fat in that. You're not going to wear that are you?" he would say to her. He was emotionally and mentally abusive. He also started to intimidate her. She longed to vent to a best girlfriend but she didn't have anyone to turn to since she wasn't allowed to have friends. This woman who professionally had it altogether felt her life at home was a mess. She was torn.

"I want to leave my husband because he loves me, loves to spend time with me and doesn't want me to wear revealing clothes? " She knew she was trivializing his actions. She couldn't deny it any longer. After years of trying to talk with her husband about his behavior, only for it to get worse, Lillian moved into her own apartment and filed for divorce. She and her husband both secured lawyers and divorce proceedings began.

"This is getting so ugly. We haven't spoken in months except through our attorneys. We loved each other. I still love you. We were married 12 years. This doesn't have to be so nasty and unpleasant. Let's take the horses out this weekend or better yet how about heading to the croquet club to play a few rounds and settle this ourselves. You can have the house and whatever else you want," Lillian's husband told her that Wednesday afternoon when he, out of the blue, called her on the phone.

At the crack of dawn Sunday morning Lillian loaded her equipment into her BMW. She drove to the country club and saw her soon to be ex-husband standing by his Mercedes there in the parking lot. They had played croquet together here, it seemed, millions of times before but this time was different. Lillian had no idea just how different this day would be but she was about to find out. Tom seemed so excited to see Lillian. He didn't move as she drove up. He only stood there watching her, smiling big as she got out of her car.

"Don't get the mallets. That bag is heavy. I'll get them for you," Tom continued to smile at Lillian as he almost skipped over to her.

"Here you go gorgeous. I bought some coffee for you. One sugar, one cream, just the way you like it," Tom announced with a massive grin.

"You're happy this morning," Lillian smiled at Tom. The sentence came out with excitement.

"I'm glad to see my beautiful wife." He bounced from one foot to another. Then he suddenly stopped and stood still again.

"I'm serious. It really is good to see you Lil'," then Tom smiled again. He grabbed the bag of clubs and they headed to do what was, for years, their favorite pass time together. He was giddy with excitement, smiling, laughing, and flirting with her. Lillian hadn't seen Tom this way in years, maybe even ever. Come to think of it Tom had never been giddy, even when he was happy, no one would have ever described him as giddy but on this day he was. They were both playing well and doing a little trash talking as usual.

"I see some things never change. A double tap? Since when is that allowed? Wouldn't it be easier to just nudge the ball along until it goes through the hoop? Is that the best you can do?" Lillian teased. Tom laughed out loud.

"Watch this sextuple peel." Tom teased back.

"Don't talk dirty to me." Lillian laughed.

"Ok, so you think you're going to win? You win, I'll give you a two-hour full body massage. I win, you'll give me, well, I can show you what I want better than I can tell you," Tom said smiling and whispering into Lillian's ear as they brushed bodies.

"You really do look beautiful. I miss you. I miss us," Tom told her. Now Lillian was getting giddy. Maybe the fear of losing her had been a wakeup call for him. Maybe he was ready to be the kind, gentle, thoughtful husband Lillian wanted. Now she was the giddy one. She blushed like a schoolgirl. With all the talking, touching, flirting and laughing the couple played only one game of six-wicket croquet over the course of about seven-hours. Lillian was having a great time.

"Hey, I'm not ready to call it a day. Let's grab a bite to eat. How about dinner?" Tom asked Lillian. She smiled and agreed. They walked into the steakhouse and Tom turned to Lillian. "Hey do you want your prize tonight? You won remember? Why don't we order to go and eat in bed like we used to?" Tom said sweetly to his wife. Lillian looked at Tom through slowly blinking eyes. She saw him through her fluttering eyelashes as she paused and wondered what he was up to. She was just about to say she was going to have to take a rain check and she was going to head home. Just then Tom held her hand, softly kissed her neck and said, "Come on my lovely Lilly flower". She loved when he called her that. He hadn't called her his lovely Lilly flower in years.

"So we're going to carry out? Potato crusted Sea Bass, lobster, roasted veggies and my lovely Lilly flower in my bed?" Tom smiled. He looked so handsome, so gentle, like the man she fell in love with all those years ago. Lillian grinned and nodded her head yes. Tom seemed overcome with joy. He was smiling so hard he could hardly get his next sentence out.

"This is the perfect day. Lil' you know what? I'm never going to forget this day," Tom smiled then laughed.

"Want to hear a joke?" Tom asked the hostess as she came over to take their carry out order. The young curly haired hostess giggled.

"Knock knock," Tom grinned as he made a fist and knocked on the menu.

"Who's there," the hostess' soft voice laughed.

"Atch," Tom's cheeks were round as he tried not to smile and his face looked so happy.

"Atch who?" the short, slim, brown-haired girl asked.

"Atch-choo? God bless you. Did you sneeze?" Tom's face was red and he was laughing even before he got the punch line out. Tom, Lillian and the fresh-faced young lady laughed out loud. "I made that one up myself. That's pretty good huh 'Lil?" Tom asked Lillian. He was still laughing at the joke and high on excitement as they walked into the beautiful home they once shared but for the past three months it was where Tom lived alone. Before you know it they were filling up the bed with food and the floor with clothes. Unpacking carryout never looked so sexy. Every time a dish was removed from the bag an article of clothing was peeled from someone's body. Tom turned on soft music and lit candles on the dresser. The flame, flickering and dancing in the darkness, played with its reflection in the mirror. Tom and Lillian kissed and touched, sharing an amazing meal, sometimes holding hands and relishing a romantic love scene. After eating a few bites the food was finally set aside and there was nothing left on the bed but two bodies that became one. After getting intimate, while cuddling, embracing and hugging they fell asleep in each other's arms.

"Hey sleepy. Sleeping Beauty? Wake up Lillian," Tom called to Lillian. She opened her eyes and smiled at him.

"Don't you want to know why I've been so happy all day?" Tom asked Lillian as he climbed out of bed and walked to the closet. He came back out and around the door with a shotgun pointed at her.

"I've been so excited because I've been waiting all day, actually, heck I've been planning for two months to do this," after being all grins all day Tom wasn't smiling now. Lillian was looking down the barrel, she found herself on the wrong end, of a shotgun held by her own husband. The world seemed to stand still but Lillian heard an unmistakable sound. "Kook-CHOOK" Tom cocked the shotgun, loading a round into the chamber.

"Tom?" Lillian didn't see her husband anymore. There was pure evil on his face and in his eyes. She knew there was no talking to him. So she came up with a plan to save her life. The bedroom door was partially open. She was going to bolt from the bed, out of the room, out of the house, running as fast as she could. She visualized it. Now she was going to make it happen. Lillian leapt from the bed and "POW". She heard a deafening noise that left her ears ringing and then her naked body went numb. She fell to the floor and was left slumped on the Berber carpet like a pile of dirty clothes. Lillian had just been shot. She took a shotgun blast to her belly and she was still alive.

"Look what you made me do," Tom yelled at his wife as she lay there bleeding.

"Please don't let me die. Tom you have to call for help for me," Lillian begged. So Tom picked up the phone, pressed some buttons, put it up to his ear and started talking. He told Lillian help was on the way but she didn't believe him.

"You didn't really call 911 did you?" Lillian asked.

"No I didn't. You want to get out of here? Why? So you can go back to him? You're going to die tonight you whore," Tom growled. After forty-five long minutes of Lillian begging and Tom ranting, threatening and yelling at her, Lillian had had enough. She was in excruciating pain. She couldn't move and the mental torture was unbearable. She didn't know if she would live or die but she was ready for the torment to be over. Tom was right in the middle of hurling insults and telling Lillian how she would soon be dead.

"Shut up and let me die, shoot me again and put me out of my misery or call 911 and get someone here to help me," Lillian ordered through clinched teeth. She was serious and something about that sentence got through to Tom. He picked up the phone and called for help for real this time.

"My wife has been shot. I did. The gun is right here," Tom said into the phone. Perhaps he thought she would die before paramedics and police arrived and he could say it was an accident.

"You'll tell them it was an accident, right?" Tom demanded. Almost instantaneously Lillian could hear knocking at the door.

"Houston police," the officers shouted. The ambulance arrived moments later. Lillian's stomach and her intestines had been ripped out in the gun blast. After a long stay in ICU and months in the hospital, life for Lillian would never be the same. Unbelievably life was actually better in many ways. She could still walk and she was soon more than happy to head back to work. She had good friends, a great deal of happiness and plenty of peace. Her ex-husband, meanwhile, was sent where he belonged, to prison for the rest of his life.

My words were strong, powerful and commanded attention as I told Lillian's incredible story of abuse, violence, betrayal and amazing survival. My report, which aired on the 5pm news, wrapped up with me asking the lieutenant over the Houston Police Department domestic violence unit "So it seems abusers rarely stop. Their behavior only escalates. If there's a man watching now who is an abuser. What is your message to him?" I asked.

"Come on and get yourself some help, man. If you call now on your terms I have plenty of assistance available for you. If I come see you because someone else makes a call after you've committed abuse, then I have something else for you. I have a pair of handcuffs and jail time for you. You lose your freedom, your family, your marriage, your kids," Lt. Mark Hayes answered.

"So you're saying if an abuser is watching right now, rather than using his fist or his hand to solve things his way, he should pick up the phone instead, call you and solve things the right way? He should use the phone right now, as opposed to using his hands later, and call for help immediately?" I asked the lieutenant.

"Exactly. Abuse always gets worse. You're using your hands now. What's next a gun? Don't let that happen. You can stop the abuse right here. I'm talking to someone right now. You are welcome to ask for me personally and I'll take your call and assist you in getting the help you need," explained Lt. Hayes. The number to the phone bank appeared on the screen and the phones started ringing almost instantaneously. I knew the story was going to make a difference for women all over Houston, dozens were calling every few minutes but what happened next I wasn't expecting. A man's voice was on the other end of the hotline phone. The director of the "Abuse Stops Here" program could barely hear him.

"Hello, sir? Are you there?" Annabella Ortiz said into the large black, plastic, old-fashioned looking phone bank telephone. The man's voice on the other end was soft and barely audible.

"I'm using the phone instead of my hand," the soft spoken man said into the phone. Annabella snapped her fingers to get her assistant's attention. She slipped her a note that read 'Get Lt. Hayes on the line'.

"I've been beating my wife for six years and I don't want to lose my family. I love my wife and kids," the man continued.

"Hayes is ready to take the call," Patsy Penamint whispered to Annabella.

"Can I talk to that cop who said he can get me some help? I don't want to be like this no more," the man said.

"Of course. May I have your phone number in case we're suddenly disconnected?" Annabella asked and the man gave it to her. "What's your name? So I can give it to Lt. Hayes before I patch you over to him and what's your wife's name? Is she ok?" Annabella asked.

"I'm fine and much better now that my husband wants to get help," a woman's crying voice came through the phone line. "We're at home here in Northwest Houston. I'm on the phone in the kitchen. He's right here in the family room. I want to thank you all for running that story. We were just sitting here watching the news. My husband saw that lady's awful ordeal and heard the officer and tears started streaming down my husband's face. He said that could've been us. I've never seen him react to anything like this before. I was shocked when he dialed the hotline number and I picked up the phone after he started talking," the woman's words trailed off as her sobs replaced anything you could understand. The man gave Annabella his and his wife's first and last name and she transferred them to Lt. Hayes. When Annabella called to tell me about the phone call tears filled, first, my eyes and then my face. I was so thankful to God that families and lives were being saved because of a story that I knew I had to tell. The family went in for counseling the very next day. Just think, that videotape had been deleted, erased. That powerful story came so close to never being told.

THIRTY

"*It just isn't working* out. You just don't do a good job," my boss said to me. That was sort of my norm these days. If I did a really good job where people actually took notice, I could expect to soon be informed that I 'just don't do a good job'.

"What exactly was wrong with my story yesterday? It generated hundreds of calls for the domestic abuse hotline".

"It just wasn't any good," he informed me.

"The story was excellent. It was well written, compelling, it evoked emotion. People are blogging, emailing and calling about it and it saved lives. You can't ask for much more than that," I responded.

"That's your opinion and it's one I certainly don't share," he softly shot back. After calmly going around and around and not getting anywhere I soon found out he was saving the best for last.

"I hear you are inconvenienced by working nights," he sarcastically squeezed the words from his unpleasant lips.

"Well, it's a little difficult and a lot expensive to secure child care at night but it isn't a big deal. If the schedule calls for me to periodically work nights I'm fine with that," I told him.

"Well, we need you to start working nights every night. Your schedule is changing next week," he smirked.

"I'm sorry but that won't work for me. Not only would that be a pretty pricey adjustment, it would also mean someone else would have to raise my daughter. Someone else would have to pick her up from school, help her with homework, give her a bath, have dinner with her and put her to bed, every night," I explained.

"Well, it's simple. You either work nights or you're being taken off the anchor desk and you'll be reporting full time," he smiled.

"I've been with this company for fourteen years. For more than a decade I have worked ANY schedule that was needed. I worked 2:00 a.m. to 10:00 a.m. for a year and a half without one complaint. I worked weekends for eight years without so much as a moan. Now because I'm a single mom and I need to be home in the evening to take care of my daughter you're threatening to demote me if I don't hire a nanny to raise my daughter for me? Is anyone else being demoted or punished if they can't change their schedule and work nights or is this special just for me?" I was livid but remained professional.

"It isn't up for debate. Work nights or you're off the anchor desk," his lips were tense, his face was beet red and beads of sweat were forming on the bald spot in the middle of his head, which was like an island of skin surrounded by a horseshoe of brown hair on the sides. I wondered why he didn't just cut it all off. He seemed very awkward, uncomfortable and frankly, unhappy. I suddenly started to feel sorry for him. Are you kidding me? I wanted to ask myself right there in front of him. I wanted to be mad at him but anyone who got this much pleasure from attempting to make someone else miserable had to be miserable themselves. I said a little, silent prayer and peace came over me. Then his misery was confirmed. I had never seen him like this before.

"This is ridiculous. Lots of people leave their kids. They do what they have to do," he was waving his arms and jerking his hands to punctuate certain words.

"I'm not fourteen days, weeks or months into my career and waltzing in here demanding a certain schedule. After years of being a valuable employee I am now asking you to regard me as such. That's one reason why I haven't jumped around to different news stations, because if I remain loyal to the company I thought the company would remain loyal and value me. I do a good job here. I have for years. I'm simply asking to keep my current schedule so I can raise my six-year-old daughter. May I please keep my present schedule?"

"You would give up anchoring for your daughter? You are juvenile and immature and I don't need an anchor at my station like that," he ridiculed. He started saying things to agitate me, attempting to make me blow my stack but of course I never did. He became angrier and by the end of the meeting he was furious, enraged even, but I didn't understand. If I was the one being demoted why was he the one so doggone upset? He was normally so calm.

"I don't want you on the anchor desk and frankly I don't want you at this station or in my newsroom. You will begin reporting five days a week and you will no longer be on the anchor desk beginning next month. You will become a field reporter as I work to move forward with firing you." He said each syllable with emphasis and squinted eyes.

Two weeks later he called me into his office again. His words were flying out, sort of sounding the same as someone holding the trigger of a machine gun. His words just seemed to be a bunch of non-stop noise. So many sentences but what was he saying? Have you ever been in a conversation with someone and you know they're beating around the bush? You know they want to say something to you but they won't come out and say it? I knew he had a point but he just wasn't getting to it. Was this guy about to fire me? I started praying a 911. You know that's what I call Psalm 91 verse 1. It's my 911. Psalm 91, verse one through sixteen, is a mighty and powerful prayer of protection but in a pinch I at least utter the first verse, Psalm 91, 1...my 911.

'(S)he who dwells in the secret place of the most High shall be safe under the shadow of the Almighty.'

And Lord knows I needed the safety of His protection right now. After about a good solid twelve minutes he finally said, "How do you do that?"

"How do I do what?" I asked slowly.

"You have plenty around here to frown at but instead you come in here and you smile every day. You speak to everyone. You're the happiest person I know and it seems genuine. It's like you shine. You light up a room. The viewers love you." If I was, in his words, "genuinely happy", he seemed genuinely puzzled. He wasn't complimenting me. He truly wanted the answer or more like the formula for happiness, for smiling. Plenty of people have noticed or asked me about my happy-go-lucky attitude but this was different. It was almost as though he was declaring 'I have done everything I possibly can to hurt you, to wipe that smile right off your face, dealt my best blow of disrespect and humiliation and you're still not miserable. How is that possible?' After a few moments of silence I realized he was truly waiting for an answer.

"It's Jesus Christ. He has blessed me with peace and joy and only He can take it away. It's His light you see in me. Say these words 'Jesus come into my heart. I accept you as my Lord and Savior' and he'll bless you with this type of peace too," I smiled but my boss then looked at me like I was a lunatic and he shooed me from his office as he sat there wearing a baffled gaze. I glanced back and even his mouth looked perplexed. Was he daydreaming or deep in thought? I don't smell anything burning so I'm pretty sure he's not thinking. He was caught in confusion and I couldn't help but stare. I jumped when I heard someone call my name.

"Daf the police commissioner, sheriff, mayor and district attorney are holding a news conference. Can you go?" the assignment manager Chris McDougal asked me. Great job, by the way, on your story yesterday."

One last look back at my boss and I'm telling you I saw his office filling up with spongy, large yellow question marks boinging and bouncing off one another. You know how in cartoons when someone is in love and fluffy red pulsating hearts fill the screen? Yes, exactly. That was happening here with question marks. There was clearly confusion coming from that room.

"Of course I'll go. What are they holding a news conference for?" I asked and the assignment manager shrugged his shoulders. "Who's my photog?"

Paul Ainsley was a real lead foot, good photographer but an awful driver. He arrived at the station six months after I did. So I had known him a long time. Over the years I used up most of my prayers begging God to get me to and from each news story alive but Paul wasn't the only one. I think to become a photog you first have to take and pass a "bad driver's" test and I'm pretty sure there's a section on the application that reads "Awful Driver" with a little box next to it. If an applicant gets a check in that box then the next step is "Come on in. You're hired".

Another prayer answered. Paul and I made it to the news conference still breathing with all of our limbs and still among the living. When we arrived at the DA's office I found out today's big announcement is about the police officers and sheriff's deputies caught on surveillance tape a few days earlier using force to arrest a teenaged suspect they had been chasing. As I wait for it to begin I start reading comments on social media. "There's about to be an update on the officers caught on camera beating up on that kid".

"Kid? How about criminal? He got what he deserved".

"They're just going to say let the investigation uncover the whole story and 'we can't comment until then'. It's the same tired script every time".

"I have the utmost respect for law enforcement. I am thankful they selflessly serve and protect us every day. It's a job I could not do. Criminals are whacko. They'll hurt, harm or kill to keep from going to jail. I pray for our officers every day".

"I love our police officers but anyone with eyes can see those officers are beating, not arresting the suspect and they are wrong. The guy is face down on the ground with his hands behind his back when they walk over and attack him for two whole minutes. I've wanted to put on brass knuckles and make over bad guys' faces after hearing about their horrible crimes but it isn't allowed. The law says criminals have to be tried in court, not beaten to a pulp. If we do that we are no better than the criminals".

"How can anyone say those officers did anything wrong? What about that thug? Did he do wrong?"

"If those officers were on tape beating a dog like that they would be in more trouble".

"Don't commit crimes. Don't run from the cops and you won't have to worry about them roughing you up". The debate went on and on.

I was partially annoyed the late starting news conference was now getting underway before I could finish checking email and right in the middle of an important flirtatious text message with a guy whose face I can't even remember (sounds like he played an important role in my life). Just then another text came in from my source on the Texas Rangers, the law enforcement agency not the baseball team. Ranger Kyle Lohman was the epitome of a Houston cowboy. He's tall, dark (in a George Clooney way), handsome and one of the most intelligent beings you ever want to meet. He's from old oil money and has a massive horse and cattle ranch. Any who, Ranger Lohman told me the news conference was starting late because the sheriff was refusing to share a podium with the commissioner and wouldn't you know it, suddenly security was dragging a second podium into the room. This new police commissioner had only held the title for less than three months but he'd been on the force since somewhere around when Jesus was a small boy. He approached the podium on the right. The long time sheriff walked up to the podium on the left. Sheriff JB Trotter was a good old boy whose family owned so many businesses, nearly everything in town carried his last name. The two ladies stood in the middle, Houston's newly elected Mayor and a, no nonsense, speak-her-mind district attorney. Police Commissioner Keith Harrow, at 6'7" tall, towered over the group. The commissioner began to speak.

"I am deeply disturbed by what I saw on the video. The actions of those officers are troubling, upsetting and their behavior is not indicative of the thousands of hard working and honest Houston police officers who I am proud to have protecting and serving our city. Those officers' actions go against policy, training, violate the suspect's civil rights and is criminal conduct. Assault and Official Oppression charges have been filed against them. I will not tolerate such behavior in the Houston Police Department," the commissioner explained but was then interrupted.

"My deputies are not dismissed and didn't do anything wrong. I'm sick of this group of loud mouths trying to force officers to cuddle, coochie coo and caress colored suspects. The thug on that tape is a criminal. That's the profession he chose and he's in the hospital with broken ribs, lacerated liver and a fractured skull because of, let's call them, hazardous working conditions on the job that day," Sheriff Trotter had tears in his eyes.

"Colored? Okay. This isn't about race but a matter of right and wrong and those 'loud mouths' are simply pointing out a pattern of black suspects being taken into custody with the use of unnecessary excessive force and they're asking for it to stop," the commissioner calmly expressed his point of view. The sheriff wasn't used to being publicly challenged.

"That's a bunch of crap, just malarkey, and they're trying to bully law enforcement into treating black criminals special in some way," the sheriff's face was red and angered.

"You'll have a hard time convincing the teenaged criminal beaten in this video until he was unconscious, he received special treatment," the commissioner slowly said each word. "Come on sheriff just off the top of my head I can think of six unarmed suspects who were recently so brutally beaten they required long hospital stays. I became an officer to stop crime not to contribute to it," argued the commissioner. I was shocked. Then the commissioner actually convinced the sheriff to partner with him for a town hall meeting to reinvest in the relationship between cops and the community. I couldn't believe the commissioner's charm and ability to deescalate such a tense situation. "Let's end this thing man. This stuff is separating us. Let's bring everyone together and erase this problem". Whether you agree with him or not you found yourself willing to listen and go with him on his journey for a solution. How did he do that?

He seemed genuine. The commissioner looked tall and handsome standing there. I was smitten. I was like a lovesick schoolgirl who wanted to pass him a "do you like me yes or no" note. I've always been attracted to good, kind-hearted people who stand up for what is right but I think my encounters with Oxford and such mean spirited supervisors also had a lot to do with what I was feeling for the commissioner. After all, bosses who seemed to always do the wrong thing inundated my news station. They abused their power and did things to harass and humiliate whenever they didn't like someone personally. Their decisions to punish, pester and badger were personal and didn't have anything to do with someone's job performance. Their conduct was so unprofessional. So to hear the commissioner make this decision, not because it was popular or easy but because he felt it was right, I had the utmost respect for him. In fact, I knew there would be people all over the country who ridiculed him for making such a call. I could see it on his face, in his eyes, hear it in his voice he was conflicted about breaking the blue code of silence but at the same time he was determined to do what he felt was right. I wanted to stand up and give him a round of applause. Well, to be honest, I wanted to give him a lot more than that, a hug, a big kiss, my hand in marriage. I had met thousands upon thousands of people in my life and no one had ever had this effect on me. I don't fall easily for guys and I wasn't quite sure what was happening here but my heart was pounding through my chest.

Immediately after the news conference I found my friend and colleague Isaac Caney. He is a well-connected reporter who always knows everyone's business. Sure, that's another way of saying he is nauseatingly nosy and he's darned proud of it. "Isaac, Isaac" I called as I rushed to him across the room. "Is the commissioner married? I didn't see a ring," I asked with urgency as if I was about to break into programming once I got the answer and immediately deliver the news.

"Did you hear a word that was said in this news conference? Five officers are being charged with crimes. I've got to get my camera inside that jail somehow where these crooked cops are being housed," Isaac rambled about some jailers he knew who could help him get cameras inside. Our reporting styles were clearly different. The thought of officers being on the other side of the law made him salivate, while the thing that I got most excited about was this commissioner throwing away the script everyone expected him to say and offering up real solutions to an awful problem.

"Isaac, focus on the task at hand."

"Apparently I'm not the one who needs to focus. My mind is on work," Isaac shot back.

"Work, clerk, smirk. Just tell me is he married. I need to know," I begged.

"Why you wanna know?" Isaac gave me a sly look.

"Why do you think? Did you see how handsome he looked? His beautiful brown skin, big hands, broad shoulders," it was like I was daydreaming and forgot I was saying these things out loud.

"Shoulders? Why are you talking to me about the commissioner's shoulders? Before you fantasize about any other body parts, I don't know if he's married. I'll find out." "Thank you Isaac," I blushed. I made it through my 5pm report without once calling the commissioner gorgeous. Weeks went by then Isaac informed me the commissioner is married. A day later he told me he isn't sure. Finally, he said the commissioner, for sure, is not married. So I decided to ask him out, only I didn't know what to say. I had never asked a guy out before. Well, there was that one adorable NBA player. He was five years younger than me and was great to look at but that wasn't the same. He was like a toy and boy did I have fun playing with him. Ok, now I need to take a quick moment to pray and ask for forgiveness. We were young and good friends and we were both Christians who sometimes had to ask for forgiveness after we hung out together but I was interested in the commissioner for much more than that. I wanted to get to know him to possibly build a life together. That had never happened to me before. So my cousin slash best friend Nora told me "stop talking about calling him and call him. Tell him who you are then tell him you have two questions. Are you married? If he says no then ask the second question. Would you like to go to lunch with me? Call him now. Ok bye" she hung up. I sat for a few seconds with my cell phone still held to my ear and then I dialed his number.

THIRTY-ONE

A woman answered the phone, a mean woman at that. She wouldn't let me speak to him.

Well, it was her job after all. She answered the phone "Houston Police Department. Commissioner's office."

"Hi. Good afternoon ma'am. Is Commissioner Keith Harrow available, please?"

"Who is calling?" she asked me. Oh no. I didn't think this through very well. I identified myself, telling her my name and which news station I work for.

"Oh you need to call our media relations department if you're trying to set up an interview."

"Actually," I responded. "I'm trying to speak with the commissioner about attending a luncheon this month, a benefit luncheon" I didn't want to lie. I did want to invite him to lunch and it would certainly benefit him if he accepted.

"Send me an email with all the information and I'll check his calendar," she said in an Asian accent. I imagined a short, very neat woman wearing a business suit decorated with a shiny broach and she would have even shinier hair, which happened to be an every-hair-in-place bob haircut.

"Ok, great," I perkily responded and she hung up the phone. "Great," I said again this time lower, slower and with disappointment. "That did not go as planned," I said out loud to my silent cell phone. I wasn't giving up that easily. The first time I decide to ask a man out and boy this is difficult.
This is work. I decided on plan B.

"Hey Chief. How are you today?" I called one of the deputy commissioner's on his cell phone. After a brief few minutes of catching up I asked him, "Will you pass my cell phone number on to your commissioner and ask him to call me, please?"

"Of course" the deputy commissioner responded. "I'll call him right now." Within five minutes my cell phone was ringing. It was a number I didn't recognize. So I started to blush. "It has to be Commissioner Harrow," I told myself but I didn't have a whole lot of time right at that moment. I had just hung up my office phone after security called to tell me my two guests were being escorted to Studio B. So I was about to head out of the newsroom and into the studio to interview a middle school teacher who had very publicly been suspended from work for drug possession.

"Commissioner is that you?" I asked my still ringing mobile phone. I was nervous about talking to him. So I didn't answer. As I walked to the studio I wondered what the teacher would say, how she would explain herself. On the phone her attorney told me she was wrongfully accused and I felt sorry for her. Her name and picture had been plastered all over the news as a horrible excuse for a human who was supposed to be a good influence on the children not some drug addict who kept a stash close by in her car. She was giving me an exclusive interview in an attempt to clear her name. As I made my way to the studio and thought about this teacher it reminded me of a time a few years earlier when I was forced to do a story on a student who was accusing a teacher of raping her. I came in to work that day and my bosses were super excited that our morning photographer had captured a captivating confrontation on camera. The girl along with her family had gone to the school and our photographer caught on tape this mob of relatives yelling, threatening and nearly physically attacking the teacher who was arriving for work. I watched the videotape and I couldn't believe we were doing the story.

"I don't believe this man raped this girl. This will be very irresponsible for us to go on the news tonight and tell the whole city this teacher is accused of raping this student," I told my news director and assistant news director but both women revealed they didn't really care if he did it or not.

"We have this great video and we're not going to pass up the chance to put it on air. We're not playing judge and jury. We're not convicting or acquitting him. We will simply state the facts. He is a teacher accused of raping a student. Legally we can run the video and the story because there is a police report. We are allowed to report whatever is in a police report," the two women were alternating sentences and words and both sounded completely idiotic to me.

"I am aware of the law but I'm telling you the way this girl is behaving on this tape, I don't believe she is the victim. I think he is," I seemed to be talking to heartless, deaf, cold corpses. Not one word got through to them. After about an hour of debating I asked, "Well, can someone else do the story? I don't believe this is a story. I don't want to have any part of putting this, in my opinion, innocent man on TV."

"If you don't do this report you'll be written up for refusing an assignment. Your contract is coming up and it won't be renewed" my news director informed me. I was young and maybe I should have fought harder or just walked out and suffered the consequences but I didn't. After all, I didn't know for sure if this teacher was innocent but everything in me was telling me he was. I went to his house and rang the doorbell, praying he would give me an interview because I knew he didn't do what he was accused of but I was asked to leave his home. I talked with police investigators and I did the report, showing this explosive video of the furious family members verbally attacking this teacher accused of raping his 14-year-old student. It aired on the news that night. Well, what do you think happened the next day? The girl admitted to police she made the whole thing up. She was a troubled teen from a broken home who was lost and headed down the wrong path. The teacher knew she didn't have a father in her life, so he tried to be a positive influence and what did she do to repay him? She made up horrible accusations about him. Then the angry phone calls started pouring into the station from the teacher's family members. My boss called me into her office.

"It would be unprofessional and immature if you try to blame someone else for putting this story on the air and if you don't own up to the responsibility that this is your story," she drilled me on how I needed to take the phone calls and she instructed me if I so much as imply she was behind putting this story on I wouldn't have a job much longer.

"And don't forget this could get nasty and go to court. If you apologize that is seen as an admission of guilt. Do not apologize to these people. Simply tell them there was a police report and you decided to do the story." She is such a snake. I don't know how people like this get hired and in jobs of authority. She was forced from her last TV news station after the community found out she made a decision about a certain story. There was a huge scandal involving accusations that she ignored and didn't put an important report on the air. Several leaders in the community didn't let it go. They met with the General Manager of that TV news station and demanded an internal investigation to find out why the station disregarded a story and eventually the truth came out. She had been lying for weeks saying she wasn't aware of the news conference until after it already happened. Turns out, in the morning staff meeting they discussed covering a news conference that area leaders were holding to address alleged discrimination in the black community. My boss, there at her old job, supposedly said, "We're not covering that. They're always complaining about something especially about being black," this was a black woman herself and no matter what color she was, she likely would have been just fine choosing not to cover an event but it was the lying about her decision that got her in big trouble.

Now she was at it again. She had with great enthusiasm, force and a great deal of arguing, made the decision to air the story about the teacher accused of rape. Once again, she was not standing behind what she had decided. I started answering the calls from the teacher's family. His daughter must have called me a dozen times and I spoke with her every time. Well, I didn't exactly speak. She was livid and can you blame her? She told me off and called me just about every name in the book. Yes, that one too. I said a prayer for that family, again, as I arrived at Studio B.

I introduced myself when I walked into the very cold studio. The teacher accused of drug possession and her attorney did the same. Lights in the large, mostly empty room, had just been turned on less than five minutes earlier for my interview. Studio B wasn't where we actually shot the newscasts. We only used this spot for periodic interviews. So it was usually one of the coldest places in the building.

"Gosh it's freezing in here. I'm so sorry you've walked into the North Pole," I laughed.

"It's ok. I'm nervous. So I'm kind of hot," Roxanne Moore told me. She went on to say she had a habit all right but it didn't involve drugs. The middle school teacher told me she would routinely leave her car doors unlocked and her sunroof open and someone must have slipped the drugs into her car. The marijuana was found in the glove box by drug sniffing dogs. These random searches in the teacher's parking lot were new for the school district. Half a dozen teachers were busted in just one month. Roxanne was the first. She was suspended and charged with drug possession in a school zone but she was insisting the drugs were not hers and she was innocent. I didn't believe a word she was telling me. That surprised me. Before

I met her I fully expected to like her and trust everything she told me but just the opposite happened. I felt like this thin woman, who didn't look healthy, was either high even as she spoke to me or headed to get high as soon as she left the interview with me. She had the mouth of a habitual drug user. Her lips were jet black and her mouth was off center and twisted to the left. One doctor told me that happens when drug users favor one side of their mouth to routinely smoke out of. The physician also told me there's something called "meth mouth" where a methamphetamine user's jawbone can lose its alignment because of constant sliding of the jaw back and forth while smoking, not to mention the awful decay drugs do to your teeth.

"Anybody could have put those drugs in there," the suspended teacher said loudly and awkwardly at a point in the conversation where the sentence didn't even make sense. She was looking me in the eye and lying to my face. After nearly two decades in the business I'm used to that. I have come face to face with murderers and others I knew were guilty but they were still walking free to offend again. Just three weeks ago I covered a story of a missing brother and sister, only five and eight years old. I have a little girl myself so my heart ached for the parents. I arrived at the apartment complex around 9:00 a.m. The children had been missing about eight hours but their disappearance was just reported to police three hours earlier. I had spoken with the mom on the phone and as soon as the photographer and I parked she came out of her apartment and started walking toward me. She was dazed with tears in her eyes. Pain covered her light mocha colored face and her huge hazel eyes. Just then a man burst out of the front door. He grabbed Paula Bateaux's thin arm hard, stopping her in her tracks. He was tall with dreadlocks and a cloud of evil hovered around him. His eyes were wild and wicked. I silently said my prayer of protection. "She who dwells in the secret place of the most High shall abide and be safe, under the shadow of the Almighty".

"Hello Paula. I'm so sorry about your babies. We spoke on the phone," I said softly.

"Don't say nothing to her. Come back inside right now," the man said to Paula as he yelled, yanked on her arm and tried pulling her back into the apartment.

"Stop Mike. She can put our babies' pictures on the news so the whole world will help me look for them. I need my babies back home with me," her words came out slowly. She broke down sobbing and her pain hurt me to the core. Her head was slumped with her face in her hands. He stood staring right into my eyes. It was like seeing a snake on two legs. He was creepy. Most people would probably look at him and think he's good looking but I could clearly see what he really was and it wasn't at all attractive.

"I just want to help. The more people you have on the lookout for your children, the better the chances of having them returned to you," I explained.

"Shut up. Don't say nothing else to her. Get away from us you effing b-word," Mike jabbed his finger at me, pointing in my face, as he shouted.

"I'm not afraid of you and I'm not talking to you. Paula do you want to go somewhere and talk?"

"If you say another word to my wife, I swear," Mike got louder. I knew right then this guy had harmed the kids.

"Paula," but before I could get my sentence out Mike was pulling a severely sobbing Paula back into the apartment. I didn't know if Paula, like the kids, was also now in danger. I immediately called investigators but they were already on to this monster. Cops told me Mike and Paula were married but lived in two different apartments in the same complex. Her apartment looked like a family home full of children's belongings, neatly stored toys and a tidy environment. His apartment wasn't only dirty but filthy and disgusting. There was no clear walkway throughout the entire apartment. You had to walk on trash if you took any steps and much of what officers stepped on as they searched the place were pornographic magazines. The repulsive publications littered every room including the kitchen. There were also mounds of filthy movies stacked knee high on just about every wall. Even officers who had been around the block a few times had never seen anything like this. They said the smell in that apartment, the pungent stench, was horrific. The police officers told me they couldn't believe a father would expose his children to such a dreadful, awful environment. Mike had been telling detectives the kids were sleeping over at his apartment and in the middle of the night around 1:00 a.m. the kids wanted to go back to their mom's place. So he says he let them leave alone, his eight-year-old daughter and five-year-old son. Mike told investigators he assumed his two small children made it around the corner, in the pitch-black of night, safely to their mother's apartment.

Four hours after I spoke with Mike, he confessed to an area activist that he had killed his kids. Mike took the community leader out to a field and showed the man how he had beaten, burned and buried his own children because he was simply sick of them being around. What a monster but I knew he was seconds after I first encountered him. My feeling about the middle school teacher with a drug problem was just as strong but I felt she needed help immediately. I certainly wouldn't want her teaching my kid, not in her current state. After the interview I thanked her for coming in and I wrote down the name and phone number of a very reputable drug treatment doctor. She thanked me when I handed her the paper.

"He is quite a successful substance abuse rehabilitation physician. He's discreet, respectful and has great bedside manners. If you ever come across the person who put the drugs in your car, they might need this info. Addiction is a disease that can be cured. God bless you," I smiled and security led the teacher and her attorney out of the studio.

"Eight voicemail messages? Why do I have eight messages? Who's calling me?" I asked my cell phone and soon got my answer. I looked at my missed calls list and skipped right over the phone numbers I recognized. I listened to the message that came in from the one number I didn't know.

"Hello there. This is Keith Harrow. You can call me back on my cell phone," and he left his cell number. I knew who it was but I never called him by his first name. I always called him commissioner. Big smile. What do I call him when I phone him back sir, commissioner, mister? I laughed and dialed his number ready to ask my two questions.

THIRTY-TWO

He was even more handsome than I remembered. The commissioner was wearing a suave black suit, matching shiny well-polished leather oxfords and the most gorgeous green Hermes tie. His skin was smooth like dark chocolate and his 6'7" athletic body seemed ten feet tall. He looked distinguished in his glasses and he smiled at me when I walked in. I'm telling you I don't know what he was doing to me but I promise it was love at first sight. We met for lunch at a seafood restaurant near my house in Sugar Land. So obviously he had answered my two questions no and yes. No he's not married and yes he would have lunch with me. I wore a beige Chloe silk peplum tie-waist blouse with sheer cap flutter sleeves and a peach Valentino eyelet above the knee A-line skirt. My vanilla colored leather Chloe Marcie bag rested on my shoulder and my four-inch Gucci patent leather nude stilettos clacked as I walked over to the hostess stand where the commissioner was waiting for me. My sweet perfumed lotion slathered on my silky skin made it to him before I did, at least, the smell of it anyway. We greeted one another with a quick hug and he too smelled amazing. His cologne was masculine, clean and just as attractive as he is. My bangle bracelets sounded like wind chimes as my arms reached around him for our brief but nice embrace.

"Hi. How are you today?" I smiled as I asked him.

"I'm great now," Keith smiled back. "Your smile is just as beautiful as you are".

"Thank you," I blushed. "You look handsome". I was glad I had spent the last week whitening with those little toothpaste strips. We chose to be seated outside and followed the hostess to our table by a beautiful dancing waterfall on a duck pond. The sun was shining. The afternoon breeze kissed my face and gently played with my hair. It was a perfect October day, warm but not hot and no humidity. Over sea bass, scallops, lobster tail, spinach with shredded cabbage, au gratin potatoes and warm buttered French bread we got to know each other. We talked for three and a half hours. Our conversation was the best and it left me wanting more. He was funny, gentle and considerate. I also learned he was a native Texan, raised by his devout Christian parents. Keith also has two sons, is divorced and is fifteen years older than me. Yikes, is what my head told me about his age but my heart was saying something else. How had he so quickly gotten through to my heart, already? Maybe after my relationship with Oxford and encountering his violence, perhaps I felt I needed to date the whole police department and the commissioner came close to that I guess. He represented the entire police department. Not to mention I longed for someone who was sweet and who I simply enjoyed being around.

"Oh my gosh. I can't wait to see him again," I called my two best friends on conference call. After playing a game of twenty questions and answering each with how awesome the commissioner is I remembered what I hadn't told them yet.

"There is sort of a 'but' though," I said.

"What? What?" their voices chimed in harmony.

"He's fifty-three."

"Fifty-three what?" Paige asked.

"Years old," I answered.

"You can't date him. He's old," Nora said.

"That's the thing. When I think of dating an old guy I think no way would I date an old man but when I look at him I don't see old. Sure he's older than me but I didn't feel as though I was interacting with or looking at an old man. I think I like him and I want to get to know him better. Actually, I can't wait to see him again."

"Well, it's your choice. If you don't think you have a problem with him being fifteen years older, then it doesn't matter if someone else does," they told me. The commissioner and I went out again and again and we became an item. He was respectful, warm, honest, so kind and he treated me like the princess I think I am. He treasured and adored me and I him. Like me, he was not an arguer. He didn't yell to solve things. As a woman who communicates for a living, I love that our conversations only got better with time. We always had a million stories we couldn't wait to share with one another. I also loved that he valued my opinion. Before he made any serious decisions professionally or personally he always talked it over with me first, weighing his options and hearing what I had to say before reaching a resolution. Keith had a beautiful brown leather bible in his office and kept his favorite verse close to his heart, especially if he was facing a tough task. He would always recite Psalm 23, "The Lord is my shepherd I shall not want. He maketh me to lie down in green pastures. He leadeth me beside the still waters. He restores my soul. He leads me in the paths of righteousness for His name's sake. Ye though I walk through the valley of the shadow of death I will fear no evil for though art with me. Thy rod and thy staff they comfort me. Thou prepares a table before me in the presence of my enemies. Thou anoint my head with oil. My cup runneth over. Surely goodness and mercy shall follow me all the days of my life and I will dwell in the house of the Lord forever". I think I clapped a little more forceful, sat happier and sang along louder with the choir when he started taking me to church. I loved having him seated next to me in the pew. His hands are huge and I love the way he holds the bible between us as we read along with the pastor. Before you know it we were best friends and in love. I was terrified to introduce him to my four-year-old daughter. I wasn't about to parade a bunch of men in and out of her life but I felt like the commissioner and I were getting serious. So I hesitantly arranged a meeting. My daughter was used to going to luncheons, dinners and charity events with me when I had to make appearances. So she had met a lot of my colleagues and we had eaten a number of meals with men and women whom I have professional relationships with. Some of them she would see over and over at the different functions and she knew them by name and they knew her. Therefore, I didn't believe dinner with the commissioner would be that out of the ordinary for her.

"Hey honey bunch. We are going to have dinner with my friend the commissioner of police tonight. What dress do you want to wear?" I asked her. She always loved to choose her dress, frilly socks and hair barrettes when we were going out. Keith arrived to pick us up with flowers for both of us, red roses for me and a bouquet of pink, yellow and orange daisies and carnations for my daughter. He also gave her a small goody bag full of doll clothes complete with a couple of Barbie dolls. Her eyes lit up when she saw what was inside. That first dinner went incredibly well. So did the second, third, fourth, you get the picture. Their conversations seemed to be just as great as ours. I adored watching the two of them together. One Sunday morning the three of us were in church and the time I was a little girl at the newly integrated swimming pool popped into my mind. I remembered wondering why those people were all leaving and why they were all so aggravated at the very sight of us. Now my last two bosses seemed to do the same, become aggravated at the very sight of me. Well, as we sat there in the big beautiful stained glass filled sanctuary the pastor was speaking from the bible, Matthew Chapter 5 verse 44. "Love your enemies and pray for those who persecute you". That's what I had then and that's what I do now. My mom raised me reading and believing the bible and that's how we live.

"You're able to do that because of Galatians 5:22. Keep your bibles out please. Let's read it together. The nine fruit of the spirit are love, joy, peace, forbearance (tolerance, patience, without a quick temper), kindness, goodness, faithfulness, gentleness and self-control," the 2,000 people in the congregation read along with the pastor. He continued, "Those nine types of fruit from the spirit only grow in those who believe. Without the Holy Spirit you can't have those things. You can't buy them, steal them or con your way to them. It's just like growing peaches, apples, avocados or oranges. There's only one way to produce that fruit and the same is true for spiritual fruit. You only get peaches from a peach tree. You only get love, joy, peace, patience, kindness, goodness, faithfulness, gentleness and self-control from God, no other way," the pastor's voice resonated through the less than two-year-old building. The Fort Bend Church Head Pastor Benjamin Sparks is a really likable man. His face looks honest and he's kind of a hefty guy with sort of a jolly look and a commanding voice. He and his beautiful wife Sarah are great people. Just about every Sunday Pastor Sparks incorporates food into his sermon.

"Let me make it real clear for those of you having trouble understanding," he would say. "It's just like hot, homemade buttered biscuits on a Sunday morning. You don't ruin those biscuits by slathering on imitation butter. It just isn't the same. That's what some of you are doing with life. You're getting all dressed up in imitation happiness. You're looking for joy in bars, money, drugs, drinking. Try the real thing. Try Jesus Christ for joy and peace, anything else just isn't the same." The entire congregation always goes rushing from the building after service and speeding to brunch. This Sunday wasn't so bad. Stomachs weren't growling in service as he spoke about the nine fruit of the Holy Spirit. "People who aren't believers, who aren't blessed with this fruit will be perplexed at how and why you have it and when they try in the wrong ways to get it but can't they will hate even the sight of you," Pastor Sparks continued. "The bible tells you right here in John 15:19. If you were of the world the world would love his own but because you are not of the world and I have chosen you out of the world, therefore the world hates you," my mind started to drift toward what was going on with me at work. This explains everything.

Although, things were getting better for me at work now that God had sent an angel to me at my job. Graham Fordham had to have come straight from heaven. One of the last conversations I had with my boss was, "I would really like for you to continue working here but ahhhh it just isn't looking good," he had told me then I went on a two-week vacation. When I returned we had a new Assistant News Director. He was the second man in charge of the newsroom behind my boss. He was Graham Fordham. He had been in TV News for decades and was a true journalist. My first day back from vacation in a meeting after the newscast, meetings once reserved for verbal assaults, Graham actually said to me in front of the whole room, "That's the way a story should be done. Her writing is brilliant. The story opener caught my attention right away and kept it until the very closing line," he actually said that to the group about me. I wasn't used to compliments around here. Then the next day, the next week and the month after that Graham did the same thing over and over. "You know, I'm not an emotional guy and her story actually put tears in my eyes. What an amazing way she chose to tell this story. It grabbed you and didn't let go," he said in the open meeting then looked right at me. "Your writing is brilliant and your sincerity shines through as genuinely caring about the people you're telling the audience about. That makes your stories even more compelling and interesting".

Graham's compliments could only mean one thing. He's planning to kill me, run me down right in the employee parking lot. I quickly got to know what car he drives so I could stay far away from him at quitting time. Okay maybe I was being a little extreme or paranoid. I guess I had become conditioned to expect insults, bad treatment, poor reviews and write-ups especially anytime my story drew compliments or positive attention. The day or so after, my bosses would then follow up with a sucker punch to the gut and if Graham was going for months saying good things about me then uh-oh his blow was going to be a doozy. Those were my human thoughts but deep down in my spirit God told me he had sent someone who was fair, respectful, honest and smart. He valued having good people on his team and Graham wasn't afraid to tell you so. He, too, was a man of God and it showed. I loved having Graham around and wherever I go from here I will forever keep him and his family in my prayers. I appreciate Graham more than he will ever know and I'm so thankful to God for sending Graham to me. Sitting there in church I, again, said a prayer for the Fordham family.

THIRTY-THREE

"This is the worst waste of a perfectly good paper bowl I've ever seen," shouted my colleague and friend Michelle McKissling as she pointed to a newspaper reporter. Michelle wasn't exactly one to hold her tongue. She actually once asked a man "Who killed a cat and stashed the body in your mouth right next to the carcass of the skinned skunk?"

"Michelle!" I yelled to try to quiet her. I always seemed to be there when she was her most abrasive. "That's just rude".

"What? Actually he's the rude one. When did he last brush his teeth 2010? That's rude and offensive to lean in and whisper in my ear when he knows his breath smells that way. I could see if there was nothing he could do about it but he can. It's called a ninety-four cent toothbrush," she rolled her eyes at the high-ranking Houston city administrator as she walked away and refused to conduct an interview with someone who was so offensive. That's my Michelle for you.

Now she was starting in on this poor newspaper reporter. "Michelle! She can hear you," I mouthed with wide eyes and a please-be-quiet look on my face. Michelle was tall and beautiful with the shiniest reddish brown hair and the smoothest milky latte colored skin I'd ever seen in my life. She was so kind but her strong opinion sometimes came across as harsh.

Every station in town was covering a news conference about a new law cracking down on child predators. This updated legislation would make it legal to use details of prior accusations, in a trial against an accused child molester. Some, now adult, victims had already spoken here at the news conference. Now we were all seated for lunch, then the conference would continue with some of the lawmakers weighing in on the new legislation. The delectable spread was unbelievable. There was everything from seafood enchiladas to beef burritos to shrimp fajitas and lump crabmeat nachos. The menu was obviously Mexican food. The best Mexican restaurant in town was catering. So what did Reporter Tiffany Fantler come to the table with? A paper bowl full of lettuce, nothing but lettuce.

"Who would do that? Why would someone eat lettuce when all of this wonderful food is here?" Michelle threw her napkin onto the table as she pointed with her fork at the bowl full of lettuce and Michelle isn't a quiet girl. Her voice carried throughout the dining hall. She seemed offended, as if Tiffany's meal choice was an insult to her.

"Why is her lunch bugging you? Will you leave her alone please?" I scolded Michelle. She rolled her eyes and without missing a beat started right in on a different topic and she began placing bets on what we would hear coming from the podium after the meal. She was making a good point. These things were so predictable. Whatever happened to people actually caring about others and people actually believing what they say? These things were always full of "talking heads" saying what they think people want to hear rather than saying what's right or speaking from the heart. They were always campaigning instead of caring about the topic at hand.

"Please continue your meal as we resume the program," a voice announced over the loud speaker. One phony after another approached the microphone.

"Because when you mess with children in Texas you mess with me," one of the politicians said. The statement on paper seems pretty heartfelt but he delivered the line in the most robotic insincere voice I have ever heard. He had a plastered fake smile on his face during the entire speech, which was clearly written by someone else. What was he smiling about? Now I was bugged and offended. I was so aggravated and even angry. These are the people running our country. I looked at the agenda. We were only two speakers in. There were six more to go. Are you kidding me?

"It's just like my bill on nutrition I passed last year," said one woman.

"So if you want to vote for someone who will take care of the kids you vote for me," smirked a man who looked like he was now about to try to sell all of us a broken down used car.

"What's wrong with you people? This law will save and change lives. It will get child sex predators off the street and protect other children from being hurt by these monsters. How can you people stand here and campaign like uncaring zombies". I realized I was out of my seat and saying this out loud. Uh oh!

"I've been in government for twenty-three years. You think you can do a better job?" barked one lawmaker.

"I know I can. I at least care about what happens to others. You people could care less. If it doesn't affect you, your pocketbook or your votes then you really aren't bothered by it," I shot back. The politicians were giving me looks like they were night-of-the-living-dead and would soon be coming after me in that slow sleepwalk like chase. Then, shaking and trembling on my leg startled me. It was my cell phone vibrating telling me I had a text message. The audience was clapping as the Lt. Governor stepped away from the microphone and I realized my confrontation with the pathetic politicians in the room was just a daydream. Now yet another selfish bigmouth was at the podium patting himself on the back and reading a prepared speech, saying words he didn't seem to mean. I read my text message and realized my station was sending me to a different story. "Thank God". I made eye contact with the photographer and slid my straightened fingers from left to right in front of my neck. He knew that meant 'cut', stop rolling, it was time to go. We were being sent to a news conference at police headquarters. As much as I wanted to leave this place, I couldn't accept an assignment covering the police department. I was dating the commissioner, and I didn't want anyone to think I would write a biased or favorable story for HPD because of it. I had been successful at avoiding police stories for more than a year until now. I sent a text back instructing the assignment desk they would have to send someone else and why. The desk manager replied back saying I wouldn't have to write the story. The photog just needs to record the news conference. It was really the photographer who was needed. No one else was available.

So I agreed.

We were seated in the large, newly built police headquarters conference room. It was more like a museum, stocked with law enforcement memorabilia. Reporters were seated filling the middle of the room. Photographers were lined up behind the chairs with their cameras on tripods ready to record the action and a couple dozen police officers stood on each side of the tall, towering police commissioner who was standing behind the shiny cherry wood podium. My sweet baby looked so handsome and I blushed as we locked eyes. He winked at me and smiled showing his beautiful white teeth. He gestured for me to meet him half way. There was still plenty of chatter and lots of people were standing and talking as we awaited the start of the news conference.

"Hi beautiful," he smiled.

"Hey handsome," I said slowly as I studied his beautiful skin and oh so gorgeous face. We only had a few seconds before he would walk back to the podium and get things started. So I wanted to flirt with him, you know, just mess with him a little to see if he could then re-gain his composure and focus on the business at hand.

"Remember the movie we saw over the weekend? Remember how nice it was sitting that close to me in that dark theatre? Remember..." the smile was wiped off my face and I was stopped in my tracks.

"Don't say another word," the words came from clear across the room. "I can hear you," Maurice Stern blushed from behind his camera. I had forgotten the wireless microphone had already been clipped on the commissioner's lapel. So Maurice, who was standing right there at his camera, checking the audio, could hear everything we were saying. I blushed back.

"Oooops. Sorry Maurice," I sang. Although he worked at a different news station I had known Maurice for more than a decade. He had been a news photographer longer than I had been a journalist. Maurice was so likable. He was the biggest family man I knew. He wore a small family portrait of himself, his wife and their two sons tucked inside a little square plastic holder around his neck. In one side there was the family picture, the other side held his employee id. The picture was clearly displayed hanging down the front of his chest attached to a thick blue ribbon like necklace with the words "Best News In Town" written on it. He always had that thing on. It was like his power. The room was silent for a few moments then Sgt. Spragtini's voice filled the room. I had known the sergeant professionally for years, an attractive Italian man with the best head of hair I've ever seen. I called him spaghetti. His last name sort of sounded like that. He was the leader of the

"Houston Cop Chorus" they called themselves. They would go to hospitals and sing to sick children and go caroling at senior citizen communities at Christmas time but now he was belting out the line "My love, my dream come true. That's you".

I looked confused and mouthed "Spaghetti? What are you doing?" The other officers joined in. In harmony they sang, "With your love, life is good. Wonderful feels like it should". Without music these beautiful voices were melodious, hit every note and the song was upbeat and bubbly. I realized this was the entire Houston Cop Chorus. They wore their blue police uniforms, their hats and white gloves. Their hands were clasped in front of their bodies as they sang this catchy tune. "One day without you would be too much. I love you so much, your smile and your touch. Like sun to the sky you are my (light). My night with bright stars, you are. My heart beats for you my thoughts are of you. I am a better me thanks to you. With you I want to share my life. Please be my wife. My best friend, my love please be my wife". The singing officers looked right at me as they harmoniously delivered the line over and over. "With you I want to share my life. Please be my wife". Tears filled my eyes. The commissioner walked from behind the podium. He nervously smiled as he walked over to me. I couldn't believe my eyes. The chorus sang softly now. The commissioner reached into his pocket and pulled out a small box. My mom, my aunts, several of my cousins and my two best friends then walked into the room smiling. The commissioner kneeled on one knee and opened the box.

"Will you make me the happiest man alive and agree to be my wife? I don't want to live without you. Will you please share the rest of my life with me? Will you marry me?" he smiled looking into my tear filled eyes. The ring was beaming from the box. It was beautiful and massive.

"Here, take it. Take it. Take this ring. Isn't this yours?" A nasally sounding voice squealed out. "You dropped it," I was baffled as I looked and saw a short, scrawny, pale man handing me a ring. I felt completely disoriented. I was still at the news conference with the zombie politicians.   No I want my daydream back. I tried to finish the fantasy but it was too late. Ok, so I admit. Sometimes this happens. Sometimes vivid daydreams take me away from boring, long, drawn out news conferences but apparently this one was finally over and the singing proposal at police headquarters had never actually happened but fantasizing about it was downright entertaining. By the way, the commissioner wasn't as smart as I thought he was after all. He let me get away. We are no longer an item.

 "Thank you. I took off my ring to put on lotion and forgot to put it back on," I explained to the little man as he placed my sparkly diamond ring in the palm of my hand. "It must have fallen from my lap. I would have been devastated to lose it," I told the skinny man who was smiling as he asked to take a picture with me. Maybe I was consumed with all this wedding stuff because one month earlier I went to Atlanta for my best friend Paige's engagement. Her fiancé is an awesome musician. So he took her to the hottest jazz club in town. At one point Joseph went to the restroom and the next thing you know he's on stage playing his saxophone, singing to Paige and we're pulling up chairs at her table. She cried like a baby as he proposed. It was super sweet. They met a year earlier when Paige took a job with a package delivery company for the holidays. She decided to stay on after Christmas to fatten up her savings account. There was a music studio on her route where she delivered packages. For two months she was making deliveries to this famous and awesome music producer. He finally got up the nerve to invite her inside for coffee. She accepted the invitation but told him they would have to gulp and not sip the java because she didn't have much time.

 "Hey how about dinner tonight?" he called out to her as she thanked him for the mug of "deliciously-the-best-Joe-Iever-had" and prepared to walk out of the studio.

 "What time are you picking me up?" Paige smiled. Just the day before, another studio employee was saying hello to her as she dropped off packages and Joseph overheard Paige saying she could sure use a French vanilla coffee with a twist of caramel, crowned with whip cream. So what do you think Joseph did? He rushed right out and bought several different brands of French vanilla coffee, extra creamy whipped cream and enough caramel to top off two hundred cups of flavored coffee.

They are such a sweet couple. It's like God made them for one another. My special creation from God can't be far away!

THIRTY-FOUR

"It was a day of tragedy. Fire spread through the city. There were explosions. People were hurt. Police were catching bad guys who were doing bad things," my six-year-old daughter reported to her cute pink camera set up on a plastic tripod as she talked into her microphone pretending to be me. Ok, no more watching mommy on the news for this girl.

"So why did you do those bad things?" she pointed the microphone at my mouth waiting for an answer.

"I wasn't thinking clearly," I played along.

"Wait. Say that again. Let me zoom in this time. I don't want Sarah in the video. It would look like she's there by the bad guy. Don't worry my baby. I won't take you anywhere dangerous like where my mommy goes," my princess promised her stuffed doggy Sarah.

"Where does mommy go that is dangerous?" I asked Daniella surprised to hear she thinks I frequent danger.

"To work," she announced.

"Why do you think mommy's job is dangerous?"

"Well, because it's the only place I'm not allowed to go with you. You take me everywhere except to work and every day on the news you talk about bad and dangerous things like fires and police taking people to jail," she grinned at me. "That's dangerous, right?" Daniella was looking for me to confirm.

"Yes. I suppose that does sound pretty dangerous," I agreed. My daughter is such a smart little something. I'm sure every parent says that, right? No, seriously she can hold a conversation with the best of them. Daniella has the amazing ability to figure things out and as a first semester first grader she's reading on the level of a second semester second grader. In addition to all of her smarts she's kind, considerate of others and she is as cute as all get out but I may be a little biased, only slightly. James 1:17 "Every good gift and every perfect gift is from above from the Father of light". God definitely gave me my perfect little gift of glowing light. For that, I am truly grateful.

"Come on Oprah MiniMe. It's time to get ready". Daniella is Oprah MiniMe (you know like Oprah Winfrey) when she is conducting videotaped interviews on-camera and pretty good interviews I might add. She is the Toddlerazi when she is snapping still pictures of every person in sight. She earned those very appropriate nicknames a few years ago.

We were headed to the convention center for Family Fun Night. It was a huge effort for our church and several Houston area religious organizations. We all came together for a day of ministry, music, sermons, singing, dinner, dancing and my favorite, DJ B.A.A.D (DJ Born Again And Delivered), pronounced DJ Bad. He leads his own choir and comes complete with dancers but as a gospel disc jockey he also has hundreds of albums that he plays and mixes on a couple of turntables. They all perform on stage for some of the best entertainment ever. DJ B.A.A.D is really good (no pun intended. Ok a little pun intended). He's just an amazing musician and music director who can also play any instrument he picks up. My daughter is his biggest fan. Families are always packed in the place and ready for a good time when DJ B.A.A.D. hits the stage.

"This one or this one?" Daniella asked me holding up a frilly pastel pink dress in her left hand and a frillier soft pink dress with fuchsia colored roses decorating the bottom in her right hand. "You have to wear pink too mommy," she declared. "I think I'll wear this dress. This one is better right? The flowers make it look really pretty and fancy. Anyway if I wear this one with the flowers I can wear my matching tights and headband," she smiled. I put my thumb up and smiled back.

"Sounds like a good plan. That is a beautiful dress and you will be super-duper pretty and fancy in it. I'll get your pink patent leather Mary Jane shoes from your closet shelf," I kissed her nose.

Before long we were walking into the beautifully decorated convention hall. The white crisp tablecloths and matching napkins didn't have a wrinkle in sight. The tables were stunningly set and decorated with yellow peonies. Yellow is such a happy color. I guess that's why there was so much of it adorning the event. There were also hanging baskets of white lilies and a lovely large calla lily arrangement on the baby grand piano. Exquisite music massaged our ears as we smiled and laughed with families we had not seen since last year's Family Fun Night. The piano player, dressed in a long silk white gown that spilled softly off the sides and back of the piano bench, had perfectly polished nude nails and flawlessly tanned bronzed skin. She stopped playing after we were all seated and a pastor took to the stage.

Several different preachers delivered encouraging words. Then we were in for a dreamy dinner. There were succulent lamb chops, lobster tail, white truffle macaroni and cheese and baby candied carrots. We started with French onion or loaded potato soup and fresh from the garden tasting salads. After a little more mixing, mingling and games for the kids we all headed for heaven, sort of. Right at sunset on the rooftop DJ B.A.A.D.'s heavenly concert was getting underway. When the elevator door dinged open at the top of the convention center I was amazed. The sunshine glistened off the serene swimming pool water where floating floral arrangements took my breath away. The pool was full of Texas bluebonnets, blue hydrangeas and morning glories made it tough to tell where the water ends and the flowers begin. The breeze sent my soft blush pink floor sweeping silk Catherine Deane dress gently wafting behind me. I wore matching Lanvin strappy patent leather stiletto sandals and carried my Judith Leiber crystal Hot Fudge Sundae clutch handbag with a thin chain strap. My metallic pink nails almost glistened here in the sunlight.

"You look like a stunning, elegant angel," a masculine deep voice called out. If the face on this man even remotely resembles this gorgeous voice then I pray that sentence is for me. I turned around and saw Dwight O'Neal smiling at me.

"Oh my goodness!" I almost screamed. Dwight and I went to college together. I hadn't seen him since college. Then, "Thank you Lord for my Nightlife" popped into my mind. Nightlife, of course, is my favorite eye shadow by LAMIK makeup. It makes my eyes look mesmerizing. Dwight is 6'6" and still all muscle. In college he played basketball and ran track. We were really good friends. We had some seriously good times together.

"You look beautiful. I'm glad to finally see you. I moved to Houston two months ago," Dwight told me.

"Look how handsome you are. Wait a minute, two months? And you haven't called me?"

"I did. I called the newsroom. I was trying to surprise you. When the guy asked my name I told him just tell her an old friend is on the phone".

"Dwight! Do you know how many people call and say 'I'm her old friend'? I run from phone calls like that," I said.

Dwight went on to med school after undergrad. He's been a cardiologist, a world-renowned heart surgeon in fact, for some time now. I had read a number of the articles he published in medical journals and I even saw him interviewed quite a bit on national news shows. Dwight did a lot of mission and pro bono work here in the U.S. and internationally. He told me he and his two children moved to Houston after he accepted a directorship position in the Texas Medical Center. I was sad to hear he had divorced three years earlier.

"Why did I let you get away?" he smiled.

"Um maybe because we were friends and I knew you very well and I was smart enough not to date you," I laughed.

"You are right about that. I was not even close to being ready to settle down in college. That was the key reason for my divorce. My maturity didn't come until long after my marriage was already in big trouble".

"We live and we learn. When we know better, we do better. Right? That's all we can do," I said as I gave him a half smile.

"Hey you're the doctor who fixed Praensa," my daughter said smiling to Dwight as she and my mom stepped off the elevator.

"Now how could you possibly know that?" Dwight said with a sincerely shocked look on his face.

"I watch the news. I saw your story. Well, it was actually Praensa's story of how she wasn't expected to live when she was a baby. Her heart just wasn't strong enough and the doctors in her country only operate if you pay them a lot of money but you gave her a new heart for free. You're a kind man," my daughter said.

"You are a smart, intelligent, impressive little girl". My daughter blushed and looked up, emphasizing the tiara she was wearing. She wanted to make sure Dwight noticed it. "And you're a beautiful little princess all rolled into one," Dwight smiled.

"I like to think of myself as a princess. That's how I remember Praensa's name. It sounds like princess. She's my age you know?"

"You're only six years old?"

My daughter grinned and nodded her head "Yes".

"That makes you even more extraordinary. Your conversation is remarkable. I've met plenty of adults who can't converse as well as you. Oh, now I know why you watch the news. I know who you are too," Dwight picked up my daughter and studied her face. "You look exactly like your mom," Dwight proclaimed. My mom and Dwight hugged and were glad to see one another again.

The music was starting. DJ B.A.A.D.'s band began playing as the lights dimmed; the sun was nearly a memory. All but a few pieces of the glowing ball had vanished into the purple, orange and sapphire colored sky. Spotlights shined on the stage highlighting the drummer, guitar player, pianist and even a harpist. We sat at a table near the pool with a perfect view of the concert. The choir slowly marched out singing and with a poof of smoke DJ B.A.A.D. appeared on stage in front of his two turntables. The music and singing stopped and DJ B.A.A.D. asked in his melodic voice "Are you ready to rejoice? Has God been good to you? If He has, let's celebrate. Let's have the biggest praise party anyone can imagine," he called out as the crowd responded in harmony to his questions. He dropped a couple of records on the turntables and out of the speakers came "I'm so glad" then there was a pause "trouble don't last always" the song continued but was interrupted by "I know God my God, God is good. God my God, God is good," the crowd was screaming and going wild. Then came "with the Earth all around me sinking sand Christ the solid rock I stand". DJ B.A.A.D. was mixing gospel songs perfectly in a way only he could. The choir began to clap, the music stopped and they started singing a capella "When I call on Jesus all things are possible" then "How Great Is Our God". They nearly made it through the entire song when very fast paced music started to play. It was "Jesus Will Work it Out". Everyone jumped out of their seats and we danced all night.

As Dwight and I danced my princess twirled, hopped and pranced around with a group of little girls right next to us. I caught a glimpse of my mom right next to the girls cutting a rug with a man from church. She looked absolutely lovely. Her brown hair hung down her back. She wore a sheer silk mauve, yellow and cream bohemian style Tory Burch blouse, emerald green cami and off white Dolce and Gabbana high waist pants with Derek Lam strappy sandals. Her skin was flawless and at 65 years old she had more energy than most twenty something's. She was so slim and beautiful as she joyfully danced here with the rest of the happy crowd. I thought to myself "Thank God I have her genes".

THIRTY-FIVE

"*I had a small* accident," my mom whispered awkwardly. "Will you please wash these for me," she said handing me a bundle of clothes.

"That's the second time. I'm going to make a doctor's appointment," I told my mom.

"I'm fine. I just waited too long to go to the restroom. I tried to hold it and I shouldn't have," she explained but I picked up the phone anyway and scheduled an appointment for my mom to see my doctor.

Two days later my mother was getting a clean bill of health, sort of. Dr. Shrader said my mom's heart, blood pressure, lungs, weight and cervix were all perfect. Here's where I was surprised. My mom didn't have an incontinence issue nor did she have a bladder or urinary infection. So why was she urinating on herself? I was puzzled.

"Well, if it will make you feel better I'll recommend an ultrasound of her abdomen so we can see if there's something going on in there," said Dr. Shrader. An ultrasound? What could possibly be going on in there?

"Hi there. I'm Mindy calling from Dr. Shrader's office with your mother's ultrasound results," said the voice on my cell phone. This was four days later. I was at a SWAT scene standoff. "Is this a good time?" she asked. I glanced around at the black army looking tank type SWAT vehicles, the officers in what looked like riot gear. Six police snipers with sharp shooter rifles were on top of four houses, each with one eye closed and the other carefully focused and seeing everything through the gun's scope. A man had taken his soon to be ex-wife and their toddler son hostage. When she escaped their house he shot at her, caught her in a neighbor's yard and dragged the woman and the boy into the neighbor's home. The neighbors soon came running out and called 911.

"Sure this is a good time. What's up?" I said into the phone. I was fully expecting one of those routine we-have-the-lab-results-and-everything-is-fine telephone calls but boy was I wrong.

"There are two fairly large masses one on each of your mother's ovaries and three more tumors in her abdomen and liver," Mindy told me. I had not even come close to being prepared to hearing this news. I was afraid and stunned and caught off guard and hurt and heartbroken and sucker punched and overwhelmed and kicked and "Ma'am?" I heard the voice say. I looked around and wished there was someone here to hug. I felt so alone. I saw a line of officers move from being shielded behind the protection of a patrol car to taking cover by an SUV in the driveway. Each wore a helmet with a face shield and the officer in front carried a heavy bulletproof shield.

"Ma'am?"

"Yes I'm here. What size masses are we talking about?" I asked her.

"The two growths on her ovaries are each about the size of baseballs. The other three are equal to about the size of large oranges or even good sized grapefruits". Are you kidding me? I thought to myself.

"And all of this is pressing on her bladder? No wonder she had trouble holding her urine." I said to Mindy.

"Yes and this is probably quite painful for your mother. Three oranges, grapefruits and two baseballs take up a lot of space. Carrying that in your tummy isn't an easy thing to do. It's also pressing on her intestines."

Certainly mom must have felt something different. She must have felt something. Why didn't she tell me?

"Ok so let's schedule surgery immediately. Is that the only way to find out if this is cancer, when these tumors are biopsied in surgery?"

"I have also scheduled a CT Scan for tomorrow. The CAT will be able to take better pictures, better images of the masses. Looking at density and a few other things will give us a better idea of what we're dealing with. Your mom's surgery will be next week Wednesday or Thursday. I will have the exact day confirmed by close of business today."

I could hear screaming coming from the house and a commotion. Then I saw the baby in the window hollering, crying and banging on the glass. The window blinds behind the toddler were flying all over the place, as he appeared to be trying to come straight through the glass. The baby's face was so red. His blonde hair was covered in sweat and pasted to his head. Then with a huge crashing blow the front door flung open and the woman was literally thrown out of the house. She was begging the man to let her take her baby. Her back hit the top of the porch and she rolled down the six concrete steps. As quickly as the door opened it closed again even before the woman hit the bottom of the stairs. Inside the house the man yanked the baby from the window. The woman, with hair like her son's, was bloody and bruised. As she staggered to her feet the sound of a gunshot forced her back toward the ground. She ducked and officers who were moving in toward the house were telling her to run to them but she turned back to the front door banging and begging for her son. Then another gunshot and officers stormed the house. The man had shot his son and himself. Fortunately the baby survived. I was absolutely emotionally drained by the time I made it home that evening.

The next few days were a blur. The CT Scan showed what appeared to be ovarian cancer and it had clearly already spread. Only surgery would reveal for sure. There in the family waiting room I was surrounded by forty-five of my closest loved ones. That may seem extreme but I was really thankful they were here. They were very comforting and supportive. We prayed a lot during my mom's six-hour surgery. There was still a chance the tumors would be biopsied and they could turn out to be nothing more than cysts, benign masses and not cancer. That was my prayer. I had faith and I truly believed my mom did not have cancer.

"Good news. Your mother is strong. Her heart is strong. The surgery went very well. It was a little more complicated than I expected. Your mother does have stage four ovarian cancer. There was a lot of cancer in there. I was able to get most of it but some of the masses are in hard to reach areas. One has grown into the outer wall of her intestines, another is attached to a major artery at the top of her abdomen and can't be cut but I took the bulk of the cancer away. She'll be a bit groggy when she wakes but you can see her as soon as she's brought out of the OR and taken to her room," my mom's gynecological oncologist announced to the room full of listening family members. Tears filled my eyes. I was heartbroken but not defeated. My mother really has cancer? How can that be? She's the healthiest person I know. She doesn't smoke, drink alcohol, eat chocolate, she never consumes soda because the caffeine isn't good for you and she snacks on fruits and veggies because she loves how they taste. It just doesn't seem fair. Just like that, in the blink of an eye, my mom went from being the beautiful, healthy, energetic woman who was dancing the night away at Family Fun Night to a very ill woman in the fight of her life battling terminal ovarian cancer. I felt so deceived, so betrayed. My Father knew this would happen? God kept this secret from me all these years, all these decades? How could He do this to me? I guess parents do have a way of protecting their children and not unnecessarily burdening them. Well, this only changes the words in my prayers. I know God will heal my mother.

I made it my mission to learn everything about ovarian cancer I possibly could. It turns out the symptoms are very vague and could be signs of simple indigestion. The symptoms include abdominal bloating, feeling full quickly when eating and a protruding belly. So my mom's tummy hasn't been the flattest lately but what 65 year old has a six pack? Women who have one or no children are more likely to get ovarian cancer, as well as, women who give birth later in life. Nearly all women diagnosed with ovarian cancer die within one to five years of diagnosis. Because the symptoms are so vague it's almost always diagnosed too late and usually has already spread but my God is a miracle worker. After my mom's diagnosis I interviewed a woman who had beaten ovarian cancer. She had been in remission for fifteen years. Back when Wendy Laitner was first diagnosed she wasn't expected to live more than a year. Then she took part in an experimental stem cell transplant therapy study. She believes that saved her life but if that's the case why isn't this treatment being offered anymore? One well-respected physician, who would not go on the record, told me a stem cell replacement is very costly and the country's top researchers made a deal with insurance companies to shelve this expensive breakthrough treatment because who was it really saving after all except "a few thousand old ladies who would die of something else within ten or so years anyway". I couldn't believe my ears. Well, I'm not giving up that easily. If this treatment worked for one woman certainly it could work for others, including my mother.

There was also research I read about where a Michigan doctor studied ginger and found ginger kills ovarian and bowel cancers. The study finds that is also true for turmeric, which is in the ginger family. I'm telling you I don't sleep these days. I fall asleep in bed every night with the laptop open researching cures for ovarian cancer. If I wake during the night I continue researching until I nod off again with my fingers still curled on the computer keys. My mom is consuming plenty of ginger root and turmeric root these days and lots of wheatgrass because some believe the chlorophyll in it helps kill cancer. I mostly make fresh fruit and veggie smoothies for us with these ingredients. Yes, everything I suggest for my mom to eat I also eat it with her, to give her all the support I possibly can.

"Honk. Honk. Honk. HONK! HONK! HONK," screamed my cell phone alarm. It seemed to get louder with every "honk". Clearly my daughter had changed the alarm tone from the soft sweet harp sound I normally wake up to, to this obnoxious old truck horn that startled me awake and scared me half to death. It was time for my mom's doctor's appointment in Michigan. I would be there via conference call. I said my prayers, brushed my teeth, took a shower and prayed some more until the phone rang.

"Good morning," the voices of my aunt, my mother and her doctor sang in unison. "So after this third round of chemo therapy we have the recent CT Scan results back and chemo doesn't seem to be working. You have two options; continue with a fourth cycle of chemo or my recommendation would be to go where you're happy and live out the rest of your life. I know you enjoy your daughter and granddaughter. So you might as well go to Houston with them and enjoy the time you have left," said the doctor as if she was telling my mom to go to Neiman's because there was an amazing sale going on that she wouldn't want to miss. Did she just tell my mom to come to my house and die? I don't know how but I ended up on the first floor of my house. I had descended two flights of stairs and didn't know it. I was standing in the bedroom where my mom sleeps when she's in town. I was just staring at my mother's room, at her belongings. This is the way it's supposed to be. I can't imagine my house without her stuff, my life without her. I suddenly found myself on the second floor standing at the kitchen counter sipping sweet caramel coffee.

Then I was back on the third floor in my master bathroom. I decided I'd better start getting ready for work. I was still dazed and I stared at myself in the mirror. I felt confused and couldn't snap out of it. I found myself standing holding my pink and green plaid toothbrush in one hand and my minty whitening toothpaste in the other but I couldn't figure out for the life of me what I was supposed to do with these two items. I knew I was supposed to know. I was getting frustrated that I couldn't remember. I looked at the toothbrush and toothpaste as if I was holding a live porcupine and a computer motherboard. I just didn't know, I didn't remember what I was supposed to do with these two things in my hands. I put them down, sat on my bed and cried.

I found myself somehow in the morning meeting at work. We meet daily to discuss which stories we will cover for the day. I had no idea how I had gotten here. I glanced down to make sure I was wearing clothes. Whew, thank God I had gotten dressed but when? Just then I heard my name.

"So, you missed the mark big time with your story yesterday. First of all, tell me about the story you did yesterday," said my Chief Executive Officer. Was he kidding? I can't tell him if I ever figured out how to use that toothbrush and toothpaste I was holding in my hands just an hour and a half ago. I can't tell him how or when I had gotten dressed and driven to work. I can't tell him how in the world I ended up in this meeting. I can't tell him anything that happened after my mom's doctor announced she should just come to my house and die. Did he really have to do this now? Apparently so.

"Tell me about your story," he repeated. I couldn't remember for the life of me what story I had covered the day before and frankly I didn't care. I was still aching inside from the devastating news about my mom. The entire meeting was silent. Everyone stared right at me.

"I'll tell you about your story from yesterday. It was," my executive producer Jeff Wright tried to help me.

"No. I asked her," my CEO insisted. Why was he being such a jerk? I hope his midlife crisis or whatever is cured soon because recently it seems his motto is 'The more chaos in the newsroom, the better'. Once he gets something locked in his mind there's no changing it, no matter how ridiculous the idea. Sort of like when he jumped down my throat after I reported during breaking news "I'll get clarification on exactly what trinitrotoluene is and bring you that information". So here's what happened. There was an evacuation at a high school because of rumors of a student with a gun. All day we, and every station, had been reporting this "gun scare" and then seconds before I went on the air in the beginning of the 5pm newscast I received information there was no gun but what was found was "extremely dangerous trinitrotoluene". After a little research I was reminded trinitrotoluene is commonly known and abbreviated as TNT, explosives. When my CEO told me I should never admit I don't know something, I told him anyone who tries to pretend they know everything is ridiculous because no one is all-knowing. Why would someone even want to pretend they know it all? "I am an intelligent person who isn't afraid to admit when there is something I don't know" I told him. He promptly told me "Only one of us here has the power to hire and fire. Therefore, only one opinion in this room matters". Wow, really? Huh!

On this day I clearly didn't have an opinion because I clearly didn't have a memory. I thought my CEO liked my work but recently I can't tell. "I'm sorry I don't remember what story I covered yesterday. Someone's going to have to remind me," I said.

"Well, that speaks volumes. If you don't remember, how is anyone else supposed to remember your story? It must have been poorly done if you can't even remember it," said my CEO.

"You did the story on the proposed law that would allow bosses to legally ask an employee for his or her social media passwords," blurted out my executive producer.

"Thank you Jeff," I said and then I thought to myself 'I will keep you in my prayers forever'. "Yes I remember. That was actually an excellent story. I received several compliments on it including from people in this room. The story was extremely well written and I included comments from my social media pages. My story generated hundreds of comments," I explained.

"Well, yes I know that's true but where you missed the mark is at the end. You failed to say 'Find me on Facebook, to solicit comments," said my CEO.

"That line would have been redundant. I talked in my story about the 'really interesting and compelling conversation' I was having on Facebook and Twitter. I even included comments from my Facebook post and told the viewers they were comments from 'the engaging discussion I was having on my Facebook page'. So that line wasn't necessary nor is your groundless and very public reprimand. For you to call my report poor and to say I missed the mark is untrue and unfounded," I defended.

"I feel like a crazy person. How does this keep happening?" It was suddenly after work and I was walking into my daughter's school to pick her up. Where did the day go? My mom has to get well soon, for her health and my sanity but the truth is since she's been sick I haven't, at all, been myself. I'm a shell of who I once was. I used to be a person who smiled 99.9% of my day. Now when someone is joking with me or greets me with a grin I have to remind myself "Self, do that thing where you make the corners or your mouth curl up and sometimes show teeth". Odd, I know.

I never thought I would see the day where laughing and smiling were not natural parts of my life. Now I don't even remember how to be that jovial girl I once was. How do you laugh and smile when the person who loves you most in the world is battling a potentially deadly disease and doctors over and over again tell you there is nothing else they can do?

Straight from her school my daughter and I drive to The Women's Home, a shelter for ladies and children of domestic abuse.   A big event, put on by TWH and The Honey Brown Hope Foundation, had women packed into the auditorium. I was one of the speakers for this annual special affair. The children were in a separate room enjoying games, face painting, food and storytelling. My friend who runs the shelter was one of the chaperones in the kids' room. My daughter was acting as her little helper. There in the open auditorium I looked beyond the faces and into the eyes of these women and they were broken. Their spirits were shattered and it showed. Just then it hit me. I had the perfect fix. The obviously sincere psychologist wrapped up her speech with "Ending domestic abuse is as simple as parents teaching little boys that hitting another person is unacceptable and let's not forget some women are abusers as well. Abuse will not be tolerated. We must raise our children and instill in them it is never acceptable to strike anyone else for any reason. Let's end domestic violence together," the pretty freckle faced woman with red-framed glasses, matching curly hair and wearing what looked like a tailor-made mauve pencil skirt suit said with enthusiasm. Her shiny wavy long hair was piled on top of her head in a really cute messy bun. The warm round of applause continued as I walked to the microphone.

"Ok who's ready for a party?" I asked with just as much excitement as the speaker before me.

"I could certainly use a party. It's been too long since I've enjoyed a party". The voices called out from the audience.

"Well, me too. I think it's time to get out of our seats and turn this auditorium into a dance floor. Let's celebrate being independent, strong, wise and blessed enough to have escaped the grips of a monster.   This is only a small obstacle that we will get over. We have the rest of our lives to enjoy and to be excited about. One question I ask myself every day to ensure I'm the best me possible is 'What kind of place would this be if everyone here was just like me?' Would this place be full of people who are part of the problem, who are weak, violent, selfish, full of backstabbing and gossip or people who are caring, respectful and people who are part of the solution? Always answer that question honestly. Too many domestic abuse victims blame themselves and hang on to that blame too long. 'If I had only done this, he wouldn't have done that'. Well, today let's realize that just isn't true. There are many reasons people grow up and become abusers. They are often abused themselves as children or maybe they're just mean. Perhaps Taylor Swift says it best," I said and then I connected my smart phone to the auditorium speaker and played the song "Mean". "You, with your words like knives and swords and weapons that you use against me. You have knocked me off my feet again. Got me feeling like I'm nothing," the words sang from the speaker. The women smiled, sang along and danced. "Someday I'll be living in a big ol' city and all you're ever gonna be is mean. Someday I'll be big enough so you can't hit me and all you're ever gonna be is mean. Why you gotta be so mean?" With every word sang the women were getting and feeling empowered.

Some women pointed their finger, clearly visualizing, seeing her abuser's face in front of her, as she sang the words right to him. I was thankful to be wearing my cute and comfortable pastel pink Tracy Reese dress, which gave me plenty of room to dance. When the song finished there were lots of tears, hugs and the sentence "You will never hurt me and my children again", echoed throughout the place. "Play Chris August Unashamed Of You" one woman called out. So I did. "I will sing about Your love. I will shout it to the sky. I will tell of what You've done when the people ask me why," the entire auditorium sang along.

"Let's leave that abuse in the past and go on to live healthy, happy lives. Let's look at ourselves and make sure we aren't gravitating toward abusive men, just as the doctor spoke about earlier in the program. We have to teach our children what the red flags are, a controlling person, someone who treats and views them as a possession, a person quick to anger. A person who first hits and destroys property will likely graduate to hitting people. Every nine seconds in the U.S. a woman is beaten. An abuser will attempt to isolate their partner from others, often has shallow relationships with others and will get very uncomfortable watching a movie or show about abuse because it's like looking in the mirror. Life with an abuser is often filled with extreme emotions and actions that most people never have to encounter. A domestic abuse perpetrator is usually a better liar than his victim is at telling the truth. Let's teach our kids, encourage our friends to immediately leave the relationship at the first sign they are dating an abuser. A victim should not be ashamed to reach out and ask for help. Let's work together to end domestic violence. We have to encourage abusers to get help and stop that behavior. We have to stop the cycle. Abuse in even one family is too much and unacceptable. Let's vow right now to fight, not one another, but battle this awful thing called abuse. Let's also remember when we look in the mirror every day to look past the physical. Take a deep look inside. We know ourselves better than anyone else. We know what we've done, what we haven't done. We know every thought we've ever had. When you look in the mirror if you like the person you see staring back at you, keep up the good work. If you don't, you still have work to do. Every one of us should look in the mirror every day and say 'I like that person looking back at me'. One of my favorite bible verses gives me strength every time I recite it. 1 Corinthians 13:4,5,7 'Love is patient. Love is kind...it is not easily angered ...it always protects'. Proverbs 3:3, 4 'Let love and faith never leave you. Bind them around your neck. Write them on the tablet of your heart. Then you will win favor and a good name in the sight of God and man'. Serve the Lord with gladness. Remember praising God is not an event but an entire lifestyle. God bless us all today and always". I finished to a standing ovation.

THIRTY-SIX

"*I've done enough* crying, crying, crying," Mary J Blige blares from the SUV's speakers. "Did I do that?" asks Mariah Carey melodically. "Can I just spend my life with you," requests Tamia. "No matter what you're going through remember God" Yolanda Adams reminds me. "I need just a little more Jesus," announces one of the Mary sister's. Then "I love me some him," Toni Braxton declares.

"Mommy why is this playlist called 'My Girls'? Are these your friends?" my daughter asks from the backseat as we leave the carwash and she plays songs through Bluetooth from my cell phone.

"Well, sort of but not exactly," I smile and my daughter lowers her bright pink sunglasses, squints her eyes and twists her face at my answer.

"They are singers. I've been listening to them for years. I find myself praying for their kids, rooting for their marriages, buying their CD's just to be supportive. I guess it is proof I've grown as a Christian".

"I-I-I know my redeemer lives," my daughter sings along. Tears fill my eyes as she then belts out "I can only imagine" with Tamela Mann. She skips to The Clark Sisters and Kim Burrell and "Oooh is this song by Aunt Janet and what do you mean you've 'grown as a Christian'?" she asks.

"I suppose she's an aunt to some kids with the last name Jackson but no that isn't your Great Aunt Janet," I grin. "Growing as a Christian means praising God continuously, graduating to having prayers of substance, having stronger faith, a deeper relationship with God. You learn to pray about everything and worry about nothing".

"Pray about everything? Sort of like when that police officer stopped you and you prayed he didn't give you a ticket and you told him the Range Rover has such a smooth ride you didn't realize you were speeding?" asks my daughter with an as serious as a heart attack look on her face. Boy, kids certainly watch every move you make, don't they? I laugh on the inside, tell Daniella speeding is never a good idea and explain to her how, yes, you should always include God and pray no matter how small something seems.

"Praying is just talking to God. It's a way of staying close to Him. Remember to always pray for other people as well, for families, your neighborhood, community, your country and the world we live in. It's important to pray that everyone has food to eat and somewhere safe and comfortable to live. Pray to protect everyone from evil. Pray that God's light will shine in you and that you will be a blessing to others. Prayer is powerful," I try to explain in the most basic, child friendly description I can. "As you become a bigger and better Christian you work hard to make the world a better place," I explain.

"Oh ok," my daughter says as if I had just told her to put on her sweater. I was certainly still praying for Oxford, praying he would become the wonderful father my daughter deserves, praying he would let God guide his life so he could be blessed with the nine fruit of the Holy Spirit (love, joy, peace, patience, kindness, goodness, faithfulness, gentleness and self-control). She loves him so much. I know every day there's air in his lungs there is another chance for him to get it right. I forgave him a long time ago. He just needs to forgive himself and move on with the life God intends for him. It's funny how we can become the only thing standing in the way of the biggest blessings of our lives but it happens all the time. I instill in my daughter the importance of forgiving, not only others, but yourself. Some really bad things can happen when you don't. Unfortunately, those people discover self-destruction is alive and well. I also teach my daughter what happens in secret gets revealed in public. Luke 12:3 'What is spoken in darkness shall be heard in light; what is spoken in the ear in closets shall be proclaimed from rooftops'. I had recently found out from Gerta's sister a longtime family secret. Gerta had been pretending to be pregnant with a pretty lumpy pillow for about six months. Then suddenly one day the plumpy padding was gone and baby Oxford was there. No one knew where he had come from. Gerta thought a baby was a good way to hang on to a bum of a man she had been seeing. Of course the plan turned out to be just as bad as Gerta herself. I feel bad for Ox. I don't think he knows. I've been trying to find his real family.

My daughter shuffled through a few more songs pausing on "It's the God in me". She sang with the beautiful soulful sisters and then she was pretending to be a DJ on her favorite radio station. "You're listening to God Listens KSBJ. Don't forget to pause for prayer with us at noon. Now here's Blessings by Laura Story". She blared out in her best radio disc jockey voice. Then Daniella placed her little finger on the phone's touchscreen and shuffled to the middle of a song. I knew what she was doing.

"Get your microphone ready," she laughed. It was a challenge to see who knows the most lyrics. "There'll be days I lose the battle. Grace says that it doesn't matter cause the cross already won the war." We sang along with Mercy Me into invisible microphones. We battled it out for a few bars and finally Daniella decided on listening to Nicole Mullen's "Call On Jesus".

On this beautiful hot Houston Friday afternoon the sun is shining, there is an inviting breeze and not a cloud in the sky. Daniella and I are headed to another one of our daily escapades, to the clear blue water and white sandy beach at South Padre Island, a six-hour drive from Houston. She doesn't have school Monday or Tuesday and I took off work. So we are in for a few days of fun, sun, swimming and relaxation at a breathtaking resort. Every day is an adventure for us. We frequent parks, museums, malls, restaurants and waterparks. Our journey yesterday took us on a 10-mile tour down a Houston bike trail along the bayou. The day before that, Daniella played dress up while I wore my Chloe ballet flats for the first time. I put them on to vacuum. I know, right! I learned you haven't truly lived until you slide on your favorite pair of shoes and do housework in a home that is certainly a blessing from God. We cranked up the music, listening to Israel Houghton's Saved By Grace about twenty times as we thoroughly cleaned our house from top to bottom. We never leave for vacation until our home is spotless. Sometimes when we're feeling really adventurous we slip on pretty fancy dresses, such as, my green one-of-a-kind Danny Nguyen Couture dramatic peplum waist backless gown, and we go for a walk or a bike ride over the footbridge and we put on an all-out photo shoot in the big park across the way. It brings smiles to our faces and to every person who happens by.

As we drive to Padre I catch a glimpse of myself in the rearview mirror. I almost don't recognize the lady looking back at me. Beyond my purple Prada swirl arm sunnies (that means sunglasses, of course) I see my diamond stud earrings and my short haircut. I recently cut off my hair to support my mom when she lost hers to chemotherapy. God is healing her and taking such great care of her. My mom has only been back in Michigan this time for two days, just long enough to get another chemo treatment. She is in her fifth round of chemo and getting monthly treatments. Mom is flying into Corpus Christi and we are picking her up on the way to Padre Island so we can all have some much-needed fun in the sun. My cut is really tapered all over. The longest part of my hair, my bangs are swept to one side and fall right at my eyebrows. It's a really edgy, elegant haircut. "This color, Deep Copper Downtown Brown, looks fantastic in the sunlight" I mumble as I admire my new cut.

My daughter and I stop for drinks and snacks at a massive and super clean convenience store.

"Oh this is Buc-ee's gas station. I heard they have the fanciest and cleanest public restrooms. Let's check it out. Can we do a photo shoot if the restrooms are super clean and extravagant?" Daniella smiles.

"Extravagant? Where did you learn that word?" I laugh. As I walk, my pastel lavender knee length Vanessa Bruno silk strapless sundress softly glides in front of me and floats behind me as if I'm walking the runway. My leather ankle-wrap mustard Chloe espadrilles, matching bag and arm full of silver and gold bangles in unison sing. I quickly fish around reaching in my large leather Marcie bag for my ringing phone but just as I grab it the sound stops. It was Dwight. "I'll call you when we get back in the SUV," I say to the now silent cell phone. Things between us are going well. He even took me to the jewelry store to look at rings but I am certainly proceeding with caution. No way am I going to parade a bunch of men around Daniella. If Dwight is my heaven sent husband then he will be here when I am ready to give him my hand in marriage and we will jump the broom, as they say, in God's time.

I smile as I grab the sour cream and onion potato chips, a massive almond-chocolate bar and an ice-cold bottle of pineapple juice and I realize it's a great day to live. Sometimes that feeling will come naturally. Some days you'll have to choose to have a great day no matter what. Then there are times you may have to decide to fight to stay alive (Psalm 118:17) "I shall not die but live and declare the works of the

Lord". Jesus Christ has brought me this far, I know He won't leave me now. I've learned whatever life throws at me the only way to deal with it is to pray, have faith, put on my best outfit, suck in my stomach, straighten my spine, roll my shoulders back, hold my head high and decide the world is my stage. I'll choose what play I'm putting on today. Sometimes supporting characters, cast or even extras on the set will send the production in an unexpected direction but that's all right. In my script there's always a happy ending. After all, (Psalm 118:24) this is the day the Lord made. I will rejoice and be glad in it.

1 in 4 women will become a victim of domestic violence in her lifetime, according to the Houston Area Women's Center.

From 2001 to 2012 **11,766** American women were murdered by abusive husbands, boyfriends or exes. During the same time, **6,488** American troops were killed while at war in Afghanistan and Iraq. (Stats from a Huff Post Women article)

15% of domestic abuse victims are men. If someone you know needs help escaping domestic abuse help is a phone call away. Nat'l Domestic Violence Hotline 1-800-799-SAFE (7233).

Get to know God and Jesus Christ for yourself by praying and reading the Holy Bible.

Looking for someone to pray with? Christ based radio stations and churches offer prayer partners in person, by telephone and emailed prayer requests are also accepted. God is always listening to you. He also accepts emails and in person prayer requests!

Damali Keith is an author and has been a TV News Journalist for more than 20 years, employed at Fox News in Houston for over 15 years. Damali began honing her broadcasting skills at CNN Headline News and CNN Sports while attending Clark Atlanta University in Atlanta, GA where she is a graduate.

For appearance requests please visit www.AGreatDayToLive.com.

Originally from Wayne, MI Damali now delightfully dwells in Houston, TX with her daughter.